Gus Busbi

(Father Tom #2)

A Novel

by Jim Sano

Full Quiver Publishing
Pakenham Ontario

Gus Busbi
copyright 2020
by James G. Sano

Published by Full Quiver Publishing
PO Box 244
Pakenham, Ontario K0A 2X0

ISBN Number: 978-1-987970-21-0
Printed and bound in the USA

Photo courtesy: iStock
Cover design: Emily Sano, James Hrkach

NATIONAL LIBRARY OF CANADA
CATALOGUING IN PUBLICATION
ALL RIGHTS RESERVED

Copyright 2020 James G. Sano
Published by FQ Publishing
A Division of Innate Productions

I would like to dedicate this story to:

All parents, especially single parents, who work hard every day to teach, care for, provide an example to, and show their kids what unconditional self-giving love and virtues are all about.

And to all those other mentors who see the value of being there, being God's hands on earth to care about and encourage a younger person, letting them know that they were created with self-worth and purpose.

When a young person knows that they are noticed, worth the effort, and that they matter, that relationship with an adult can make all the difference in the world.

Chapter 1

Gus Busbi slowly opened his eyes to the early spring morning's sunlight streaming through his bedroom window and muttered, "Crap!"

Gus hadn't always felt this way, but, these days, he went to bed each night hoping he wouldn't have to face the raw emptiness of another day. Why should he have to face another day without meaning or joy and the same nightmare each evening? Gus and his wife Julia had been married for forty-three years. It was three years ago today she died of a failed heart and, as Gus was painfully aware, a broken one as well.

Sliding his long legs over the side of the bed, his feet then touched the cool wood floor. With elbows resting on his knees, he rubbed the sleep out of his eyes then stood to be greeted by the early morning arthritic stiffness of his bones. His six-foot-two lanky frame was unusually tall for his Italian heritage. The lines and character of his masculine face reflected a life of joys and tragedies but now seemed empty, like an old abandoned home that had once been filled with the life of its family and friends' deep relationships.

He methodically began his routine of washing his face, shaving, combing his short salt-and-pepper-colored hair, and pulling on his gray pants, red flannel shirt, and jacket. After locking the worn door to his apartment, he made his way down the narrow staircase and out the back door of his two-family house, to the chilly early March morning. Like most people in Boston's modest South End neighborhood, he yearned for the end to the long, cold winter. The early morning sun melted the ice on the rooftops and the sidewalks as Gus walked several blocks to the Eastside Café, his regular breakfast spot for the past thirty years. Every Monday and Thursday, he met with a group of seven other men to share breakfast, stories, company, and to give their favorite cranky waitress, Linda, a hard time. Most of the men were retired from the same factory where Gus had worked since returning from the Korean War.

His best friend, Mike, glanced up and smiled as Gus's silhouette appeared at the front door of the café, then waved him over to the table full of men already engaged in talk of spring training and the upcoming 2004

Red Sox season. For years, Gus had typically been one of the more outgoing talkers at the table, but a distant quietness had settled over him since Julia passed away. Mike made sure Gus continued to come to breakfast but would often find himself glancing across the table into Gus's empty-looking eyes.

The group's fun started when Linda came to their table with a pencil in hand, an order pad at her hip, and a sarcastic greeting for her favorite breakfast crew. "I spent all morning wishing—I mean worrying—that my favorite table of admirers wouldn't show up. Let's see if we can get through this before the kitchen closes, shall we, men?"

Andy quipped, "Since I'm your number one fan, I'll order first." Linda shook her head and stared straight at Mike for his order, leaving Andy opened-mouthed, with his palms raised in the air, getting a chuckle from the rest of the guys at his mocking expression of disbelief.

Mike quickly replied, "I'll have two eggs over easy, rye toast, and some of those sweet Italian sausages." Just as Linda turned, Mike reached out and said, "Never mind. I'll have my usual instead."

Linda looked up from her pad and rolled her eyes. "That *is* your usual, Mike."

He said, "Linda, that's my usual usual but—" Linda promptly ignored Mike as she turned to the next wise guy. Several of the guys kept changing their minds until they finally ordered their usual breakfast just to get a rise out of her—and she never disappointed. Finally grabbing menus out of their hands and shaking her head, she scurried back to the kitchen.

Mike had made a point of sitting next to Gus, and Gus knew it was because today was the anniversary of Julia's death. The rest of the table entertained each other with their usual banter and stories that had been repeated more times than any of them could count. When they finally left the Eastside, each man wished a happy day to their favorite waitress, who stood by the register, her thin arms crossed over her chest and a priceless expression of bemusement on her face. The group continued to talk for a while on the sidewalk outside the café, and then Mike walked with Gus back towards Gus's house. The two walked in silence during the handful of blocks as they passed office buildings, storefronts, and apartments until they approached his street with its few remaining two-family homes in this part of the city.

Mike Carbone served with Gus during the Korean War, had been the best man at his wedding, and worked with him for forty-five years at Dennis

Corporation, a manufacturer of jet-engine parts located in the South End. Mike was shorter and stockier than Gus and still had jet black hair despite being only a year younger. He stopped for a moment and put his hand on Gus's shoulder. "Gus, I'm glad you came this morning. I know it isn't an easy day for you. How are you doing?"

Gus's gaze remained fixed on the cracks in the cement sidewalk, and no words came in response.

Mike's voice choked as he uttered, "I miss her too." Mike was Julia's brother and a steadfast friend and brother-in-law to Gus. "I miss both of them."

Gus's eyes squeezed tight. He felt as if a bullet tore through his chest as his son's short seventeen years of life flashed before him. Mike was Danny's godfather and had spent many days with Gus and Danny remodeling the house, working on cars, fishing, or just sitting on the front porch on summer nights chatting and listening to the Red Sox on the radio. Mike was as close to his nephew and sister as an uncle and brother could be, so the pain of their absence was no stranger to him.

Continuing to walk, Gus was in no mood to talk about Julia or Danny, not now, not ever. Mike deserved some response, but once they were in sight of the front porch of the house where he had lived for so much of his life, a sudden rush of emotion overwhelmed him. A few months after Julia died, Gus moved to the smaller upstairs apartment of the Victorian and put the main part of the house up for rent. He had left the renting up to a friend who ran a local real estate agency, who quickly found him a tenant, a single mother, Celia, and her teenaged son, who remained tenants ever since— almost three years. The realtor told Gus that Celia had been actively looking to get her son out of the Lenox Street projects, and when she first learned of the chance to rent the light blue Victorian and its welcoming porch, she was brought to tears at the prospect of a healthier life and a better school for her son.

Celia couldn't have been a more hardworking and devoted mother, nor a more respectful and gracious neighbor. She kept the inside and outside of her home impeccable and seemed determined to connect with Gus, leaving him gifts of homemade bread, cards on the holidays, and thank-you notes.

She and her son had been dream tenants, which left him totally unprepared for what met his eyes as he rounded the corner of the house. Celia's son was on the front porch with a gang of six other black youths in their teens and early twenties wearing their hooded sweatshirts, baggy jeans hanging from their hips, flat-brimmed baseball hats, oversized shoes, and an attitude of nothing good.

Despite Celia including it in her many notes, Gus didn't even know the boy's name nor did he care to. He and this group of thugs represented everything that had taken his son's life and broken Julia's heart. Danny was only one victim among hundreds over the years, but the vast majority of the tragedies seemed to be caused by gangs like the ones now at his very own home. Gus turned with an expression that had apparently become familiar to Mike over the past seventeen years since Danny's death. That look had once been filled with rage but was now resigned to resentment and despondency. Gus's competitive, self-giving, and energetic personality had been buried with his family. Now he merely existed. With urgency in his voice, Gus said, "Mike, I gotta go. I'll see you some other time."

The day was already emotionally loaded, but Mike obviously knew that the sight of this crew on the porch where Gus shared so many moments with his family had pushed him over the edge and didn't argue with him. "Make sure you're taking care of yourself and let me know when you're ready to work on that roof."

Gus quickly disappeared around the back of the house without acknowledging the existence of the young men, nor did they seem to even notice him.

Once in his apartment, Gus quickly found paper and pen, and hastily wrote a note to his downstairs tenants.

Mrs. Russell,

If you can't get your son to keep those gangsters from hanging around on my porch like a brood of vipers, I'm going to have to ask you to think about renting elsewhere.

Busbi

Chapter 2

When Julia died, Gus could no longer live in his old downstairs rooms or sit on that porch, so he decided to rent the first floor out to a nice family at an affordable rate. Gus was well aware of the area Celia grew up in the Lenox Street apartments, historically the very first affordable Boston housing project blacks could move into. Lenox Street was also home to one of the oldest and most violent gangs in Boston, known as the Lenox Street Cardinals or sometimes the Lenox Street Boys. The gang terrorized the local shop owners and were involved mainly in trafficking drugs, robbery, and murder. Growing up in the seventies and eighties, Celia would have been surrounded by street gangs from the South End, Roxbury, Mattapan, and Dorchester, each protecting their turf. The local racial friction and gang violence permeated the air with a palpable tension that would have been Celia's childhood. Tensions were at their peak on hot summer Saturday nights when revenge shootings occurred, and neighbors would often wake up Sunday mornings to the sight of yellow crime scene tape.

Due to comprehensive neighborhood programs such as Operation Ceasefire put into place after a brutal stabbing during the wake of a gang member at the Morningstar Church, gangs and gang violence had noticeably subsided by the late nineties. But, as members of the programs moved on and gang members were released from prison, less organized gangs emerged, and the deadly turf battles erupted again.

Celia had sought an opportunity to get her son out of the projects and away from the local gang that was pressing him to join. The answer to those prayers came out of Gus's loss and suffering, and this fact was not lost on Gus. It appeared that Celia believed she was called somehow to help this man who had lost his son while she was carrying her own son, Jamiel. Gus knew his note likely threw her into a panic.

On Friday, when Gus opened the door to retrieve his morning paper, he found a white bag with its handles twisted around the outside doorknob. He looked at first with caution and then curiosity as he lifted the bag and ascended the back stairs, then placed the paper and the unexpected bag down on the kitchen table. He watched the bag as if it might move on its own while he poured his morning coffee and arranged his toast and eggs onto his plate. If Gus had a dog, he might have asked him, "What do you think could be in the bag, boy?" but he was alone and sat staring at the mystery package while he dipped the corner of his toast into the egg yolk. He took a sip of his coffee and peeked at the sports page to see if the Bruins had won against the Maple Leafs.

Finally, he tipped the bag, and two freshly-baked blueberry muffins and a folded paper slid onto the kitchen table. Lifting the note with two fingers, he unfolded it and recognized Celia's handwriting: *Mr. Busbi, I hope you like the muffins. I was wondering if you might be around to talk about something when I get home from work at 5:30? Leave a note if that doesn't work, otherwise, I'll drop by then. Thank you and have a good day. Celia.*

This was a response to the note he had left her. He was in no mood to hear any complaints or to talk to anyone about anything at the moment. He thought about leaving another note to say that it wasn't a good time for him but instead went for his usual walk, picked up a few groceries, and spent most of the day replacing a pressure valve on the boiler in his cellar. He was surprised when he climbed the stairs to his apartment to find that it was already 5:30 and saw Celia standing outside his door in the gray wool skirt and white blouse she had worn to work. "I hope this is a good time for you, Mr. Busbi?"

Gus grunted, "It's *Buzz-bee*," as he opened the door with his key. "I must've lost track of time working on the boiler. It's supposed to get a little nippy next week." Celia stared intently at Gus as they entered the kitchen, but he didn't look at her when he pulled out the old wooden chair from the table for her to sit. She didn't move to sit down. "Mr. Busbi, thank you for being willing to talk."

After three years of avoiding this moment, Gus peered down at Celia's face. She was probably in her mid-thirties, if she had become pregnant as a teenager like many girls from the projects, and was quite striking. One thing he knew, from his distant observations, was that Celia was a hard-working, dedicated, self-sacrificing single mother. Gus never saw any men come to the house, and there were times he heard Celia reading out loud to herself on the porch. She worked a full-time job at a local company that was a twenty-minute walk from the house and dedicated the rest of her time to raising her son, improving herself, and taking pride in how her new home looked inside and out. Gus didn't often take the time to think about his renters downstairs, but he had to admit that she impressed the hell out of him.

Gus shrugged.

Celia said, "I came to apologize for my son—well, I want Jamiel to come over to apologize and help you with some work you have around the yard as part of that apology."

Gus sighed. "Just tell Jamil to stop having those hoodlums hang out on that porch."

"It's *Jamiel*, Mr. Busbi. I've told him that already. They shouldn't have been here, never mind hanging around on your porch and making it look like a—well, I've told him to stop hanging around with those boys, and he didn't do that."

Gus hesitated. "I'm not sure apologizing to me is going to help him listen to his mother's rules. Shouldn't he be in school on a Thursday?"

Tears rolled from Celia's dark brown eyes as she dabbed them with the tips of her fingers. "It was a holy day at the St. Francis School, so he had the day off. I think it had something to do with Mary. I've just been so afraid of him getting involved with the gangs, and drugs, and such. I grew up in those neighborhoods, and it would—" She stopped a moment, taking a deep breath and putting her hand to her face to calm herself. "It has been an answer to a prayer to be able to move to your home and a new school, but I'm afraid he's being pulled in by a gang that will rob him of any chance he has for a better future."

Gus shook his head. "I can see why you're worried, but I don't know what this has to do with me. I don't know the boy and I don't think he's going to listen to some stranger about what friends he should have. Have the priest at the school talk with him."

Celia stared down at the wooden kitchen floor. "I thought he owed you more respect than the sight of those boys on the front porch of your home, and it just seemed like a chance for a man to teach him some responsibilities and skills. He hasn't had the father he needed and deserved. That's my—"

Gus grunted, "I'm not interested in filling in for his father. That's not my problem, and I don't think he's looking for some old guy like me to be one either. I can't help you, Mrs. Russell."

"It's Miss. And please, call me Celia. I'm sorry to burden you with all this. I really do apologize for what happened, and I've just been more than a little desperate lately thinking about Jamiel. I thought—oh, never mind.

Thank you for your time, and it won't happen again. Have a good night, Mr. Busbi."

He watched her from the open doorway as she stepped slowly down the dimly lit back stairs.

Gus quickly clamped down on the warring emotions of anger and empathy so that he could move to a safer place where he could keep his distance. Three years of living in the same house with the Russells, and he didn't know if he could even pick Jamiel out of a line-up of the gang members hanging out on his porch. Why would Celia want to solve her problem through him?

Despite going to bed early to put the day behind him, he couldn't manage to fall asleep. Until Danny died, he had never had a problem sleeping, but this was more of restless energy keeping him awake as compared to the deep emotional emptiness that he'd been haunted by for the past many years. The more he tried to shift his thoughts to other things, the less he was able to relax. Before he knew it, the rays of morning light made their way across his face without a wink of sleep.

Chapter 3

The slower Jamiel tried to open the door to the back stairs leading to Gus's apartment, the more the door hinges seemed to squeak. Climbing the steep staircase, he cautiously tried to find the spot on each step that creaked the least, but the nails in the old wood wouldn't cooperate as his heart pounded fiercely against his chest. The next step creaked even louder than the previous one. He froze in panic as he thought he heard the door at the top of the stairs opening, but it remained shut. Adrenaline rushed through his veins. Never in the three years that he had lived in the same house had Jamiel met Gus face to face, and, at this moment, he assumed the worst.

After what seemed like an eternity, he finally reached the top. There wasn't much of a stoop, so he stood one step down and knocked gently on the door, hoping that Gus was out early on this rainy Saturday morning. He almost fell backward as the door swung open, and Gus glared down at him from the opening. "What do you want?" Gus grumbled.

Jamiel had argued repeatedly with his mother since the previous afternoon about having to talk to Gus, but Celia was determined. He knew he couldn't win when he saw that look in her eyes.

Gus peered down, appearing perturbed and impatient.

"My mother—I mean, I wanted to say I'm sorry for using your porch the other day."

"You rent the apartment. It's your porch to use."

"Okay, but there were friends over that don't pay you rent."

"Those hoods are your friends?"

Jamiel shook his head and snapped, "So, just because they're black, you assume they're no good? Thugs, bangers, crack-dealing jacks!"

"And you're here to tell me they were over to discuss Chess Club strategy for your next meet?" Gus's arrow had hit a nerve.

Without a good retort, Jamiel turned and raced down the steps letting out a muffled, "Peckerwood," as he reached the bottom. He tried to walk off his frustration and his inability to follow through with his mother's instructions to stay respectful and sincere in his apology. He was supposed to offer to do some work for Gus around the house. In his gut, he knew that the gang was exactly what Gus thought, but he also knew them in ways that he thought Gus never would—as human beings trying to survive an impossible set of obstacles as young black men in neighborhoods they did not choose to be born into.

Jamiel knew his mother would ask about his discussion with Gus, which was one reason he didn't groan as he normally did when she woke him up for Sunday morning church services at the Hope Baptist Church located halfway between their old and new neighborhood. Even though it was unlikely he would see any of the guys from the old neighborhood on a Sunday morning, he still worried about running into them as he and his mother walked to the church he and his mom had attended since he was born. Attending church and building his faith was non-negotiable for his mother, but he finally convinced her to let him out of Wednesday evening Bible study classes.

The Hope Baptist Church was mainly a black congregation deeply devoted to Christ, family, and character. This was one of the few places where Jamiel was exposed to men who believed that manhood looked very different from the gang credo on the streets. These men were committed to their marriages, to being fathers to their children, and following Christ's example. Most men dressed in their best and often only suit, tie, and shined shoes to show respect and honor to God. Women wore dresses and hats to show that same example to their children.

As much as Jamiel felt it was time to stop attending church as so many of his peers had, once inside, something attracted him to the place. Here he felt community, humility, decency, and had his only exposure to male mentors and father figures that were absent in his daily experience. The man who made the deepest impression on Jamiel and many other parishioners was the pastor, Reverend Richard Obasi. Reverend Rich had not only built up a vibrant and active community within their church, but courageously involved himself in the streets, with the youth and families of the neighborhood to foster a healthier place to raise a family. He walked the streets, talking with black youths both in and outside of the gangs. He had become close to Jamiel over the years and was as concerned as his mother about the strong influences that may impact pivotal decisions Jamiel would make in the coming years.

As Jamiel and Celia approached the front entrance of the small, attractive stucco church, Reverend Rich smiled, greeting Jamiel with a handshake and Celia with an embrace. "Good as always to see you, Jamiel. How's your college search going?"

"I have to make sure I get through high school first, Reverend Rich, but I'll let you know if I can find a college we can afford." Jamiel always knew that his mother believed in him, but it felt different knowing that someone else cared and had confidence in him.

"The right college is going to be very lucky to have you."

Celia gave the minister a smile that Jamiel knew held the years of gratitude she had for his mentorship and example to her son. "Looking forward to your sermon as always, Reverend Rich, especially since it's Palm Sunday."

"If I hear that beautiful voice of yours singing, that will be inspiration enough to let the Holy Spirit guide my part. Take care of that good man with you." Celia nodded and returned a hesitant smile that seemed to communicate concern more than happiness.

His mom greeted the many supportive friends she had been blessed with in this place over the years. Jamiel thought about the contrast of the unadorned interior of the church compared to the Catholic church at St. Francis School. He had asked his mother about this, and she told him that a Baptist was more about a strong individual and decisive commitment to being a Christian, which was an emotional and unambiguous experience for many of the parishioners that Jamiel had yet to experience himself. What he experienced was a connection to his African heritage through the rhythm and cadence of the music, the strong sense of community and belonging, and the feeling that all aspects of life were part of a sacred way of looking at the world. Reverend Rich's sermons were heartfelt, sometimes emotional, and always connected to the struggles of everyday life. Today's sermon was about preparing for Holy Week and Easter Sunday.

After the service, there was a social gathering in the adjoining hall organized by the Fellowship Committee, of which Celia took an active part. As she busied herself with greeting parishioners and serving coffee and donuts, Jamiel stood against the wall observing the boisterous social scene in front of him. The church had no ethnic restrictions, but everyone at the service and in the hall was of color. When he was at church for these few hours a week, he didn't think about himself being black, but just another person in the hall. While he didn't want to get up early to go to church every Sunday morning, he did feel more relaxed and at home here than in a world where he was primarily defined by the color of his skin, "the black boy." He kept playing the scene over in his mind of Gus Busbi glaring down at him from the top of the stairs, judging his value as a human being because of the color of his skin, another worthless hood from the projects. He could feel the anger rise in him again, and now he knew why he had felt that way so intensely the day before.

Out of the corner of his eye, Jamiel caught Marnie walking over to him. He suddenly felt glad that he was wearing his suit and tie. For some reason, girls seemed to love it when guys were dressed up. Maybe it was because of how the boys in the neighborhood normally dressed? At seventeen, he stood six-foot-three, with an athletic build and a handsome face.

While Marnie hadn't talked to Jamiel very much, she seemed to assume that any son of Celia would have to be a good person, something that was apparently important to her. "Hi, Jamiel."

"Uh. Oh, hi, Marnie." Although she was a year younger, Marnie knew he was shy with girls and smiled at him as she seemingly studied his features more closely. He nervously smiled back, wondering what she was thinking.

"You go to that Francis School, right?"

"Yeah. It's St. Francis, but I wish I was still going to English and was around the neighborhood."

"Yeah, right, and waste your brain on people trying to drag you down. I think you should be glad you're getting a chance to do something with your talents."

"Talents? What are you talking about, girl?"

"You know what I'm talking about—boy. You're smart. You're athletic, and you got the character to be somebody—somebody good. Don't waste it hanging with that gang I've seen you with lately."

Jamiel couldn't believe how assertively this girl was talking to him. He hardly knew her, yet she was telling him what he should be doing with his life. Before he could respond, Celia waved him over to help in the kitchen. Jamiel turned back toward Marnie and just stared at her without being able to think of anything to respond with. He noticed how pretty she looked, waiting for his response with a turn of her head, but no words came as he pointed to the kitchen and left her standing there alone. When he glanced back, Marnie smiled and shook her head.

On the walk home, Jamiel was quiet as he thought over what Marnie had said to him. Did she actually think he was all those things she had said? Realizing his mother was talking, he finally caught the end of her question,

"—did it go with Mr. Busbi yesterday?"

"It was fine. Everything's all set."

"So, what chores did he ask you to help with?"

Jamiel was stuck. Why was it always on the way home from church that she asked him about things he'd prefer to lie about? "We didn't get that far."

Celia stopped in her tracks. "Jamiel. Exactly what do you mean, 'We didn't get that far'?"

Jamiel was uncomfortable, but she was clearly determined to have him follow through on this. "Mom, the conversation was short. I apologized, and he seemed like he didn't want to hear it."

"Hmmmmm."

Chapter 4

Gus had just sat down to his freshly made sandwich of turkey, bacon, lettuce, and tomato on toast, when he heard a tapping on the door. He wasn't expecting anyone, and few people came around to see him these days. He heard the tapping again and finally got up to open the door only to see Jamiel standing there again. Although his expression didn't show it, Gus chuckled inside. *She's a very determined woman.* "What names do you want to call me today?" replied Gus with a grunt.

"I didn't—" Jamiel pressed his lips together and took a deep breath, "Mr. Busbi, I came by to apologize for the gang on the porch and for how I talked to you yesterday. I'm sorry and would like to do some work to make up for it." It wasn't until the last word that he lifted his eyes to glance up at Gus, who wouldn't give Jamiel much of a read on what he was thinking.

With Jamiel standing one step down, they both stood there with Gus looming over him for what seemed like several minutes in awkward silence. Jamiel appeared nervous until Gus finally responded, "Tell your mother that I'm not interested in babysitting a boy I don't care a lick about."

Rage and shame flooded Jamiel as his mind filled with comments to fire back. It took every ounce of energy to resist the knee-jerk temptation to let them all out. He glared back at Gus with a look of ire that seemed to leave Gus speechless. Jamiel turned and scurried down the stairs and onto the street. His whole being felt as if it had been stomped on, torn apart, and tossed into the gutter with no recognition of value. To Gus, Jamiel was no better than street trash, not worth taking the time to dispose of in a barrel. Why would his mother want to humiliate him with this hateful turd of a man?

Without thinking, he started walking and then running through the streets until he found himself back on the outskirts of his old neighborhood, the narrow confines where he had spent the first fourteen years of his young life. There were 376 apartments in the three-story brick buildings known as the Lenox Street projects. When Jamiel was born, Celia was only eighteen and dropped out of high school to take care of him, while living with her mother and brothers. Jamiel grew up only knowing these few streets around this area of Lower Roxbury, known as the South End. No matter how many times his mother had told him otherwise, growing up every day with the gangs, crime and violence, made it seem normal. When he was very young, he didn't connect the gunshots at night to the police interviews the following day. It was only when he was older that he understood, and he would hear the stories from the other boys as they hung out on benches at Ramsay Park or on porches of abandoned houses in the area.

Even though Jamiel and Celia had moved out of the projects three years ago, Jamiel continued to spend time with the boys he grew up with, playing basketball at the park or just hanging out on the corner. Daytime felt safer for those who were trying to live their lives and do the right thing, while the nighttime darkness provided a protective cover for the small minority of neighbors who committed most of the crimes in the area.

As Jamiel turned the corner off Mass Avenue and onto Tremont, he could see Lenox Street a few blocks up and wondered if he should turn around. Sweat ran down his back and forehead as he slowed down to a walk and took a left on Lenox. He spotted a group of fourteen or so boys congregated on the steps of one of the buildings, listening to one of the guys telling a story, as much with his body as with his words.

As Jamiel approached the group, he heard one say, "Jam, what's up, man?"

Then the ragging started, "What's you doin'—slummin' it?"

"Did they let you out of church for good behavior or did you break out early?"

"I think they flew him in for the game."

One of the guys, who looked a little older than the others, stood up to stop the barrage of comments, put his arm around Jamiel's shoulder, and patted him on the cheek. "How you doin', brother. Haven't seen you in a bit. Everythin' good?"

Jamiel nodded, "Everything's copacetic, Cool."

"Glad to hear you're keepin' up with your college vocab."

Cool was born Leonard James Morris. The nickname "LJ" had morphed into "Cool" after the rapper LL Cool J, and that is what most people called him. "Cool" was his protective persona to shield the real Leonard from the world. With no work and no hope, his father had left home too early for Leonard to remember what he even looked like. His mother tried to keep things going, but the drugs she'd leaned on to cope led to a heroin addiction that ended her life when he was only fifteen and his younger brother was thirteen. After living in a series of foster homes, Leonard decided it was time to take life into his own hands, living in abandoned buildings or staying at friends' houses when it got too cold out. He became a member of the Lenox Street Cardinals gang and quickly moved himself up in the ranks. He gained "street cred" early on by showing no fear with rival gang members and pulling in serious dough from robbing homes, businesses, and wealthy pedestrian opportunities. For a time, he and his brother had staked out bank ATMs near alleyways, allowing him to come out of nowhere when his brother gave him the high sign as the person making a withdrawal passed by. At an average of two-hundred dollars a pop, they could pull in four to five thousand in a night, moving from ATM to ATM to avoid the police.

In the beginning, this had been all about survival and taking care of his younger brother Ricky, but as time passed, everything became about respect and building a protective layer around the turf Leonard now ruled. The old gang leaders had either gone to jail or been killed, and this left openings for someone with Leonard's fearlessness and willingness to lead with others happy to follow. Leonard was four years older than Jamiel and had always treated him like a brother. He leaned in as he cupped the back of Jamiel's neck with his hand and asked in a quiet voice, "You stayin' clean and hittin' them books?" With half a smile, Jamiel nodded as he peered into Leonard's eyes, past the often intimidating glare, black do-rag, and heavy gold chain that rested on his chest.

While black teens in the neighborhood were pressured into joining local gangs, ballers and rappers with talent were given a pass on getting involved with criminal activity. "Ballers" were neighborhood kids that played basketball, and Jamiel was one of the more exceptional players Lenox Street had produced. Kids that tried to stay clean and take school seriously were often given a hard time and socially ostracized. Leonard made it known that he didn't want Jamiel to fall into that trap because he knew how intelligent he was, and Jamiel always appreciated Leonard having his back. He was also aware that Leonard was probably gifted intellectually despite the rough exterior he projected.

For most of these boys, the gang was their extended or only family, a community where they belonged and felt wanted. There was a strength in the group, and any member would risk their own life for another. Jamiel knew he was fortunate to have other outlets and people who cared for him.

His mother sacrificed her life for him every day, something he often took for granted. Despite his desire to stay in bed on a Sunday morning, the church was a community where he felt wanted and supported, especially by Reverend Rich. St. Francis High School was another place where he was accepted, encouraged, and supported. Jamiel was lucky to have these people who loved and cared about him, but something was missing that drew him to these boys he grew up with—a different type of bond, black male comradery, and a sense of identity that he didn't find in those other places. There was also the intensity of living on the edge that gave him an adrenaline rush and somehow tapped into the anger he felt about the injustices of a society that created ghettos like this—and men like Gus.

Jamiel stood for over two hours listening to the usual stories of what had been going on in the neighborhood, issues with rival gangs, and general bragging and ragging on each other for laughs. Most of the conversation was about the drive-by shooting that took out the front window of Fish's living room. Marlin "Fish" Jackson was Leonard's top lieutenant, and this was clearly a warning shot for the recent Lenox Street gang retaliation. The Grant Manor gang had renewed efforts to expand their drug operations to the Ramsay Park area, and this was Lenox Street turf. A few of the gang members were spotted in the area and roughed up by some of Leonard's boys. The rivalry between the two gangs had heated up, and hatred was intense. One thing that wouldn't be discussed out in the open were specific plans for break-ins, drug dealings, or retribution for rival players. Leonard ran a tight ship from the business side of the gang and also tried to run things in as organized and professional a way as possible. He didn't want emotions driving how to best deal with Grant Manor, especially since they were only two blocks away.

After the congregation started to break up, Leonard walked with Jamiel down to Ramsay Park to see how the courts were looking now that the warmer weather was close.

"Jam. How's that team of yours at Francis goin' to look next year? I mean, you've got God on your side, and you still ain't won that title?"

"I think we're coming together, but I'd rather be playing for English."

"Damn. They would've been a shoo-in for States with your talent on that team."

Jamiel smiled with raised eyebrows.

Leonard asked, "What you doing hangin' around here on a Sunday after what happened last night?"

"Cool, man, I hadn't even heard about it. What're you planning to do about it?"

"Nothin' you need to worry about. We don't need another 'Bloody April' this year too." Jamiel could tell that Leonard was bothered by the current situation. "We've got turf battles brewing all over, and things are getting damn chaotic with the new gangs of younger kids ready to pull the trigger for the smallest crap. Used to be certain guys that were shooters. Now, every jack thinks he's a banger with a gun. Nobody knows how to fight anymore! We got Lats, Asian, Somali, Jams, and CVs complicating this whole thing. It was more black and white when it was just us and the Irish."

Leonard stopped, glanced up, and smiled at Jamiel. "Stay in school, boy. It's a white man's world out there, and it's stacked against the brothers. The system's rigged, and they're goin' to fight for their turf, just like we do. You've gotta fight ten times as hard against those cracker-assed rednecks just to keep from falling further behind."

Jamiel took a deep breath as he checked out the courts he had been playing on all his life. "I don't know, Cool. I just don't know if I want to play their game. It gets me pissed just to think about it. I get crap from my landlord, and I'd take him out—if he wasn't so old."

Leonard laughed. "I can see you doing a double-six for an aggravated beat-down of some chalk-white senior ciz and becoming the girlfriend of some ugly prison wolf. I needed that laugh today. Go home and think about that the next time you pay your landlord the rent."

Jamiel walked home and thought about what Leonard had said. He definitely didn't want to do any time. He also knew that Leonard was no one to ignore. He demanded respect and had killed more than one person who crossed the line and tried to challenge him. Jamiel didn't know how many businesses and homes he had robbed, drugs he had sold, or acts of violence he had committed over the years, but he suddenly realized he should be more concerned about the conversation he was going to have with his mother when he got home.

Chapter 5

Jamiel spotted Celia breathing a sigh of relief as she sat waiting on the front porch. However, the expression he saw on his mother's face, as she tilted her head, was unmistakably one that was also looking for an explanation. What happened with Mr. Busbi, and where had he been for the last three hours?

Jamiel sat down next to her, and they were both quiet for several minutes, watching a few cars pass by, a jogger, and then a woman walking two mastiffs that seemed curious about how long her arms could stretch. The sight broke the silence as it made them laugh, and Celia placed her hand on his. "Sooooo?"

"I can't do it, Mom. I tried. He is one hard old crusty bugger."

"Sometimes, there's more to the eye than those protective prickles people let us see."

"Prickles? It's more like machine gunfire. He wants no part of us. That's pretty clear."

"I think you're right."

Jamiel felt his own sigh of relief until she followed up with, "I noticed some loose pickets in the fence next to the driveway. Why don't you see if you can't straighten them out and nail them back in?"

Groaning inwardly, Jamiel closed his eyes. "Can I grab something to eat first?"

"I'll have a great snack ready for you afterward. You know where the toolbox is."

He reluctantly got the hammer and some nails and walked over to the section of the fence where the pickets had become knocked loose. He started repositioning the first picket and pulling out the loosed nail, thinking to himself, *Why can't the neighbor's kids who knocked these out fix these? She's always talking about taking personal responsibility and not waiting for others to solve your problems.*

As he worked to nail the first picket back into position, he spotted Gus staring down at him from the upstairs window. Only seconds had passed before Jamiel felt a presence behind him. "What do you think you're doing to my fence?" Gus demanded gruffly.

"It looks like I'm fixing it. How'm I doing, Mr. Busbi?"

"If I want your help around here, I'll ask for it. I like things done right, and I doubt you're going to make that happen."

Jamiel was shaking inside because he didn't know this man well enough to figure out what he would do, but he also thought back to what Leonard said about "fighting ten times as hard" to win. Jamiel slowly got up from his crouching position with his hammer held firmly in his right hand. He thought about responding with a sarcastic, "I guess if you want something done right, you gotta do it yourself, right, Mr. Handyman," but instead raised his eyebrows and said, "Maybe you could teach me the way you want it done?"

"Look, just leave the fence, and please leave me alone. I just want to be alone."

As Gus walked to the back door and up to his apartment, Jamiel thought about Gus from a different perspective. Jamiel was not alone. He was fortunate to have never been alone, but he understood the feeling of isolation and loneliness. He'd felt alone in many places in his life because he didn't feel as if he fit in. Plenty of the kids he grew up with had no father in their lives, but he often felt as if he were the only one when he saw other families together. He had never been told who his father was, what he looked like, or if he was even alive. Part of him felt as if he belonged at school, at his church, and even with the gang from the old neighborhood, but most of him felt as if he didn't completely fit anywhere in his life. As he glanced at the old backboard and hoop over the garage door, it hit him that playing basketball was where he felt he could just be himself. For the moment, this made him forget about Gus as he walked back into his house and up to his room that, nowadays, seemed more like a prison than a sanctuary.

Jamiel didn't have dinner that night and woke up in the morning feeling restless about everything in his life. When he finally came downstairs and said he wasn't hungry, Celia must have known something was wrong.

"Jamiel, I can't remember you skipping one meal, never mind two in a row. What's goin' on?"

"Nothin's goin' on," he mumbled with an attitude.

"Well, somethin's goin' on here, and I don't know if I like it—but I'm more worried than upset. What's been on your mind, Mr. Russell? You're usually full of energy and talk more than any boy I've ever known."

"I dunno. It's nothing."

"Can you look me in the eye and tell me there is really nothin' goin' on in that wonderful brain of yours?"

Jamiel had lost his patience. "Can we just drop this?"

Jamiel could tell by her furrowed brow, that she was concerned. When a mom is worried and doesn't know what's going on, she starts imagining the worst possibilities.

"I'm sorry, Mom. I just don't know what's goin' on. I don't know where I'm goin'. I don't even know who I am."

Celia reached up and put her arm around her son's shoulders. He knew she had worked to make sure he had good men in his life—ministers and teachers, but that wasn't the same as spending time practicing a sport in the backyard, repairing the faucet in the kitchen together, or asking a hundred questions at bedtime. Once, he had overheard her tell another woman at church that the shame she felt when she got pregnant was nothing compared to the pain of knowing her son wouldn't have the father he deserved and needed. She knew she'd love him with everything she had, but there would always be something important missing, and that was her fault, not his, and he would have to pay for it his whole life. He never forgot those words.

"You've had all these hopes and dreams."

"Mom. Who'm I kiddin'? I'm never gonna be a big-time ballplayer. We can't afford school, and where would it lead me anyway? Maybe, if I'm lucky, I can work for some curmudgeonly old cracker like Busbi, who will always look down on me and treat me like dirt. I don't feel like there's any place I belong, now or ever."

His mom stood, open-mouthed, appearing not to know what to say in the minutes she had before work. "I can't imagine that any of that is feeling too good. Is there anything I can do?"

"Why have you never talked about my father?"

All of a sudden, the previous comments must have seemed like a soft-serve compared to this curveball Jamiel was asking about. Her eyes widened with a look of terror. It took several moments before she said, "You haven't really asked about him in a long time."

"I keep rememberin' you changin' the topic when I asked as a kid, and then I started believin' that I never had a father. I don't know anything about him or if he's even alive. Do you even know where he is?"

He deserved to know and she wasn't one to lie, but she didn't respond. She breathed in deeply, trying to hold back the tears but to no avail as the drops rolled down her cheeks. Jamiel would normally be moved to comfort her when anything difficult came up. They had comforted each other for seventeen years, but today it only frustrated him more. He marched up the stairs, two at a time and took a long shower to avoid saying goodbye to her before she left for work. Celia knocked on the door to let him know she was leaving but received no reply.

He stepped out of the shower and dried his hair as the steam on the mirror began to disappear. Jamiel stood and looked at himself, not as he usually did, but as the world saw him – not as a promising young man with no limits on achieving any dream he had, but as a black teen to be wary of. How many people had he walked behind who worried until he passed them on the sidewalk? How many policemen gave him a second glance to see if he might be a thief, drug dealer, or gang banger? How often had spectators seen him play basketball and thought his athletic talent would be his only way to get into college? How many negative stereotypes had passed at lightning speed through the minds of the people he passed every day? Up until this moment, he saw himself as his mother's son in that mirror, but now he saw a stranger he didn't know. He didn't know his father. He didn't know his heritage or what country his family came from. Who *was* he?

Chapter 6

The Monday morning routine of dressing for school seemed like the last thing Jamiel wanted to do. Instead of his blue dress shirt, khaki pants, and cordovan penny loafers, he put on a pair of baggy jeans and his Nike basketball sneakers. He slipped on a black hooded sweatshirt over his tee-shirt and grabbed an apple as he headed in the opposite direction of St. Francis High. He was still feeling a mix of discontent and heightened energy he needed to walk off as he strode toward the streets of his old neighborhood and spotted two of the guys from the Cardinals. "What's up, Trig?" he said as he clasped his hand and pulled him into his chest. "How you doin', Bronx?" Bronx did not like physical contact with other men.

Trig replied, "Doin' all right, man."

Bronx asked, "What's you doin' around here on a school day, Jam?"

Jamiel responded, "Didn't feel like goin' today. Weather's getting better for some games at Ramsay."

Trig was a good ballplayer. Not at the level of Jamiel, but he enjoyed playing and was more physical with his game. Jamiel had originally assumed his nickname was short for "trigger" because he liked to shoot during the game, but found out years later that it had more to do with being the main gunman for Leonard's crew. "Hope to be seein' a lot of your game this summer. You here to see anyone?"

Jamiel replied, "Nope. Just in the neighborhood."

Trig hesitated. "I probably shouldn't be askin' our star player this, but we're short a lookout today. Lenny B got detained last night for a parole violation and needs to stay low. You doin' anything?"

Normally, Jamiel's instinct would've been to say that he wasn't interested, but instead, he said, "What's goin' down? What do ya need?"

"No risk. Easy stuff, but important. We have a few apartments to do some house cleaning in and need some eyes on the outside. Just a few hours, and if you see anything, you only need to text and walk."

Jamiel knew this wasn't where he should be. While the big money for the gang was working the drugs, there was good money in robbing the right houses when people were out at work. Some of the younger members would stake out neighborhoods and watch for which homes had well-to-do owners who were definitely both working. No animals. No complicated security. And easy access through a back window or door lock to pick. At the right time, they would block traffic on that street with a phony stalled car problem for the few minutes it took them to get in, and then again when they left with the take. Trig, Bronx, and Halfway wore moving-men type of uniforms and had carrying bags to fill and load into the car once the coast was clear. It was typically Lenny B's job to let them know when they had a clear window to move quickly in and then out of the apartment, and then they would repeat the process in another staked-out neighborhood. They'd only keep the cash and quickly move all valuables through a fence and out of their hands. It was Lenny B's job they were asking Jamiel to fill in on this morning.

Jamiel knew the right answer, but he said, "We've known each other forever. If you need me, I'm there. I trust you." His heart pounded, and if he put his hand on his chest, he could feel it pulsing, but he worked to act cool on the outside.

Trig smiled. "We need ya, man." A white Lincoln approached. "Here's Halfway and Mal with the wheels."

On the way, Trig went over and over the instructions with the team. Every street and every apartment was different, and Trig was one to do his homework as thoroughly as any professional sports team would when scouting and preparing for an opponent. Before they let Jamiel out to walk the few blocks to the first target, Trig put his hand on his shoulder, looked him in the eye, and repeated his specific instructions, "Don't look suspicious, but don't look anyone straight in the eye, either. Don't panic if you see the Five-o drivin' by. That's all their doin' is drivin' by. When Mal gives you the high sign that the street is blocked, just text; '*Movie tonight?*' If there's a problem, and we need to clear out, text '*Ben's coming,*' and when Mal blocks the street for a get-a-way time, '*or Hoops?*' Got it? Should be simple if you stay cool—just like taking those jumpers, cool as ice."

Jamiel didn't feel as "cool as ice" as he walked the two blocks to his lookout station outside a small coffee shop where he was supposed to act as if he were taking a phone call. Then he noticed Trig, Bronx, and Halfway heading down the street with a two-wheeler, looking like a professional moving crew. Trig had tested the front door lock on the apartment, and they went in within seconds, acting as if they belonged there. Leonard would always say to his crew, "Act like you know what you are doing, and people will assume that you do." And Trig was a trusted soldier.

Traffic moved along as Mal restarted his "stalled" car and then made a loop around the block that was timed with what Trig allotted for cleaning out the valuables from the target. Jamiel stayed on the phone for the ten minutes it took for Mal to circle the block and then "stall out" again up the street. He nervously punched the keys with his forefinger, "*or Hopps*," and clicked send before he noticed the typo. Before he could decide if he should send a correction, Mal drove by, giving him a salute sign. He pulled in front of the apartment as Halfway, Bronx, and Trig calmly walked out with bags full, loaded the car, and got in, and then slowly pulled away as if he was on a Sunday drive.

Jamiel was impressed with how smoothly they operated and clocked everything out. He immediately crossed over the two blocks as Trig had instructed him, and the white Lincoln was pulling over to pick him up, well away from the crime scene. Trig smiled as Jamiel slid into the back seat. "I told you. No risk if you keep ya cool. Good job, man."

The next job went just as smoothly, and before lunchtime, they were back on Lenox Street while Mal changed license plates and dropped off the stolen car from the morning's chauffeuring. Jamiel was still trying to come down from the adrenaline rush as they sat on the same steps they had the previous day, acting as if nothing had happened. A police cruiser drove by, slowing down as they usually did when passing by one of the multiple gangs in the neighborhoods. Jamiel tried hard not to look up but felt only guilt as he caught the eye of the cop staring back at him. He wondered if they already knew about the robberies. As they drove off, the sense of relief increased the further away they got before disappearing. Trig surprised him as he stuffed a roll of bills into Jamiel's sweatshirt pocket.

"What's this?" said Jamiel as he pulled out a large roll of the twenties. "I don't need this, Trig."

Trig pushed the roll back into Jamiel's pocket, "Don't go flashing that around. The watch is a critical part of the operation. You earned Lenny B's share. Five-hundred large."

"What? I stood outside a coffee shop."

"Keep it and buy some new kicks or show your lady a good time." Trig didn't give Jamiel his share out of the goodness of his heart. This made him vested in the crime and would keep him from talking about it. The cops were bearing down on the local neighborhoods lately with the rise in shootings between gangs. Some of the members of Grant Manor, in particular, hated the Lenox Street gang and believed killing them off was the only solution. The Lenox Street Cardinals had allies in the Orchard Park, Holmes, and Heath Street gangs but were fierce rivals with H-Block, Franklin Hill, Greenwood Street Posse, and the Columbia Point Dawgs from Dorchester, who gunned down three Cardinals in 1991. It was a challenging balancing act to maintain a low profile while keeping the business going and not showing any signs of weakness to rival gangs.

Jamiel hung out until school would typically let out and then made his way back home. He hadn't skipped school before and hadn't planned on it. He certainly hadn't planned on being involved in robbing people's houses either. He was pretty sure he had gotten away with the worst offense but needed a story to cover for missing school. The two hours he thought he was going to have to come up with that story evaporated into thin air when he saw a man dressed in black sitting on his front porch as he approached his home. He peered up at the sky. *You're not going to give me a break, are you?*

Sitting on the steps of his porch was Father Tom Fitzpatrick, the headmaster of St. Francis School and a Catholic priest. Father Tom was a few inches shorter than Jamiel's six-three height, in great physical shape, and about forty years old. The girls at school thought he was handsome. He took the time to know all the students attending his school, but Jamiel had more of an opportunity to know him personally since he also coached the basketball team. Jamiel respected Father Tom as a coach, but more so as a man. Father Tom returned that respect to Jamiel with his trust and how he treated him with the dignity he only experienced from two other people in his life: his mother and Reverend Rich.

"Good to know our students are so excited about Easter coming that they start celebrating on Monday." He turned to Jamiel, who was now on the porch, smiled, and made a welcoming gesture with his head towards the seat next to him. Jamiel took one long step, turned, and sunk onto the porch chair next to Father Tom. They sat in silence for several moments, something which oddly made Jamiel feel more at peace. He also knew that Father Tom sincerely had his best interests at heart, no matter what the situation.

"Sorry I missed classes today."

"How've you been? I haven't had a chance to talk with you as much since the basketball season ended."

Jamiel didn't know what to say. "Everything's fine and dandy."

"Anything you'd like to talk about?"

A barrage of responses came to mind as Jamiel knew he needed to talk to someone outside of his own head, but he simply replied, "Nothin' I can think of, Father Tom."

"Jamiel, if someone took your basketball and you confronted them, and they said, 'I'm sorry,' would everything be settled?"

"He can't just say, 'I'm sorry.' He's gotta give the ball back too. Why?"

"You skipped school today, and you said you're sorry. That's important but, like you said, it wouldn't be enough to bring justice to the offense."

Jamiel knew that Father Tom must have had some punishment in mind, but he also knew that he'd prefer any punishment if it meant that his mother wouldn't have to know. "Okay, I see your point. How many hours on the rack do I get for this?"

"You're already taller than me, so no stretching on the rack for you. I've got two things in mind."

"Two? Only if you promise to keep this one-and-only time I have ever skipped between us."

"You mean, no mom, right?"

"I'd really appreciate it. She'd freak out and start worrying."

"I promise, if—if, it's indeed the 'one-and-only' time."

"Thanks. What do I have to do to satisfy the judge?"

"Trust me, I'm not your judge, but I do care about you. For the first thing, let's take a walk to school."

As they ambled down the street towards St. Francis, Jamiel grumbled, "It doesn't seem fair to hafta go to school the same day you're gettin' punished for skipping school."

Father Tom smiled as he patted Jamiel on the back, matching Jamiel's long strides until they reached the front of St. Francis Church. The brick structure, with its steeple reaching up to the heavens, was a beautiful building, but to Jamiel, it was just a Catholic church and very different from the much plainer Baptist church he grew up in. They walked down the driveway between the church and the rectory where Father Tom resided. Jamiel expected they'd be going to Father Tom's office to have a long talk, but instead, Father Tom asked Jamiel to wait outside for a few minutes, after which he emerged wearing a tee-shirt, a black pair of sweatpants, and his basketball shoes.

They proceeded down the driveway to the school entrance, where Sister

Helen stood guard as students were leaving to get rides from their waiting parents. Sister Helen stood nearly five feet in her gray habit and veil that covered some of her black hair. A strong hint of her Irish brogue came through as she said, "Well, isn't it a fine sight to see Mr. Russell finally making it to school today."

Father Tom smiled. "I'm sure Jamiel will be missing a few days as he starts visiting colleges."

Sister Helen glanced at Father Tom. "And I'm sure he will let us know when he actually starts those visits, won't he now?"

The priest and Jamiel walked down the hall and into the real cathedral and sacred space at the school, the basketball court. Tom pulled out one of the basketballs from the netted bag and handed it to Jamiel. "Your first punishment is to play me until you win a game."

Father Tom was in good shape for someone twenty-three years older, and he knew his basketball, but Jamiel had never played an actual game against him. He felt pretty confident he could win fairly easily and handed the ball back to Father Tom at the top-of-the-key, saying, "Age before looks and talent."

Tom took the ball from Jamiel and immediately sank the long jumper, getting Jamiel's attention. He faked the next shot and drove around Jamiel, who was caught in the air trying to block the original shot, and scored an easy layup to lead 2–0. He narrowly missed his next fall-away jumper, and Jamiel scooped up the rebound with authority. Jamiel dribbled to the key and tried to use his youth and quickness to drive by his opponent and dunk the ball, but Tom poked it from behind, retrieved the loose ball, and immediately scored on a jumper. Jamiel was starting to feel both surprised and frustrated that he couldn't take command of the game as he so often did at the park. He did manage to score on some pretty plays and played more aggressively on defense, but Tom hit the final shot and won the first game convincingly by an 11–4 score.

Tom won the second game by a score of 11–6, and Jamiel finally prevailed in the final game after an intense back-and-forth battle, 17–15. Tom shook Jamiel's hand to congratulate him on the victory, and they both collapsed to the ground, sitting with their backs to the wall and beads of sweat pouring down their foreheads. In between deep breaths, Tom managed to say, "I was hoping you were going to hit that last shot."

"So was I. I think I've learned my lesson," answered Jamiel as he wiped the salty sweat from his eyes with the sleeve of his tee-shirt.

"Oh, yeah? You may have learned your lesson, but a day of school is too valuable to be paid back that easily."

"That wasn't so easy, old man."

"Well, I want you to help out Angelo with a repair project on the back of the rectory. Some of the work will be high on a ladder, and we need a volunteer," Tom said with a smirk.

Jamiel mumbled, "Volunteer, huh?"

When they finally stood up and walked to the doorway of the court, Tom stopped and stared at Jamiel. "Would you be interested in working on some of your moves in this off-season? You have the talent and potential to play at a higher level."

Jamiel lifted his head as he heard the word potential. He had become one of the best players at the local courts and in the high school league.

Tom added, "That's not a compliment that I've been able to give to many players. You've got more upside than you may know— and I don't just mean as a basketball player."

"Sure. Maybe there are a few things I could pick up with some one-on-one."

Tom put the basketball back in the bag with the rest of the balls. "My mom used to say, 'The more you know, the more you know you don't know—and the less you know, the more you think you know.'"

"What?"

Tom patted Jamiel on his shoulder, "Think about it on the way home. Oh, let's plan on working with Angelo on Monday morning after Easter."

Jamiel's head popped up. "That's vacation week!"

Tom smiled broadly. "Great, that should give you a lot of daylight to help out."

Jamiel mumbled something under his breath as he headed down the driveway and then home, where he showered and dressed before Celia returned home after a long day of work.

"I'm home, Jamiel. How was school today?"

"It was good. Father Tom wanted me to stay late to work on some basketball skills, and he asked me to help out with a project next week."

Jamiel's mom would be happy with him spending more time with the people she trusted and admired. Much better than hanging around with the gang from the old neighborhood. Celia motioned Jamiel to bend down, and she kissed him on the cheek before heading into the kitchen to prepare dinner. As he thought about everything that happened during the day, he felt happy and relieved that he made it through without being arrested and without having to explain himself to a worried and disappointed mother.

Chapter 7

After school the next day, Jamiel found two of his old friends on his front stoop dressed for basketball. It was unexpectedly warm for a late March afternoon, and they were itching to play full-court games at Ramsay Park. It wasn't hard to convince Jamiel, who was in and out of the house, changed, and ready to play in less than a minute. As they started down the street, Jamiel glanced up and saw Gus peering down at the three of them with a condescending stare and a hateful scowl.

The park was just around the corner from the Lenox Street project, and there was a four-on-four game going on with onlookers comprised of neighborhood gang members, hustlers, and dealers ready for a diversion. Some young boys also watched earnestly, determined to learn how to emulate these admired players and how to be men. Jamiel and the other players were met with high fives and chest bumps as they picked sides for the first outside full-court games of the new season – for many of the players, this was their sanctuary and relief from the often-hopeless and confined world they lived in.

The game started aggressively, with two quick passes and then a hard drive to the basket for an acrobatic shot by the other team. Jamiel felt alive and free as he moved smoothly down the court. He could play with anyone. Each play that elicited a response of excitement and affirmation from the crowd made him forget about all those moments, the hugs and encouragement he longed for and needed from his absent father. He felt a sense of worth and value that he didn't experience in the world outside of his house. For most young men from the neighborhood, basketball represented one of the only paths of hope out of the ghetto prison they had felt unfairly sentenced to from birth.

The games were exciting because of the energy from the motley crowd watching and because they played as if their very value and lives depended on winning that game. For Jamiel, it was partly subconscious, but he had watched enough documentaries on TV to know that the poverty level for blacks was double the rate for whites. Many didn't complete high school, and few went on to college. The majority had no fathers at home, and crime rates were the highest of any ethnic group in the city. Blacks moving up from the South in the seventies were funneled into places such as Roxbury, Mattapan, and Dorchester, where there seemed to be few opportunities for young blacks to escape the projects, never mind survive. There were few employment opportunities, and the hopelessness they experienced from others didn't support a developing sense of worth, purpose, or direction. There was little support for students, who were often socially ostracized, and many turned to the gangs for a sense of belonging and crime as a means of making money. The only other opportunities that presented a narrow ray of hope were through rap and other pop music, or through basketball. Basketball wasn't only a way to be somebody if you were talented, but the chance to go to a better high school in the city, possibly an opportunity for a scholarship to get into and pay for college, and if you dreamed big enough, the hope of playing pro-ball.

Many of the players on the court were streetwise young men that had to hide their authentic emotions behind the protective cover of tough black masculinity, distrusting everyone, especially if they were white. On the court, Jamiel and these young men experienced a sense of freedom to let their emotions out and express themselves through their personal style of play. Jamiel was younger than the other players but had their respect because of his ability to play the game and to keep his cool when a big shot was needed. The ring of observers erupted with a roar when Jamiel hit the final shot from downtown to win the first match.

"Great shot, Jam! King of the Asphalt."

"The kid is always 'money' on those shots. Like ice."

They played for several hours, games got sloppy as players tired, and some stopped passing and started to hot dog it more. Leonard had shown up during the earlier games and was discussing business with his top guys. Earlier that day, some of the gang members from Grant Manor had fired shots at some Lenox Street members as they drove down Columbia Road while making a cocaine pick up.

When Jamiel finished playing his last game, he made his way over to where Leonard was standing and gave him a nod. Leonard smiled and patted him on the back. "Keep this up and we're goin' to be sittin' in front row seats at the Garden to watch you play for the Celts."

Jamiel lowered his head. "Let's see if I can do some damage in the States this year first. Is everything okay? You looked like you were havin' an intense meeting over here."

"Nothin' you have to worry about, Jam. You just focus on ballin' and stay clean."

Halfway jumped in, "Jam was a big hel—"

Trig thumped Halfway's chest with his forearm and interrupted, "Jam was big in the paint today."

The exchange didn't go unnoticed by Leonard, but he let it go for the time being. "He was NBA today. Great playin', man. I bet you can almost forget what's goin' on in the world when you're playin' like that."

Jamiel was well aware of the opportunities he might have that Leonard would never feel he had. "Sometimes, just for a moment."

Leonard said, "Enjoy the moment whenever you can get it. Remember, you gotta be tough and be ready to fight. We're livin' in a prison here, and we've got to stick together. It's bad enough that we have to fight with the brothers just a street or two over because we're forced to live off of the white man's scraps like rats crammed into a garbage bucket. Schools suck, no jobs, cops breathin' down our necks, and packed in like sardines in these sixty-year-old projects. All this after being kidnapped, hauled over in the belly of a boat, and thrown into the fields like animals to make redneck crackers rich. 'I'm sorry, nigga. Why don't you move up to the ghetto projects in the north and freeze your ass off while we keep livin' the American dream?!'"

Jamiel hadn't seen Leonard this worked up in a while and didn't know how to respond. It also brought back the anger and resentment he had felt just a few days earlier.

Trig responded, "Cool's right. We've got to stick together and keep fightin'. No givin' up and no selling the Cardinals out."

The large and usually quiet Bronx said, "Gotta keep it real, man. Keep it real."

Jamiel was on such a high after playing the game he loved on the courts he grew up on, but now he was brought back to reality with a million thoughts racing through his head on his walk home.

A police cruiser slowed down to a crawl next to the sidewalk. He recognized the white cop, Officer Mullen, who was in his forties and too overweight to be chasing anyone down in these neighborhoods, but he didn't know the black cop sitting on the passenger side. Jamiel worked to stay cool while he felt the tingles of anxiety and nervousness riding up his chest. *What're they pulling me over for? 'Walking while black?' I don't ever see them doing this to white kids that are just walking along.* He turned to the cruiser that had now stopped.

Seconds ticked by like an eternity before the black cop leaned over with his coffee in hand to peer directly into Jamiel's eyes. "You just playin' ball at Ramsay?"

He thought, *What business is it of yours where I play ball?* but answered, "Yeah."

"I thought that was you. That was a sweet shot to end that game. You can play, man."

Jamiel simply nodded, and the cruiser slowly drove off as he continued to feel the tightness in his chest and the pounding of his heart. He was relieved, but on the way home started thinking that he shouldn't have to feel that way for just walking down the street. He started talking to himself and then answering, *"Did that guy look suspicious? Yeah, he looked very suspicious. You mean because he was very black? Yeah, like I said, he looked very suspicious."* It hit him that he was always going to be looked at suspiciously simply because he was black. Maybe, if he were a lighter-skinned black, it would be less intense and less often, but it would still be something he would be either thinking about or experiencing. He stared down at the dark skin of his arms and hands and shook his head. *How does that make me less? If you are lily white and fry on a beach and turn beet red with a sunburn, are you a different person? Stupid, maybe, but you're not more or less than you were an hour ago.* When he reached his house and peered up to see Gus sitting by the window, he scoffed. *And I don't hate you 'cause you're white. I hate you 'cause you're a bigot. That's a more thoughtful kind of hate.*

He went into the house, kissed his mom on the cheek, and started helping her cut some vegetables for the dinner salad. His mom once told him that her favorite moments in life were simple ones like this, making dinner or doing the dishes. She smiled and leaned against him. His mother would do anything for him and loved him more than anyone else in the world. Deep down, he wondered if he deserved it.

Chapter 8

Jamiel was lying on his bed with his eyes closed as he moved to the rhythm of the music. He jumped when his mother lifted one of his headphones from his ear. "I didn't mean to startle you. Good tunes to dance to? I called up but just got nervous when you didn't respond."

"You'd make a good thief. I didn't know you were home. Good day workin' for the man?"

"Luckily, a good man to work for. I'm going to heat the meatloaf and potatoes for dinner. Remember we got church tonight."

"What? Church on a Thursday?"

"You know it's Maundy Thursday. You'd think, going to a Catholic school, you'd know it's Holy Week."

"But I'm not Catholic."

"No worries. We're going to a Baptist Church," said Celia with a smile in her eyes as she left his room.

On the way to Hope Baptist Church, Jamiel thought that no one was going to be at the church tonight, but when they arrived, the pews were full of the parishioners he had come to know. The hymns and singing were filled with emotion to commemorate the beginning of the Passion of Jesus. Reverend Rich reminded everyone why the day was called "Maundy Thursday." Jamiel was wondering why they called it "Holy Thursday" at St. Francis.

"I'm so glad to see all of you here around our table. Jesus celebrated his last meal with his closest friends that he loved. Maundy, not *Monday*, is from the Latin word *mandatum* or command. Jesus gave us a new commandment that we find in John 13:34, '*A new commandment I give you, that you love one another as I have loved you.*'"

Jamiel felt a little embarrassed that he thought it was *Monday*, but the affirming responses from the congregation made him not dwell on it.

Reverend Rich continued, "When I think about this night, I try to pay close attention to everything Jesus said and did. These were the last moments of His life, the last moments with His closest friends. What message was He giving to all of us to know that He wanted us to hear and follow?"

Jamiel thought it made sense that He'd want his disciples to understand the meaning behind His journey.

"There were three things that stood out at this night. First, Jesus called His disciples to the Upper Room for the Last Supper and knelt down to wash each of their feet. You know He served them in so many ways during the three years He spent with them, but this was different. He took a simple cloth and basin of water and washed their feet. How can the Lord humble Himself on His knees to serve us in this way? He prepared them with love for this last meal as if they were priests who were ordained to prepare a sacrifice, a sacrifice only He could make for us out of nothing but self-giving love."

Reverend Rich talked about Jesus going into the garden to pray, and how He sweat blood because of the level of stress and anxiety He experienced as a human being, knowing what He was about to face. He asked the apostles to stay awake with Him, but they fell asleep.

Jamiel thought he would never have fallen asleep, nor would he turn his back on Jesus as Judas had. He felt that he'd be more loyal as he was with his own friends. How could he rat him out for money? Reverend Rich's next words brought back his attention.

"Greater love hath no man than this, that a man lay down his life for his friends—" Jesus didn't only say it, but he backed it up by doing it. Jamiel thought, *Talk about keeping it real.*

They were back at church again the next day for Good Friday. He still didn't want to be there, but he did feel moved when one of the older men in the choir with a tight gray beard sang, "The Old Rugged Cross," and then again when Reverend Rich preached about what Jesus went through that day to take away our sins, not His, offering us eternal life. He talked about Jesus's life experiences from a very human perspective.

Then, Reverend Rich had each person in the congregation carry a stone to represent one of their sins and come up to the foot of the cross to let it go. Jamiel had never really thought about the things he shouldn't have done as sins and figured he should be coming back with a pile of rocks.

Finally, Easter Sunday was a celebration. Everyone dressed in their best clothes, men in suits with colorful ties and handkerchiefs, women with floral dresses, gloves, and colorful hats. The choir sang with joy and emotion. The celebration filled everyone with joy, but when Jamiel collapsed on the couch in their living room after three days of church sermons and songs, he was glad it was over. "Mom, couldn't they do this Easter stuff in one day?"

She didn't bother even acknowledging his question as she plopped herself next to him and put her hand on his. "All you need to know from these days is this: You are now immortal, you are now God's son, and you will always be loved."

Jamiel suddenly remembered that he wouldn't be immortal if he didn't keep his promise to show up at St. Francis in the morning. Some vacation. He told his mom that he offered to help out, and she seemed glad that he would be doing something safe with people she trusted.

When he got to the rectory, he could hear the clanging of the metal ladder being moved as he walked around the back to see Angelo already setting up for a day of work. He was familiar with Angelo working around the church and school, taking care of all the maintenance needs.

Angelo Salvato, a short Italian man, with rough, olive-colored skin, a large nose, and facial lines marked many years of a hard life, showed up at the church one day and started helping with repairs and maintenance in return for the small quarters of a converted shed, meals, and regular chess games that Father Tom rarely won.

Angelo glanced up at Jamiel. "Good afternoon."

Jamiel shot back, "It's nine o'clock!"

Angelo responded, "Like I said, good afternoon."

Just as Jamiel was ready to respond, Father Tom came around the corner. "Good morning, Jamiel, and Happy Easter."

Jamiel turned to Angelo with a smirky smile and then back to Tom.

"Angelo will show you what he needs help with. The tough winter loosened some of the siding and roof shingles. It looks like a good week to take care of it, and we appreciate the help."

"I didn't think I had a choice."

Tom smiled at Angelo and then at Jamiel. "Sure you did, when you got up last Monday morning and made a choice."

Angelo's eyes shifted towards Jamiel. "Choices have consequences. Working with me will help you remember that."

Angelo was very patient with Jamiel, showing him how to use tools to remove and replace the siding, and explaining how the overlapping system and the tar paper underneath stopped any water from leaking into the house or causing rot. They primed the wood and then painted the repaired area to match the house. Jamiel hadn't gotten up in time for his normal breakfast and was starving by lunchtime when Tom came out to let them know he had sandwiches made for the carpenters. There was no argument from Jamiel. His eyes widened when he saw three plates stacked high with grilled sandwiches of turkey, cheese, tomato, and basil pesto, chips, glasses of milk, and chocolate chip cookies that a parishioner had baked and brought over.

Sitting at the kitchen table, Jamiel dove right in and then stopped in the middle of his first bite as he noticed both Tom and Angelo make the Sign of the Cross and say a short prayer before joining him.

Even though Jamiel had seen Angelo taking care of the grounds and maintenance for the past two years, he hadn't spent time directly with him like this. They talked about the Red Sox, Easter week, and looking forward to spring weather. Tom told stories about growing up in nearby Hyde Park, and Angelo shared his own stories about moving to Boston to be with his dearest friend in his last days. Jamiel found himself enjoying the conversation and the company of these two men, so he was in no hurry to get back to his work sentence.

"Father Tom," Jamiel said, "this past weekend, there was a lot of talk about Jesus having to die for our sins to be forgiven and to open up the gates of heaven again."

"That's right."

"Why was God cruel and unforgiving, making His only son die to satisfy Him?"

"Great, great question, Jamiel."

Jamiel was surprised that Tom thought it was a great question and that Angelo's nod seemed to concur.

"Remember, with anything in faith, understanding the full picture helps to see how the pieces of the puzzle fit, how they make sense where they didn't before. Make sense?"

"That does, but the dying part doesn't, especially how brutal it seemed. Why did He have to die if God is all about love and forgiveness? I don't know that He is."

"At one level, this is one of those questions that often takes years of learning and experiencing life to understand. I'll try to give you a *Reader's Digest* version."

Jamiel's eyes narrowed. "Huh?"

"*Reader's Digest*—the magazine? Never mind. It means the short version that will hopefully make you want to spend more time thinking about this." He took a sip of his drink and then peered into Jamiel's eyes. "God is love and created us only for love. He has a plan for us and wants us to live an abundant life, but we have to trust Him and His plan for us. He gives us free will so that we can truly choose to love Him back and enter into a real relationship with Him, the most important relationship in our lives."

Jamiel had never heard that before.

"We are made in God's image, and once we realize we are sons and daughters of God and part of His family, we start to see who we are and what we were made for. Our self-worth, our purpose, the only real meaning for our existence can only come from knowing who we are and why we are here."

Jamiel tilted his head. "What does that have to do with Jesus dying?"

"Well, God gave Adam and Eve everything you could imagine, but they didn't fully trust God, and that was their real sin. Instead of knowing who they were and how much they were loved, they wanted to be the deciders of right and wrong, to be gods themselves. Remember when we talked about the difference between saying you're sorry for something and the justice of paying back the debt? If you steal someone's money, saying you're sorry is important, but giving them back the money and paying your debt would be justice."

"I get that."

"So, Adam and Eve sinned against God, who is infinite, which makes it an infinite offense."

"Huh. So, human beings needed to pay the debt but—" Jamiel noticed Angelo nodding as he put the puzzle pieces over the right spot, "they couldn't because humans are finite."

"Soooooo—" said Tom.

The wheels were turning for Jamiel as he replied, "So, only someone who was infinite like God could pay the debt, but since it needed to be paid by a human, wait a minute. That's why Jesus is both human and divine at the same time?"

"Yes! Fully. He fully experienced what it was to be human. He entered into our suffering. He was willing to sacrifice everything, humble Himself, and even die to show how much He loves us and forgives us. Have you heard the story of 'The Prodigal Son' before?"

Jamiel was a little embarrassed for only knowing part of the story. "I've heard of it."

"Jesus always taught profound wisdom through relatable stories. 'The Prodigal Son' is probably my favorite. In this story, the son dishonored and disgraced his father, turned his back on him, and even wished him dead by asking for his inheritance while his father was still alive. After squandering his inheritance on sinful living, he returned to repent. Unexpectedly, the father had already been looking for him to return every day, and when he saw him, he ran to him, hugged him, and treated him like a royal son. That's how God sees us and loves us and forgives us, every time. We are His royal sons, and He is always waiting for us with open arms. There is no greater act of love than—"

Jamiel finished Tom's sentence, "—to lay your life down for your friends, right? I never thought of God as a friend. He seems more like a scary, distant, angry judge ready to send us to hell if we slip up."

"Far from it, Jamiel. He likes you way too much not to be rooting for you every day. You always have a Father waiting for you and who loves you, but unfortunately, you also have a hard-driving boss who's looking to get you on the roof to take care of those shingles."

Angelo was by the door, so Jamiel stood up to go back out with him but turned toward Tom and stared at him, wanting to believe what he said.

Jamiel spent the afternoon learning to shingle roofs and how similar the concepts were in protecting the house. It was clear that Angelo enjoyed how Jamiel caught on so quickly and gained confidence with the tools. When he reached home, Jamiel felt beat and was fast asleep on the couch when his mother opened the door.

"So, I can see you've been loafing on the couch all day."

Jamiel knew she was kidding and just opened one eye to let her know that he didn't appreciate it.

Chapter 9

The next day was finally a day off from school, from church, from everything. Jamiel was tired from the full day he put in working with Angelo and slept in. After fixing himself breakfast and wandering around the house, he quickly got bored and decided to see what the Lenox Street crew was doing. When he got there, a handful of the guys were sitting on the stoop and greeted him, "What's happenin', Jam?"

"Nothing at all, which ain't so bad." His days had been full, and he looked forward to a day with nothing to do, but then it hit him that most of the guys he knew in the neighborhood had nothing to do, all day, every day. No school, no work, no yard or house to take care of, and no money for any diversions. Jamiel knew how much of a struggle it was for those guys who faced each day without any sense of self-worth—without hope. Jamiel was suddenly grateful for his mother, Reverend Rich, and Father Tom. At least they gave him hope and a sense of purpose. Even the slightest possibility of hope made all the difference in the world to people living in poverty.

Soon, Trig, Halfway, and Mal joined, and the conversation became lively, which made him feel as if he belonged. He was certain they weren't the influences his mother wanted him spending time with, but these were boys he had known his whole life.

Most of these young men didn't think they'd make it to thirty years of age. Many gang members died young as victims of shootings, drugs, or sickness. The real possibility of dying young changed the way they lived, the way they thought.

They never talked about life, but Jamiel was certain they thought about it. They hid their feelings and fears behind tough masks that dared not show the vulnerability that existed beneath their tough personas nor the tears that flowed at night. He knew, all too well, they secretly craved the intimacy they avoided exposing, partially satisfying it through their comradery and loyalty to each other. They wanted to let down the protective armor they built, to be different and more authentic, but the risk seemed too great around this band of friends and the girls they were beginning to pursue.

45

Trig tapped Jamiel on the shoulder and motioned him over to the curb. "We're short tonight and could use your help."

"What's up?"

"Lenny B is becoming unpredictable these days. He's been freaking out with the drive-bys lately and won't come out of his house. We just need some eyes for a sweet gig tonight. Can you help us out? Less risk on this one than the last."

Jamiel turned toward the street as if he wasn't responding to Trig. "I thought you said the last one had *no* risk?"

"Right and this one's even less. Do you know Sam on the fourth floor, who was part-timing at the P.O. in Back Bay?"

Jamiel nodded.

"He's been gettin' more hours sorting mail, processing packages, and crap like that, so he's back and forth at the postal counter and sees the requests from people that want their mail held for a week or two while they're on vacay."

Jamiel quietly asked, "So?"

Trig smiled, then chuckled. "So, we know which houses are empty for a week. No worry about surprising anyone sleeping or coming home early. We have all night to pick over these cracker-assed Richie Riches and share the benefits of the country that was built on our backs. That's what Cool always says. There's no way this country would be where it is without your great-grandaddies' blood, sweat, and tears, and the beatings that went with it. Now they won't even let us have a chance like all the other immigrants that came over after us."

Jamiel had already decided to say "no" this time, and any other time Trig asked him to help out again, but Trig's words sparked something inside of him, another compartment that felt angry and impulsive to exact some justice. "When are you talkin'?"

"Tonight, around eleven-thirty. We've checked this place out for any type of alarms, dogs, and traffic, especially cop patrols in this area at night. We can slip in the back, fill the bags with the bling-bling, and be off while everyone in the neighborhood is snoozin'.'"

"Geez, I don't know if that time works for me."

"I'm sure your mama won't mind if she doesn't know. Be right here at half-past, and I can show you where your post is when we drop you. No chance of bein' caught. Wear your black hoodie and shoes."

Jamiel couldn't believe he was saying yes to another robbery. He wasn't stealing anything or selling it. He was just watching out for his friends. Any cop would believe him when he told them he just liked to walk white neighborhoods at night on his school vacation. Sure, they would. Luckily his mother was tired at the end of the day and was fast asleep by eleven o'clock, so he could quietly slip down the stairs and out the front door with ease.

Surprisingly, the watch was fairly uneventful. Trig, Halfway and Bronx got into the brownstone apartment with no problems and filled the black canvas bags with an array of expensive jewelry, watches, cash, memorabilia, antiques, and artwork that they could sell to a fence that night. There was only one patrol car that made its way down the tree-lined street and a few other cars during the half-hour that they were in the house.

Those thirty minutes seemed like an eternity compared to the daytime break-ins.

When they were done, Trig texted Mal, and he drove slowly down the street, first picking up Jamiel and then the other three as they crept down the alleyway and loaded the car before driving to Quincy to get rid of everything that wasn't cash. As they turned the corner on this quiet night, lit only by the full moon and a few street lamps, Jamiel's heart jumped into an immediate panic, pounding so strongly, he wondered if it would bruise his chest. There at the end of the street, two police cruisers were waiting for them.

There was nowhere to go as another car now approached them from the rear, and the street was a narrow one-way lined with parked cars on both sides. They just had to hope that the police were there for another reason, and everything depended on them remaining cool as they removed their black hats and pushed the smaller bags deep down on the floor. Jamiel knew Trig probably had at least one gun in the car for protection and felt another wave of panic as he envisioned them trying to shoot their way out of the situation.

Mal asked, "What do we want to do here?"

Trig answered, "Shhhh. Shhhh. Let's chill. We're just on our way home from a few clubs where we had no luck with the ladies. That's it, okay? No panickin'. And let me do most of the talkin'."

Just then, the officers shined their flashlights into their vehicle, front and back, to see what they were contending with. The light blinded Jamiel's vision, and he couldn't see the faces of the officers holding the flashlights. Mal rolled down the driver's side window of the black 1975 Chrysler

Cordoba with a red interior. He waited for the officer to speak first to make sure he didn't sound like a wiseguy. You never knew how different police officers were going to react to the most innocent questions from a car full of black teens that looked like gang members.

"You boys are out late for a school night."

Jamiel started to say, "It's vacation wee—" until Halfway pressed his elbow into his rib cage to stop him from answering.

Trig glanced over at the white officer asking the question. "It is late, Officer. We were just heading home." He didn't add any additional information or ask any questions.

Jamiel guessed that more information would only create tension and more questions, and all they probably wanted from them was to see that there were no issues, no drunk driving or drugs, and let them move along.

Jamiel recognized the police officer from the other day when he was walking home and tilted his head to see the same partner with him. The officer was still shining his light into the back to make sure no one was pulling any weapons or if he could spot anything suspicious. As he shined the light on Jamiel's face, he said, "Hey, I recognize you. Weren't you playing some great ball the other day at the park near Lenox? Is that where you boys are from?" He moved to the driver's side window and bent down to look at Jamiel in the back seat, "That was you the other day, wasn't it?" Jamiel nodded but didn't say anything.

The white officer was a bit pudgy with a round face. His skin was Easter lily-white with a red nose and cheeks. He was most likely part or all Irish. "Would you boys mind stepping out of the car—one at a time?"

The tension in the air rose several notches, and Jamiel, who, for a moment, felt as if they'd let them move along as they had with him the other day, was now feeling anxious and sick as his heart pounded rapidly again. He stepped out, and the other cop took his arm, turning him to face the car. "Hands on the roof and legs apart. What's a baller like you doing with this crew?"

Jamiel noticed that the other officer was thin and tall like himself, and had a dark beard, but the gun on his hip is what stood out the most. He didn't respond as the officer moved his hands down his chest, along his sides, across his waist and down the outside of his legs and then back up the inside until he reached his crotch. The officer didn't stop where Jamiel had prayed he would, but at least he was clean.

They frisked each one of them and found no guns or knives, which made

Jamiel feel more hopeful that they'd be done soon until Officer Mullen pulled a handgun out from under the driver's seat. He held it up to inspect it in the light. "Well, now, what's this? A Baretta 81?" Everyone kept their heads down, still standing with their legs spread and hands on the car. "Who's the Scarface fan?" Still no responses as he reached over and popped the trunk button and moved to the back to see five full black bags. "Mind if we take a peek?"

The gig was up.

Mullen unzipped the bags and said, "Now, this doesn't look very good for you boys."

Trig took the opportunity to run. With four other suspects to watch, he was able to disappear behind the cars and down a dark alley. Trig had spent three years in prison when he was tried as an adult at the age of sixteen for the shooting of a member of the Columbia Point Dawgs gang. Trig had been determined to be a respected member of the Lenox Street gang and was willing to earn that respect by being one of its enforcers. He was now twenty-one, only out for two years, and he wasn't ready to return for a ten- to thirty-spot for an armed robbery conviction and a probation violation.

Everyone else was taken down to the station, along with the stolen merchandise.

The officer explained to them that this street had a neighborhood watchers' program. Jamiel hadn't seen them because they watched from their windows for suspicious activity. When a neighbor plans on being out of town, neighbors from apartments across the street would be assigned as watchers. Unfortunately for Trig and his crew, the target apartment was being watched by an eighty-four-year-old woman who had trouble sleeping at night and would watch several apartments while taking in some old movies on TCM. Despite their using low voltage flashlights, she could see that something was going on inside and called it in.

As Jamiel sat in the holding room for questioning, he blamed himself for not doing his job as the watch, but greater than that was the dread he felt knowing how much shame and disappointment his mother would feel when she found what he had done and how much trouble he was in.

Each boy was questioned separately to compare stories.

"Where were you tonight? When did you go out? How long were you there? Who can vouch for you? When did you leave? Where did the stuff in the trunk come from? What were you doing in this neighborhood?"

There was no way they could all come up with the same story. If they lied, they would get no help from the police. If they told the truth, they would be ratting on their friends. Jamiel couldn't believe this was happening and stayed silent as they asked each question.

Finally, Officer Anderson asked Jamiel to look him in the eye. "You don't seem to fit in with this crew. You're a baller and a good one. What are you doing getting involved in something like this? What were you doing? Pulling watch? Fillin' in for someone? I can't see you as being a regular part of this. Each one of your partners is stone-cold ice right now, but you are shaking in your boots under that silence."

If it had been the white officer, he might have shot him a resentful stare, but he somehow felt that this man could see the truth. He was shaking.

"Look, every one of the other guys tells us that you were not in the house and not involved at all with what was in the trunk of the car. Part of me wants to believe them, but it doesn't seem reasonable that they just happened to pick you up a half a block from the robbery at this time of night. I know you have no record, but something doesn't jive."

Jamiel continued to only stare at him, knowing that the officer, right at this moment, had power over the direction of his entire life. He froze as his mind thought of every possible negative thing that could happen— including jail. Jamiel remained silent as Officer Anderson kept talking, but Jamiel's eyes widened when he asked, "Who can we call to pick you up?"

"What?"

"You're not off the hook, and we'll be bringing you back in for questioning, but we're not holding you overnight if you have an adult who can pick you up. Who do you want to call? And it's got to be someone responsible for you."

Chapter 10

Father Tom was in such a deep sleep that it didn't register at first that his phone was ringing at four-fifteen in the morning. He cleared his throat and answered, "Hello, Father Tom speaking. Can I help you?" He had doctoral degrees in both theology and psychological counseling, so he often worked with people who would call at all hours of the night, particularly when a family member or a parishioner was dying or in a crisis.

The desk officer responded, "I have a call for you, Father."

"Father Tom?"

"Unless I'm still dreaming. How can I help you?"

"Father Tom, it's Jamiel Russell. I didn't know who else to call."

"Is everything all right? Are you okay? "

"I guess I don't have a good answer to either one of those questions. I need someone to pick me up."

"Pick you up? Where are you now? Did your car break down?"

"I wish I had a car, and I wish I wasn't where I am right now."

"Jamiel, you're not making sense. What do you need?"

"I'm really sorry to wake you up and ask you this, but I didn't know who to call. I couldn't call my mother. I'm at the police station on Harrison."

"Of course I'll come. I told you — anywhere, anytime, for any reason, you can call. Are you hurt, or is it something else?"

"Something else."

"Okay, sit tight, and I'll be there as soon as I can."

"I don't think I'm goin' anywhere. Thanks."

Tom had already shaken off the cobwebs of sleep, was dressed in a few minutes and out the door. When he reached the station, parking was easy to find as the city was still dark and quiet. Inside, he met with the station captain, who shook his hand and thanked him for coming. "Father Fitzpatrick, is it?"

"You can call me Tom, Captain. Is Jamiel okay?"

"Sure, sure. It wasn't an accident or anything. He was found riding around with members of the Lenox Street Cardinals last night just after a

51

break-in and robbery took place around the corner from where they were stopped. There was a gun in the car and the stolen goods in the trunk."

"What? That doesn't sound like Jamiel."

"We don't know the boy, but my instincts and his demeanor compared to the other boys would say that you're right. The rest of them said the same thing too. He wasn't involved, but what's he doing out at two in the morning riding around with a group of hoods who just robbed an apartment around the corner? It doesn't add up. He's not talking because of some sense of loyalty, but that loyalty might buy him a record. I don't think that's what he wants."

"Can I talk with him?"

"We're not done with him, but we're willing to let him go under your cognizance. He'd be your responsibility to keep clean and be back here when we have more questions. There may be charges that include him, depending on where this goes. I'm hoping he isn't going to be charged, but we need the facts, and he needs to cooperate. I don't want to hold him in a cell overnight, but I do want some reality scared into him. Does that make sense, Father?"

"Yes, it does. I can take responsibility for him. Do I need to sign anything?"

"The desk officer will take care of the paperwork, and then you can go through that blue door, and an officer will take you in to see him. Father, thanks for coming in. You seem like a good one."

Tom shook his hand. "So do you, Captain, and thanks for trying to do the right thing here."

As the holding room door opened, Tom could tell that Jamiel was tired and anxious after several hours of questioning and waiting. Jamiel lifted his head to see him, and he noticed a tear roll down the boy's left cheek and then a sigh of relief and shame.

"Thanks for coming, Father Tom. I wish I didn't have to call you for this."

"I wish you didn't have to call for this either, but I'm glad you did and that you're safe."

"If being arrested means being safe, then I guess I am. They said something about letting me go but not letting me go?"

"You can come with me, but you're not off the hook. They'll be asking you back to answer questions, and you're still at risk of being charged, but not yet." He put his arm around Jamiel's shoulder, "We'll figure this out. You must be exhausted."

Jamiel signed some papers and collected his personal belongings before exiting the station and walking silently with Tom to his car.

Tom might have been ready to give it to Jamiel. Instead, he glanced up and let out an "Awwww crap!"

Sitting on the windshield of Tom's car was a bright orange Boston parking ticket. He hadn't realized that he parked in a "Police Vehicles Only" spot and a cop, who liked to get his ticket quota out of the way early in the month, couldn't pass up on the opportunity.

Jamiel sighed. "I'm paying for it."

Tom responded, "You got a hundred dollars on you?"

Jamiel sank into Tom's old blue Honda hatchback, shaking his head. The passenger side door was a slightly different color than the rest of the car, which looked like it was ready for the junkyard. Most people Tom knew couldn't respect the car, but they could certainly respect the humbleness of the man who was willing to drive it.

Tom waited for Jamiel to start the conversation. "I really appreciate you pickin' me up. I know I shouldn't be hanging around late at night, but I didn't break in or rob any of that stuff. I swear to it."

"The captain thought it was quite a coincidence that you just happened to be in the neighborhood at the exact time your buddies were busy stealing that family's stuff. Sleepwalking, maybe?"

"No. No. I don't know what to tell ya. I didn't steal anything."

"Do you know if they had an outside man? You know, a lookout to tip them off if anyone was coming?"

Jamiel didn't answer. Tom wasn't a dummy, and Jamiel was too smart to try to pull any wool over his eyes. Tom pulled in front of Jamiel's house but didn't chance turning off the engine in case the car might not start up again. "Get some sleep and come by to see me tomorrow. Okay?"

"Will do, Father, and thanks. I really mean it."

Tom reached over and jiggled on the inside handle to open Jamiel's door. "And make sure you come by. I mean it." His eyes rolled toward Jamiel, and he smiled as Jamiel pushed the door open and slid out.

"I know you do, and I'll be there."

Tom watched Jamiel slip off his sneakers on the porch and gently open the door, most likely to avoid waking up his mother. Tom figured his mother knew the difference between when her son was safe and sound in bed and when he wasn't, even at this time of night.

Chapter 11

At nine o'clock, Jamiel showed up at the rectory door, ready for work and his penance. Father Tom had probably been up early to pray and say the morning 7:00 AM Mass for dedicated parishioners on their way to work.

Tom opened the door just as Jamiel was about to knock and gave Jamiel a big grin as he let him into the small kitchen.

Jamiel liked the feel of the old kitchen, and he also liked the sight of the two plates on the table, with eggs-over-easy, buttered toast strips, bacon, and some orange slices.

"I wasn't sure if you took time for breakfast this morning, but I figured you're probably always ready for a meal at your age—and after a busy night." Tom smiled as Jamiel scoffed down his breakfast. "So, my guess is that you'd prefer not to talk about last night?"

"If I have a choice."

"I'd like you to tell me everything that happened, but only when you're ready. You're going to be asked about it several times by your friends in blue." Tom hesitated, but Jamiel didn't indicate that he was ready to talk. "Remember we talked about justice and paying out debt? Well, I have another job for you."

Jamiel's head dropped as he stared at the table. "I'm sure there'll be something my blue friends will be having me do."

Tom chuckled. "There is certainly the debt to those people who were robbed that needs to be rectified, but, for this morning, I meant your debt to me for waking me up at four in the morning. Angelo is in pretty good shape here after last week, so I have someone in mind who could use some help with his house. He could use an expert roofer like you."

Jamiel was beginning to regret the new skill he had learned with Angelo and took a deep breath. "Okay, Father Tom. Let me know the address, and I'll be there today."

Tom was already writing the address on notepaper. He folded it and handed it to Jamiel. "This is a much bigger project than the one day you spent with Angelo, by the way. And it's important that you finish it."

Jamiel left by the side door, nodding as Tom held open the door. "Thanks for breakfast, Father Tom, and I'll let you know if I want to thank you after I finish this punishment project of yours."

"I'm sure you'll be cursing me before you thank me," said Tom as he laughed and stood in the doorway while Jamiel trekked down the driveway with notepaper in hand and a load of anxiety about the predicament he put himself in. Jamiel opened up the folded paper and stopped in his tracks when he read the address. It was his own house. Did he want him to tell his mother? To do something for her at their apartment that he hadn't noticed? He thought about going back to clarify, but he ambled the short distance around the block to see if he could figure out the riddle. When he reached the front of his house and faced the porch, he remembered him talking about roofing. As he looked back at the note, he noticed a small "B" next to the address. It could be for "apartment B," but the "B" was not after the address number.

Jamiel sat on his porch steps and remained confused as he tried to figure out what to do. He couldn't ignore his promise after Father Tom had "bailed" him out.

After about an hour, he started back to the church to talk to Tom. When he got to the rectory, he spotted a note on the door that read, *Jamiel, I'm in the church, FT.* Jamiel opened the heavy front wooden doors of the church and entered. He'd only been in the church with an assembly of other students to hear a talk, but this felt different and peaceful, to have the church to himself. The sunlight was streaming in through the large rose window over the entrance door and the brightly colored stained glass windows. The height of the ceilings and the carved columns gave a sense of beauty and awe that he didn't feel in his Baptist Church building. He sat in one of the empty pews next to where the light from the window shone on the floor and gazed around at the statues of the apostles and saints along the walls and the wood-carved Stations of the Cross depicting Jesus's last moments on Good Friday.

Tom came out from the sacristy and crossed the altar before noticing Jamiel sitting in one of the middle pews. He genuflected before the Blessed Sacrament, stepped down from the altar area, and sat down next to Jamiel. Tom gazed up at the ceiling. "Fancy meeting you here."

"I think it was planned. Yup, definitely planned all along."

"You may *beeee* right," smiled Tom.

"All right, can you tell me what my assignment is? I'm lost, and what's with the 'B'?"

Tom straightened the hymnal in the holder just in front of him. "I know someone who could use some help."

"I thought you were goin' to say that was me."

"We all need each other at different times in our lives. You may be at one of those points in life where you need something that isn't clear to you right now, but I was referring to someone else."

"B?" Jamiel thought for a second. "Why send me to my own house? B?" And then he turned his head quickly toward Tom. "You don't mean Busbi? Tell me you are not talking about him."

"Surprised it took you this long. That would be Gus Busbi."

Jamiel recoiled. "That cranky old buzzard is hateful, racist, and rude. He hates me and wants nothing to do with me. Why him? Why me and him? I don't get it."

"Doing something for someone you like is easy. There's no act of love in that."

"Now you're askin' me to love him? I think I would rather face the judge than that old geezer. I'm nothin' but a black-skinned no-good hood to him. Can I help Angelo out around here to pay you back?"

"I hear and understand everything you're saying. Do me this favor. Go and see Mr. Busbi and tell him you want to help with his roofing project. If he asks why you want to help, don't mention my name. Just say, 'I just want to help.'"

Jamiel put both hands on his head and ran them back over his hair. "I'm not interested in being humiliated and treated with disrespect by that old coot again."

Stepping into the aisle, Tom put his hand on Jamiel's shoulder as the sunlight from the large window warmed them. "Go home and think about it. I'd appreciate you doing this—no matter how cranky that old man is."

Jamiel sighed, nodded, and they exited the door with the rose window above.

When Jamiel arrived home, he stared up at Gus's window above the porch and felt no positive vibes about going up to see him. He sat on the porch for a while trying to understand why Father Tom put him in this predicament. He had always been fair to him before, but this was way out of line. He stood up and paced a few times and then leaned over the side of the railing next to the driveway, noticing an old red and white Chevy truck in front of the small garage. *Maybe Gus has company and I should wait?*

Then he thought, *Maybe Gus has company, and he'll have to treat me better in front of them?*

Jamiel decided to get it over with and climbed the back stairs to Gus's apartment and knocked lightly on the door. No answer. He knocked louder, and the door swung open. There he stood, long, lanky, and cranky Gus Busbi.

Gus shook his head. Maybe he admired the persistence of this kid. "What do you want today? Are you selling Girl Scout cookies or something?"

Jamiel responded, "Nope. I'm selling some cranky Yankee pills, though." Jamiel heard a loud laugh come from someone in the kitchen.

Continuing to laugh, a stocky man made his way over and pulled the door open wider. "He'll take a box of those. Come on in— if you're brave enough."

Jamiel stepped into the room with the two older men, not knowing what to expect next.

"I'm Mike Carbone."

Jamiel reached out to shake Mike's extended hand. "Jamiel."

"What can we do for you, Jamiel?" asked Mike.

Gus glared at him as if he had killed his dog or something. This isn't the kind of person he felt like he had the patience to be around but responded, "I don't know. I was just offering to help out with your roofing job. That's all."

Mike smiled. "That's a nice offer, but how did you know we were going to start working on the roof, and why are you volunteering?"

Jamiel lowered his shoulders with a disbelieving shake of his head. "Just trying to help out."

Mike responded, "I have a feeling there is something more to this but—"

"Thanks, but no thanks. We're all set," interrupted Gus.

Mike tugged Gus's shirt sleeve, pulling him into the kitchen, but Jamiel could still hear the conversation.

Mike pleaded, "Gus, we actually could use some help. Totin' those shingles up that ladder with these old legs isn't—"

"The kid doesn't know what he's doin'. You should've seen him trying to fix the fence."

"Why was he fixing your fence?"

"He wasn't. That's the point. We don't need help."

"I think we do."

Jamiel left Gus's apartment before they came back into the room. He was just outside the door when he heard Gus's muffled voice. "See what I told you. Quits too easy and doesn't know what he's doin'."

Mike replied, "Sounds like the perfect fit for the old Gus I used to know."

As he tiptoed down the back stairs, Jamiel imagined what type of glare Gus must have given to Mike.

Chapter 12

Jamiel was often measured before reacting, but lately, his patience was paper-thin when it came to his interactions with Busbi. Once outside the house, he felt ugly inside, and his negative energy steered him back to the old neighborhood. As he approached the gang congregated on the Lenox Street stoop, he felt as if he needed to commit to something instead of being on the outside of everything in his life. An animated Leonard was talking to the gang when he spotted Jamiel approaching them. Jamiel was surprised to see Trig in public after fleeing the scene, but it struck him that they may be wondering why *he* was let out from the police station so easily. Did they think he ratted on them or told the police that Trig was the one who took off?

Leonard put his arm around Jamiel's shoulders, pulled him closer, and leaned in to whisper, "Stick to balling and school, okay?"

Jamiel didn't know if Trig had told Leonard he had been involved in a few jobs recently and wanted to snap back that he could handle it, but he only nodded in response.

Leonard stepped back and said to the gang, "Everyone set for tonight?" Jamiel noted a seriousness on the faces of Fish and Trig that he hadn't seen before.

After Leonard left, Jamiel approached Trig and clasped hands.

Trig peered in Jamiel's eyes. "You okay after last night?"

"I'm fine. No problems."

"You keep things tight? How hard did they push you to rat?"

"They pushed, but I stayed quiet. I said I was just out walking and hitched a ride with some brothers from the old neighborhood."

"And they just let you go? Mal is still in because of the gun in his car."

"They definitely pushed me pretty hard. They said they weren't done yet, but let me go home if I had someone responsible to pick me up and vouch for me."

"They know you're squeaky, but you're also just another no-good jig from the junk pile to them. They'll never trust you or believe you 'cause you're a

59

brother up to no good. They can come from white garbage, and still, we're always the ones that stink. You should stay low. Probably not be hangin' around here."

Jamiel responded, "I'll be okay. Aren't you worried they may see you hangin' out?"

Trig smirked. "Hey, we all look alike to them. Someday I'll take a bunch of them pigs down before I go."

"What was Cool talking about? What's happenin' tonight?"

"Nothin'. Nothin' you need to worry about."

Jamiel slowly exhaled. "I don't like the sound of that. This have anything to do with Grant Manor?"

Trig quipped, "Look, Jam. They know this is our turf. No man is going to take that kind of disrespect. Now they're out to kill every one of us. You didn't hear what happened earlier today?"

Jamiel shook his head.

"They came drivin' by Fish's house real slow and unloaded again, but this time his sister was playing on the porch with another little girl named Bretta who was hit. She was bleedin' and everything and is in the hospital fighting for her life now. That could've easily been Fish's little sister or one of us. They need to know that ain't gonna happen again."

Jamiel didn't like the expression in Trig's eyes. He had been more on edge lately, but now he was getting wound as tight as a tourniquet. He had known Trig since he was a toddler when he lived in the apartment across the hall on Lenox Street. Spending time in prison had noticeably changed Trig. Jamiel pleaded, "Trig, don't do anything crazy. A lot of people could get killed if this escalates even more."

Rubbing his forehead, Trig said, "Jam, I'm not going to make it past twenty-five anyways. When I go out, it's goin' to be on my terms. Nobody's goin' to dis me or my boys and treat us like dirt. Crackers are goin' to crap on us no matter what, but no brother's gonna get away with it without some loud and clear response. You've got your ball, but most of us are left with fightin' for respect and holdin' on to our share of the scraps." Trig stomped away agitated, his large frame covered in baggy jeans and a black hoodie making its way down the street.

Jamiel thought about what could happen tonight. Leonard wasn't going to let anyone move in on the only world he ruled, and Trig looked like a man with nothing to lose, ready to go down in a blaze. Jamiel had no love for Grant Manor, but Marnie lived in those projects, and she'd watched her older brother get mixed up in gangs early on, causing a rift in the family that drove her brother further down a criminal road until he became the leader of this tough and aggressive gang. That gang had obviously decided that the only way to deal with Leonard and the Lenox Street Cardinals was to remove them from existence and make a statement doing it. If Leonard and the gang were heading to an evening drive-by of Grant Manor, Jamiel didn't want Marnie to be at risk, but he also didn't want to tip them off either and create an ambush situation for the Lenox crew. Jamiel didn't think he could live with himself if he were the reason that anyone in his gang got killed.

Anxiety and fear permeated his entire body again with the consequences feeling more real than those hours at the police station the night before. Heading back home, he felt exhausted, but his mind reeled with the world of things that were closing in on him. *How could he not warn Marnie? How would he warn her?* He wasn't done with the police, and he hadn't satisfied his promise to Father Tom, something that seemed out of his control with Gus's constant rejection and disrespect. He reached his house but passed right by and headed across Huntington Avenue to Titus Sparrow Park, where he could hear the pounding of basketballs on the green asphalt court.

Jamiel recognized only a few of the players on the court, and all were older and physically stronger than him, but he was used to dealing with that. One of the players turned his ankle and limped over to the metal bench as another pointed to Jamiel to take his place. Once on the court, Jamiel felt instant relief in this sanctuary. He breathed easier as he strode down the wing, caught a long bounce pass, and glided in for a pretty-looking reverse layup. For the moment, he forgot every fear that weighed on his mind and felt free to be himself.

When the games finished, Jamiel high-fived his teammates and was a good sport with the players on the tough but losing team. He headed home with a renewed sense of confidence, showered, and left his mother a note, then decided to pay a visit to Marnie. He hoped he could take her out for a walk and a burger, so she would be away from her home before any of the fireworks began.

When Marnie opened the door, her eyes widened, and her jaw dropped, but her mouth turned quickly into a smile.

Jamiel fidgeted, glancing down and then back up. "I didn't know if you might like to go out for a bite or something?"

Marnie's smile broadened as she opened the door wider and let him in to see Marnie's mother standing next to her. Jamiel had met Marnie's mother several times at church but shook her hand and asked her if it was okay to take Marnie out.

Marnie's mother, Bette, was protective of her daughter, having lost her husband to drug addiction and Marnie's older brother to the lure of crime. Bette knew Celia well and trusted that Jamiel would honor that friendship. "Okay, but no later than eight o'clock. It's a school night—for both of you."

As they headed down the worn stairs from her fifth-floor apartment, Marnie asked Jamiel, "Did you hear about that poor little girl who got shot?"

"I heard earlier today. She's in the hospital—right?"

Marnie stopped as they reached the bottom steps and, suddenly, became very serious. "My mom just told me that she died. She was only eleven!"

Jamiel was shocked by the news as he stepped silently into the lobby and could see that a gang had gathered on the front steps of the project building. On the landing, large as life, was Marnie's brother, now the Grant Manor gang leader. With his body leaning toward them, he appeared like a coach giving a pep talk to his team, only this game was a life or death one.

Pausing at the glass doors, Jamiel watched Marnie's brother, Tyrell, animated and passionate, appearing to be passing out instructions to each member. Tyrell was dark and thin, with a beard that was thicker around his chin and lips than on his cheeks. He was always well-armed. He reached down and patted a bulge on his hip, most likely a gun. Under his jacket, he wore a black shirt topped with a thick, shiny, gold chain that swayed back and forth as he spoke. Jamiel couldn't imagine meeting him in a dark alley and coming out alive, which made him want to wait until everyone left the area.

"Marnie, is there another door we can go out?" asked Jamiel. But then he heard the loud engines of cars coming down the street. As one of the cars drew closer, he could make out Ricky and Leonard in the front seat of the long Chevy Impala with darkened windows in the back. Behind them was a yellow Hummer that must have been loaded for a major hit. It was clear that Leonard wasn't going to wait for any back-and-forth battle this summer, and he had arrived to end the fight tonight.

Jamiel hadn't expected them to arrive so early, not for anything this major, but his instincts took over as he saw Tyrell pulling out the Magnum that had been tucked in the back of his pants. Jamiel burst through the door, down the steps, reaching Tyrell as his armed trigger hand began to rise in what felt like slow motion. Ricky slowed the car as Leonard aimed quickly with what looked like a sawed-off shotgun and pulled the trigger just as Jamiel came down on Tyrell's arm to stop him from firing. Tyrell's body collapsed, and burning metal exploded through his chest. Things went suddenly silent, barely hearing the back-and-forth firing of multiple guns from the Cardinals' stolen Hummer and the Grant Manor gang-members as he saw several bodies on the ground in growing pools of blood. Both vehicles were long gone before sirens were heard in the distance, and Jamiel finally collapsed to the ground, unconscious.

* * * *

While it seemed as if several minutes had passed, it may only have been seconds before Marnie raced from the lobby door screaming, not knowing who to lay her head upon in grief —the brother she had already lost years ago or the boyfriend she had hoped to have. She dropped to her knees between their lifeless blood-stained bodies. Two members of the gang lay contorted just a few yards away from them, and the rest of the boys had scattered as the sirens, and blue flashing lights approached the scene. Windows above opened with heads popping out to see what had happened, and others began to appear on both sides of the street from their apartments.

Four young men who should have been the energy and promise of the next generation now brought piercing quiet that seemed to muffle the sounds of the police and ambulance sirens.

Marnie clutched Jamiel's hand while hugging her brother tightly, and a wail escaped from a place deep in her soul. A pudgy white officer reached down and gently tried to pull Marnie from her embrace. After her initial resistance, he was able to help her up. The front of her morning blue dress and her hands were covered in blood from the open wound in her brother's chest. The sounds of the scene still weren't registering in her ears as the officer held her and leaned over to look in her eyes. "I'm Officer Mullen. Are you all right, Miss? What's your name?"

Before she made any response, Marnie heard her mother come out of the lobby door screaming as she grabbed Marnie, and dropped to the ground, caressing her dead son's cheek as she would have done when he was a baby. Tears streamed down her cheeks as she screamed.

Marnie had never imagined this growing up but knew this day might come from the moment Tyrell turned away from hope and a desire to be good.

Officer Mullen knelt down to check for a pulse for both Tyrell and Jamiel. "Ma'am, are you the boy's mother?"

She nodded.

He said in a respectful tone, "I am deeply sorry for your loss."

Then he quickly turned and waved the EMT over to Jamiel's body, shouting, "This boy is still alive! Let's get this boy some immediate attention. He still has a pulse!"

Bette continued to sob, while Marnie's heart felt as if it had split in two with the hope that Jamiel was okay and the reality that her brother would never be okay again.

The second EMT brought a small oxygen tank and placed the mask over Jamiel's face. Soon he was placed on a stretcher and raced to the Beth Israel Deaconess Medical Center.

Marnie watched her brother being photographed, covered, and then finally lifted into a larger ambulance with the silenced bodies of the other boys—Ben and Jaylen.

Chapter 13

Jamiel strained to open his eyes. The white ceiling tiles seemed blurry as he tried to lift his head to see where he was, noticing the shadow of someone sitting in a chair. He rested his head back down to ease the pain, but it didn't help, so he raised his head again

He could now make out his mother's face. Her eyes were closed, and her hair was curlier than she normally wore it. She looked tired, and he watched her as she slept in one of the two leather chairs beside his bed. He felt exhausted himself, but he was also hungry.

He smiled when a nurse entered the room.

She was short, round, with short black hair and freckles on her rosy cheeks that made her look younger than she probably was. She gently rubbed Celia's shoulder to awaken her to the good news. Celia's head jerked upward, and she gazed at Jamiel, her eyes wide. She bent over to hold her son's hand and kiss him on the cheek as tears streamed down her own. "Jamiel. Jamiel, you're going to be okay. How do you feel?"

"Besides this headache, I'm pretty hungry."

Celia glanced at the nurse, and they both smiled and laughed.

The nurse said, "Anything in particular?"

"Any chance of a cheeseburger and something to drink?"

"I'll see what I can rustle up for the hungry man." She finished checking his vitals and the intravenous tubes before leaving the room on her mission. "Now, don't go anywhere."

Celia stroked her son's hair. "How are you feeling?"

"You just asked me that. I'm not sure how I feel. Everything seems kinda fuzzy."

"Well, we have a lot to talk about, but let's focus on getting you healthy, first."

Jamiel nodded as a tall blond doctor entered the room and peered at him through wire-rimmed glasses resting on his prominent nose. "Jamiel, I'm Dr. Doane. How are you feeling?"

"It seems like that's what everyone wants to know."

After listening to Jamiel's breathing and heart, he shined a light in his eyes.

"Do you know what happened to you?" the doctor asked as he straightened up.

Jamiel became aware of the dull pain from his wounds and furrowed his brow as he tried to think about the answer to his question. "I don't know. What exactly did happen?"

"Well, you've been unconscious for four days. You were hit several times, eight exactly, with buckshot pellets from a shotgun. You were lucky that no vital organs were hit, but we removed pellets from your abdomen, chest, and arm. The back of your head must have hit the pavement pretty hard, explaining that headache of yours, but I'm hoping the recovery time shouldn't take long."

Jamiel jerked back as he recalled the muted sound of the gun blasts, a searing, burning sensation in his chest, and the sight of blood under the scattering bodies as the cars drove off. His breaths became short and quick as he felt a sense of panic. The doctor held Jamiel by both shoulders to calm him.

Celia stroked his back and pulled him close. "You're okay. You're okay."

He moved his head to wipe the tears that rolled down from his weary eyes and put his good arm around her waist. His eyes settled on the tan leather hospital visitor chairs and noticed that both seats looked like they had been sat in recently, but exhaustion overcame him as he slowly let his body fall back onto the pillow with Celia's hand behind his head.

When Jamiel woke again, Father Tom was sitting in the chair next to Celia, and they stopped talking when they realized he was staring at them.

An enthusiastic smile spread across Tom's face, and he was on his feet and next to Jamiel before Jamiel could say hello. "It's so good to see you finally awake, and I hear healing very quickly," said Tom, gazing fondly at Jamiel.

Jamiel rubbed his forehead. "I'm awake but feeling a little sore. Thanks for coming by. I wasn't expectin' to see you."

Tom leaned over so that his lips were close to Jamiel's ear. "I just wanted to make sure you paid off your debt and didn't want you thinking you were getting off that easily."

Jamiel glanced up at Tom with his lips pressed tight, and his brow tightened. He didn't want to let his mother in on their conversation, but he'd had it with Busbi.

"What's you two whisperin' about over there?" asked Celia suspiciously.

He responded quickly, "Nothin', Mom. I just promised Father Tom that I'd help him out on somethin' at school."

"Sure you did, and I was born in the day—but it wasn't yesterday," she responded with a nod and an unconvincing smile.

Jamiel glanced at Tom and then back at his mother. "Ma, why don't you go home and get some rest? You need sleep, and you can't be using up all your days from work." She opened her mouth to interrupt, but Jamiel pleaded, "Mom, like you said, I'm gonna be okay."

Tears started to flow again as she nodded.

"Please go home for a while. Will you do that for me?"

Celia touched his cheek and kissed his head before thanking Tom for being there, and then gathered her things and left, stopping to talk to the nurse in the doorway before disappearing down the hall.

Tom stayed behind and pulled up a chair next to Jamiel. "I can't tell you how good it is to see you awake. I talked to the doctor, and he thinks you'll be up and around very soon if the swelling stays down. Good thing you have that thick skull of yours to protect a brain that could be lurking underneath."

Jamiel smiled at Tom's ease in giving him a hard time instead of the sympathy he deserved. It made him feel more comfortable to push back a bit on the reminder. "Father Tom, I know I still have a debt to pay. I tried to follow through and work with that guy. He's as angry and anti-social as you can get—and I know he hates me. I don't think I came in the right color."

"What do you think makes someone angry, antisocial, and distant?"

Jamiel responded, "I think he was born that way."

Tom tilted his head and stared at him.

"Okay. Okay. Ummm—I don't know what makes people feel the way they do. How could you know?"

"That's a very good question for you to answer on your own," said Tom as he stood. "I have to go, too, but I'm glad to see you acting more like your old self."

Jamiel suspected that he had been sitting vigil with his mother over the past several days, which meant a lot to him. He didn't think of Tom as a father image, but he was a mentor, and he must have provided his mother with some comfort as she anxiously prayed for his recovery.

"I appreciate your comin' by," said Jamiel with a half-smile.

As Tom reached the door of Jamiel's room, he turned. "Oh, and Sister Helen said she prays you are well very soon." He smirked. "And she expects you to be back in school with all your homework done when you are."

Jamiel's body shook with a laugh that made him grimace from the pain it caused.

By Thursday, Jamiel was feeling much better and was getting bored with his confinement.

Dr. Doane talked with the nurse after checking his wounds and vitals. "Mr. Russell, one good thing about being young is that you heal quickly. All your vital signs are looking very good, and I think you can go home today if you feel ready."

"I'm ready and have a lot more energy than I did Monday. What do I need to do?"

"Your body doesn't have to spend so much energy healing now, and that nasty bump on your head has disappeared. Just start slow, and I think you will be doing everything you want in no time at all. No restrictions I can think of—except for staying away from the front-end of a shotgun whenever you can. You're a very lucky young man, and I wouldn't test it if I were you."

Jamiel nodded and shook the doctor's hand.

The nurse changed the dressing on his wounds and let him know how much she appreciated getting to know him, his mom, and his visitors. She informed him that Reverend Rich had visited regularly. Even Sister Helen had surprised him when she came by with a coffee frappe for him. Friends from school had dropped by too, but no guys from Lenox street, which he could understand. There was no word from Marnie, making him wonder how she felt about him now.

Father Tom came by in the early afternoon to drive him home. He shared with him that he told Celia that he was happy to stay with him until she could get home from work. As they walked together, Tom said in a hushed tone, "Interesting that you keep getting released into my custody."

They exited the front doors of the hospital to see Tom's beat-up Honda in the pickup zone. Jamiel said, "I'm lucky you made it all the way here in that blue bomber!"

His insult didn't seem to phase Tom as he drove the handful of streets from the hospital to Jamiel's house. When the car pulled into the driveway,

Tom pointed to the basketball hoop above the door of the old garage behind the house. "Sounds like you'll be playing again any day now."

Jamiel thought that he'd never dared to take a shot at the hoop above Busbi's garage. Come to think of it, he'd never even seen the garage open to know what was inside. Probably the bodies of all the people who had annoyed Busbi over the years.

Jamiel couldn't find his key to the house, and he didn't want to bother Busbi to unlock the door, so he and Tom sat on the porch and talked. They discussed how much Jamiel admired the play of Paul Pierce during another losing season for the Celtics and what the slim chances were for the Red Sox to break the "Curse of the Bambino" and finally win the World Series after an eighty-five-year drought. Tom patted Jamiel on the back and motioned to him that he was leaving and would see him soon.

They were laughing as Celia reached the porch steps and gave Jamiel a long but gentle hug. Jamiel wrapped his arms around his mother and let her bury her head in his chest. "I won't break, Mom."

Chapter 14

Jamiel took it easy for the next few days and enjoyed watching the Red Sox win their first two games against the *Evil Empire*, the New York Yankees. His house was almost close enough to Fenway Park to hear the cheers and the excitement of this fierce rivalry. Sunday came, and he was doing well enough to walk with his mom to church, and so he did.

Reverend Rich was glad to see Jamiel and shook his hand as Jamiel tried his best to spot Marnie in the congregation. He finally caught sight of her and her mother, but they left so quickly at the end of the service that he never got to talk to her. He hadn't seen her since the day of the shooting, and he wanted her to know he was wondering how she was doing—and what she was thinking. Did she blame him for her brother's death? Why wouldn't she? He was sure her mother would never talk to him or his mother again.

Jamiel's mom told him that Reverend Rich had officiated the funeral for Tyrell only days before and gave an impassioned sermon about forgiveness and loving our enemies, a tough pill to swallow when there was so much hurt and anger in the air. The gang members who had attended the service did so under the threat of a potential ambush as they left the church for the burial at the cemetery, but all was quiet for the day of mourning. Everyone worried about the coming retribution and the unending cycle of violence, a cycle that never satisfied anyone—especially because Tyrell's second in command was less measured and more emotionally reactive than Tyrell. The odds of an all-out war were high, and innocent neighbors would live and die with that reality. Reverend Rich told them that he had walked the streets and talked with members of several gangs, offering them a chance to talk, a chance for another path in life despite the incredible pressure to stay together on this road to hell.

Back home, Jamiel scoffed down two BLT sandwiches and two pieces of homemade blueberry pie topped with vanilla ice cream, which pleased his pampering mother. Jamiel tried to watch that afternoon's Red Sox game, but after the Yankees scored a run in the second and six more in the third, he felt restless and went for a stroll, leaving his mother napping, with one hand barely holding onto her library book.

As he approached Lenox Street, he thought of Marnie and wondered what she was thinking. He also wondered about the guys from the gang. He hadn't heard from any of them since the shooting. Were they being careful? He found the gang in their usual spot, guarding the entrance to their small patch of the universe.

* * * *

Leonard caught a glimpse of Jamiel from a distance but did not let on. He had been suspicious of why Jamiel just happened to be at Grant Manor at that specific time. Did he go there to tip off the intended targets that they were coming? Jamiel had overheard them talking about the plans for that night and was the only one outside of a handful of trusted members who knew.

A few days earlier, Leonard had made a point of staking out a spot on the route that Marnie walked to and from high school. She was walking with a girlfriend, too engrossed in their conversation to notice Leonard sitting on the stairs as they passed. "You should have someone escorting you home in these neighborhoods."

Marnie turned, clearly recognizing the voice and stood frozen, holding her backpack and her girlfriend next to her. "What're you doing here? Are you stalking me? You going to take care of me too?"

Leonard smiled. "Why would you say that? I'm just saying hello."

Marnie took a deep breath, seeming surprised at the words that had just come out of her mouth. "Don't you think you've done enough? What do you want?"

"I'm not the one that kills little girls, so don't worry. I was just wondering about Jamiel."

Marnie tilted her head and narrowed her eyes. "Why would you ask me about Jamiel?"

"Well, he was at Grant Manor, where you live. What was he doing there?"

"He was taking me out. Why do you care?"

"So, you had this date planned for some time, did you?"

"What does it matter?"

"Just curious. Was it?"

"No. He just dropped by out of the blue and asked if I wanted to go out."

"Had you dated before?"

Leonard could tell from Marnie's reaction that she had probably asked herself a thousand times why Jamiel had just happened to show up at that moment to ask her out instead of calling or asking her at church. Jamiel had run out to Tyrell just as the shooting started. Maybe she had her own doubts about Jamiel and why he was really there.

"I don't see what difference it makes," she replied. "No, it was the first time he had asked me out."

Marnie jumped back when Leonard pushed off the step and stood up, towering over her and her girlfriend.

Leonard smiled. "I don't know of any gentlemen who just *shows up* at a girl's door for a first date without making plans first. Be safe goin' home." He turned and walked away from the girls as they quickly proceeded back on their route home to Grant Manor, confused and still shaking inside.

* * * *

Leonard glanced up at Jamiel as he reached the crowded stoop. "Hey, brother. You're lookin' good. How's it feel to be back on your feet?"

Everyone crowded around Jamiel. "Feelin' a whole lot better today than a week ago."

No one owned up to the hit coming from the Cardinals, and Leonard didn't apologize for the errant buckshot that had hit Jamiel. No one had been arrested for the shooting even though everyone knew who it probably was. No Lenox Street Cardinal was going to acknowledge it, and surprisingly, no one from Grant Manor would provide information to the police when they investigated. They would take care of things themselves and wouldn't even rat on their sworn enemy. It was an unwritten code. They may have hated each other, but they hated the cops and outside intervention even more.

Leonard, Ricky, Trig, and Halfway were away from the scene of the crime before the blink of an eye and had probably disposed of the stolen vehicles in Quincy before the police reached the scene. Three people were dead and one wounded and unconscious. Other than that, it was as if nothing had happened when the police asked questions.

Jamiel knew Leonard was smart and paid attention to all possibilities when a war was on. Was he suspicious of Jamiel and why he happened to be at Grant Manor just at the time of the hit? Did it look too fishy, too coincidental, and could he have been there to tip-off Tyrell, who just happened to be Marnie's brother? A tip-off like that could have gotten

Leonard and his crew killed in an ambush. If Leonard were suspicious, would he act normal and try to find out the truth by bringing Jamiel closer? Leonard would need to know.

Jamiel felt as if these guys were his brothers, his own family from the beginning of his life. He realized they weren't a good influence, and it was dangerous to be around them, but he also felt they were part of who he was. They asked him a thousand questions, making him feel as if they were interested and cared.

"You feeling all right? We thought we'd lost you."

"Good to see ya, Jam. When can you play ball again?"

"The heat has been really high. Hope you understand why we couldn't drop by the hospital."

Up until now, Leonard had always encouraged his crew to lay off of Jamiel and allow him the room to pursue the rare opportunity he had to escape the often-permanent confines of the black ghetto. He also believed in keeping your friends close and your enemies closer.

After a while of talking and joking, a few of the guys, Tall Pete, Naggie, and Jamiel made their way over to the Ramsay Park courts with a basketball on hand. Jamiel wasn't ready to play, but he did shoot around with the guys, and the familiar touch of the ball in his hands felt good in a way that was hard to describe, almost magical. He glanced around at the courts he had known since he was old enough to hold a ball. The memory would have been sweeter if he had a father to bring him down to show him how to play, but he learned largely on his own, playing with the boys from Lenox Street on this very asphalt with all its patched cracks and missed opportunities for fathers to be in their sons' lives.

On the way home, Jamiel thought about all the things that had happened over the past several weeks. He was feeling confused about what direction he should be heading in with everyone pulling or pushing him in opposite directions. He thought about Gus but didn't know very much about him. He didn't know where to begin thinking about his own father. He must have one, but it never felt as if he did. What would he be like if he had a father to teach him how to do things, to talk with, to look up to? There were boys in the neighborhood with fathers, but most seemed largely absent, and the ones he knew weren't men he could see himself looking up to. Some were rarely seen, some had drug or alcohol addictions, few were gainfully employed, but others were very present, hardworking and very involved with sacrificing their lives to give their sons and daughters better ones—but none of those men were available for the boys with little hope of imagining, never mind creating better lives for themselves.

Chapter 15

Jamiel felt funny heading back to school the next morning. How many kids at St. Francis had been involved in two robberies, hung around with a dangerous gang, and were almost killed in a drive-by shooting since Easter? How many of them had even skipped school in their lives? It almost felt wrong for him to be going back to school, as if he had graduated to a new, less innocent level of life. None of them had any clue what that life had recently entailed. To them, he was one of the lucky black kids that got the chance to go to school here and had the hope of winning a coveted state championship. He was the boy who was personable, easy to get along with, smart, and usually smiled, but now he felt almost hardened. Did they notice the difference?

"Mr. Russell," sounded a familiar voice behind him. He turned and looked down to see Sister Helen peering into his eyes in a way that no one else could. She could always see through any attempt to disguise the truth. "It's good to see you back with us and appearing healthy again. Father Fitzpatrick gathered the entire school in the church to pray for you—because, you know, we can't lose someone like you before your time."

Jamiel wasn't sure how to respond. He was taken aback by the image of everyone gathered to pray for *him*. He smiled and nodded.

"And I'm sure you used that time to prep for the college exams coming up in May," she said as he walked down the hallway busy with students chattering and getting their books out of their lockers. Jamiel was left standing, shaking his head. He hadn't even thought about college for weeks, never mind the SATs.

As Jamiel walked out of his last class of the day, he saw Father Tom standing just outside the door.

He put his hand on Jamiel's shoulder. "These halls haven't been the same without you. How has your first day been?"

"Pretty good. Still feelin' a bit out of sorts."

"Let's go over to the rectory so we can talk."

Jamiel followed Tom down the short driveway to the side door of the rectory and into the kitchen.

"Can I get you something? Mrs. Quigley dropped off some tasty-looking chocolate chip cookies."

Jamiel didn't protest as Tom poured him a tall glass of milk and put out a plate of the thick cookies filled with chocolate chips. He picked one up, dunked it in the milk, and popped it into his mouth.

"Jamiel, I've been thinking about you quite a bit lately. It means a lot to me that you're on a healthy path for yourself. You mean a lot to me, and I don't want to see you getting lost."

"I'm okay. No need to worry about me."

"How much time do you spend hanging around Lenox Street?"

"I grew up there. I don't like to drop my friends just because I moved and I play ball at Ramsay. Nothing to worry about."

"Let's see. Armed robbery at two in the morning, getting pumped with shotgun pellets, being unconscious for days in the hospital, missing school—nothing to worry about, huh?"

Jamiel chewed on his cookie and stared down at the top of the gray Formica table.

"Everything that happens, and every place we end up, is largely a result of the choices we make. You just happen to be at the age where some of those decisions can have a lasting impact on your life."

"I know. I know."

"Becoming the man you want to be isn't something that just happens to you. It's a set of intentional decisions about your values, your integrity, what you care about, and, more importantly, who you care about."

Jamiel stared up as he dunked his second cookie in the glass of milk. "Are you saying that my friends aren't worth caring about? Somehow that doesn't sound like the Father Tom I know."

Tom smiled. "Not saying that at all. It's complicated because the people you hang around with at your age can have a huge impact on the decisions we make, what examples we follow, and how we look at life. I'm not saying any of those friends don't matter. I'm just not getting any good vibes that they're helping you grow into the man I can see you were made to be."

Jamiel got up. "Father Tom, no need to worry. I'll be fine."

Tom stood and extended his right hand to shake Jamiel's. "Good thing is that you're healthy enough to help out Mr. Busbi now."

Jamiel's hand pulled back from his grip. "I don't think so. That old buzzard can drown in his own misery for all I care. Talk about bad influences. I've tried my last with that dude."

Jamiel headed home the short route fast enough to work up a little sweat under his basketball jacket. He could see Mike's red-and-white pickup truck parked in the driveway with several bundles of roofing shingles in the back under two extension ladders tied on top. Jamiel flew into the house to avoid being seen by either Carbone or Busbi.

Once safely in the house, he was surprised to hear sounds from the kitchen. Was Busbi in their apartment for a surprise inspection? He moved to slip back out when he heard his mother ask, "Jamiel, are you home?"

He felt relieved. Jamiel entered the kitchen. "It's me. What are you doing home early from work?"

"It's Patriot's Day, and they gave everyone a half-day to watch the runners finish the marathon."

"Yeah. Everyone at school was complaining that we had to have classes instead of going to the game or the marathon. Do you know who won the Sox game?"

"I heard they beat the Yankees, which I know breaks your heart to hear. How was your first day back?"

"As good as a day at school can be."

Celia laughed. "Good. I was thinking about you. How would you like some milk with a couple of chocolate chip cookies I just made?" Jamiel chuckled, and Celia gave him a curious look. "What's so funny, young man of mine?"

"Nothin'. I'd love some of your homemade anything."

Celia brought out some cookies on a plate with a tall glass of cold milk and sat on the couch next to Jamiel. "Don't have too many before supper."

Jamiel laughed again. "Don't worry about that. I was talking with Father Tom after classes today. I forgot to thank him for sitting with you at the hospital all those days when I'm sure you were worried about me."

She glanced down at the plate as she broke off a piece of a cookie. "Father Tom didn't sit with me until that day you finally woke up. He had a trip out of town and came over as soon as he returned."

Jamiel's bottom lip pressed up against the upper, and he tilted his head. "Oh. Since there were two chairs, I thought someone else might have been with you."

Celia responded, "I wasn't alone. Mr. Busbi came and sat with me the first day and then the next and then the next. I was surprised to see him when he appeared at first. He didn't talk a lot but sat and watched you with me. I forgot to tell you that."

His heart almost stopped as he sat, stunned and confused. Why the heck would Busbi sit in his hospital room? Busbi wanted nothing to do with him. Busbi was rude, dismissive, and acted as if he hated him. He couldn't process what his mother had just told him in any way that made sense to him. "Are you talking about our upstairs Busbi?"

"That's the one. Like I said, he didn't talk very much, but there he was keeping watch. There's always a lot more to people under the covers than we would expect."

Jamiel walked up to his room in a bit of a daze. As uncomfortable as it had been trying to offer his help to Busbi, at least he figured it was done and over with. Now he didn't know what to do. Why was he making this so confusing?

He felt too antsy and walked out onto the porch, where he saw Mike pulling some roof jacks out of the back of his truck. Mike must have caught a glimpse of Jamiel on the porch. "Hey, kid. It's Jamiel, isn't it?"

Jamiel stepped down off the porch and onto the edge of the driveway. "Yup."

"Glad to hear you're okay. Are you feeling as good as you look?"

"Yup." They both stood there for what felt like a long awkward period of silence. "Do you need help with anything?"

"We need some help with everything," said Mike with a smile.

Jamiel helped unload the ladders and bring them to the back. As they turned the corner, his heart started thumping again when he saw "the man" standing by the blue paint-spattered tarps that had been laid out on the ground. It looked like they were trying to ignore each other as Jamiel and Mike let down the ladder, and he headed back to grab the toolbox. When he returned, he could see Mike and Gus arguing. He couldn't hear what they were saying, but it wasn't hard to imagine as he put down the toolbox and quietly disappeared from the scene. He started thinking about what Trig would always tell him: "They just hate blacks," in more colorful language. "If they can't use us, then they just see us as trash stinkin' up the neighborhood. If someone burned down Lenox Street with everyone in it, it probably wouldn't even make the news unless they were talking about how the real estate could be used. They hate us 'cause we're black, pure and simple. The darker you are, the more they hate you."

He sat on the porch staring at his arms and hands. They were dark and brown. Sure, other immigrants came over poor, feared, and treated poorly, but they could meld in overtime because they were mostly white. He'd always be instantly seen as black and always treated differently because of it—even if people gave him scholarships or other program assistance because he was black. They would still be treating him differently because of that skin. He didn't know what Busbi saw when he looked at him, but it wasn't good, and the only thing he really knew about him was that he was black. That seemed to be enough to judge him as someone not worth the time or the bother to get to know. Busbi hated him because he was black – simple as that.

Mike returned to the front of the house, where he saw Jamiel sitting on the porch. "Jamiel, what happened?"

"Look, I saw you talking with Busbi, and I know how he feels about me."

"It's not about you," said Mike as he climbed the porch stairs.

"What do you mean, it's not about me? It's obvious that he can't stand the sight of me and doesn't want my help," Jamiel felt the heat flush to his face.

"It's not about you, and we could use your help."

"Mr. Carbone—"

"You can call me, Mike."

"Okay, Mike. I'm confused as to why people are trying to get me to help this guy out when he keeps dissin' me. I'm happy to help people that want me to help, but I've had it with people that don't know me and still hate me."

"I don't hate you yet, and I want you to help," quipped Mike with a smirk.

"It's not your house."

"I know, it's yours, and your house is going to have some leaky rooms if we don't take care of it. Believe it or not, Gus is a good guy. He's just had a tough ride. He doesn't hate you."

"Funny way of showin' it," said Jamiel as he stood up and reluctantly descended the porch stairs with Mike. "What side are you patchin' up?"

"We're not patching; we're replacing the whole thing," said Mike with a smile. "That's why we need someone like you."

They lifted the first bundle of shingles onto the wheelbarrow, and Jamiel worked to balance the load as he held the handles and pushed it forward. He dropped the first load at Gus's feet. "I have a debt to pay, and I'm here to pay it."

Gus seemed to fight off a smile as Jamiel glanced up before turning to retrieve another load. In the meantime, Mike and Gus set up the roof jacks and boards to give them a safe working platform to remove the existing worn shingles. As Jamiel climbed the tall ladder, he realized this was the first time he'd climbed a ladder this high. He tried not to glance down as he carefully stepped onto the planks, something that brought a laugh to both Mike and Gus. They spent several hours scraping and removing the old shingles that slid off the roof and onto the tarps below.

The sun was setting a little bit later now, and the forecast showed a dry stretch of weather that was unusual for April.

Jamiel caught on quickly and was a hard worker. With the three of them working together, they were able to remove a sizeable section of the roof before they covered it with a new tarp for the evening. Jamiel was impressed with the strength, agility, and work ethic of these two old men that were four times his age. The silent mutual admiration society had begun as they carefully descended the ladders and called it a day. The constant effort to maintain balance, contort themselves, and get their tools up and lift the heavy shingles out of their thirty-year resting place was not as easy as it looked from the ground. Jamiel could feel aching in muscles he never knew he had, so he could only imagine how Mike and Gus felt. After bringing down the ladders and putting away the tools for the night, Mike said, "Everyone up for a beer?"

Jamiel didn't decline as they ascended the stairs to Gus's kitchen, the spot of one of the negative encounters he'd had with Gus. Jamiel and Mike literally dropped themselves into the kitchen chairs as Gus brought out three cold bottles—two Budweisers for them and a "frosty one" for Jamiel. They laughed, and Jamiel smiled at his bottle of "Frosty Root Beer." No complaints as the cool tonic relieved his dry throat, and it tasted good.

Mike talked about the plan for the next day to finish removing the old roof and begin preparing for the new one. Jamiel asked questions about handling angles and corners, which he hadn't run into with Angelo at the church when he repaired small sections of the roof. Gus and Mike seemed impressed that he knew what he did and how inquisitive he was about the system to avoid water from seeping through. The techniques were basic and ancient but probably took years of thought, trial, and error, and wisdom passed down from generations.

His mother must have been worried about where Jamiel had disappeared to. If she checked his room and didn't find him there, she might have thought that he was back at Lenox Street. When Jamiel opened the door appearing exhausted and dirty, she darted toward him. "Jamiel, are you all right?"

"I got beat up—"

"What?!"

"—by two old guys out back."

"Two old—what are you talking about?"

"I was working on the roof with Mike and Gus. I'm beat."

Celia sighed, relieved, and then concern quickly returned as she tightened her brow. "Were you safe up there? Were you careful?"

"Gus and Mike made sure I was safe. They each grabbed onto a leg and hung me over the edge to do all the work. They figured they could always find another black boy up the street to do the dangerous stuff if they dropped me."

A smile came to one side of Jamiel's mouth, and she laughed. "Let's talk about it in the kitchen. Dinner's ready if you're hungry."

"Oh, I'm hungry enough to eat a roof shingle with gravy right about now."

"Good, because that's what we've got," said Celia as she wrapped her arm around her son's waist and walked him into the kitchen where they talked about Jamiel's day.

Chapter 16

Jamiel woke up still sore but feeling good as the early morning light made its way into his room. His bedroom in this house felt a lot homier than the narrow apartment rooms at Lenox Street. It felt like a home with the wood moldings, the papered walls, a bureau with some of his basketball trophies on top, and a braided rug to meet his feet on cold mornings. He looked forward to the day as he gave his mother a goodbye kiss and wasted no time after his last class to get home, change his clothes, and join the crew already at work on the roof.

They cleaned the roof of nails, replaced a few rotted boards, and laid down new courses of heavy tar paper to act as the last guard against water leaking into the house. Gus showed Jamiel how to lay the first course of shingles and then the second right on top with the staggered notches so that any water hitting the notch would flow down and over the shingle instead of getting underneath. Angelo had taught him these same techniques, but the repetition was helping to build speed and confidence as they started moving along as a team. They talked about the Sox playing the Yankees, the bygone Celtic teams, and how the neighborhood had changed over the years. Before they knew it, they had finished half of the roof as the sunlight dimmed to mark the end of another productive day. Gus and Mike thanked Jamiel for all his help before he went into the house to greet his mother with a big hug, wash up, and help with dinner.

His mother worried about him working on the roof, but she let Jamiel know that she liked his energy and positive attitude. He realized that she had a fierce urge to protect him, especially after almost losing him. After dinner, she sat at the kitchen table and studied for her class at Northeastern.

Jamiel wanted to listen to some music before doing his homework. Before putting on his headphones, he heard a loud crack at the window and then another. Was Mike doing something on the porch roof to get ready for tomorrow? He made his way over to the window and tried to see what he could make out in the darkness of the night that had firmly set in. No one was on the roof, so he peered out towards the sidewalk below. When he opened the window, he could hear a voice below, "Jam. Jam, come on down."

"Who's that?"

"Trig, man. Just need to talk for a minute."

"I'll be down. Give me a second."

His mom was working on the computer, and so he slipped quietly out the front door and down the porch steps, avoiding the creaky one on top. "Trig, what's up, man?"

"There's been a load of heat lately around the 'hood. I can't be at my house for a while. Any chance I can stay here for a few days?"

Jamiel hesitated for several seconds, shuffling his feet back and forth. "I don't know, man. My mom's still freaked out about the shooting."

He could see the disappointment on Trig's face as they started to walk down the street. "I think the cops know that I was the one that took off that night, and I'm pretty sure there's going to be some serious retaliation from GM soon. Part of me is ready to go out in a blaze, and then I feel shaky and nervous all the time about getting my face shot off or something."

They walked the block in silence as Jamiel tried to think of options for Trig, but he couldn't come up with any. Trig was too loyal to follow through on the impulse to run, and he had no place to go. This was the only world he knew and operated in with some level of respect. Jamiel couldn't have Trig move in with them and put his mother at risk, nor would she agree to it. "Trig, there has to be someplace you could lay low. Do you have any relatives?"

"I'm like you, Jam. I don't even know my father, and my mom's family is all in Lenox. I'm not like you because I haven't got it to play or do the school thing. I was dealt my cards early. I've got to just play them, but I feel like the last hand is comin' up. You've got options I just ain't got."

"Trig, there's gotta be some options."

"Don't spend any time worrying about me. I shouldn't have asked you anyways. How've you been doin'?" asked Trig.

"I'm doing okay. All healed and good as new."

Trig stopped. "Jam, what were you doing at Grant Manor that day anyway?"

"It was a freak accident. I went over to ask a girl out and just happened to be leaving when shots were being fired," replied Jamiel.

"But I heard you were standing with Tyrell and not some girl."

"I know. She said 'no' and was walking out at a bad time."

"That's some coincidence. Did they find out who shot you?"

Jamiel gazed down at the crack in the sidewalk as he searched for an answer. "I haven't heard anything yet. I'd never seen the cars before and couldn't make out anything except a loud blast and a burning sensation before I hit the pavement. I was out cold within seconds. What's up? Why are you asking?"

Trig patted Jamiel on the tops of his shoulders. "'Cause I don't want anything to happen to you. I was just curious, that's all. You and your mom don't need anyone shootin' out your windows trying to take me out."

"I appreciate that, but why would anyone be wanting to take you out?" asked Jamiel.

"They probably assume we had something to do with it since there's been some bad blood lately. We need to keep things tight. Real tight." As Trig took off into the cool night air, he said, "Take care of yourself, brother. Don't trust anyone."

Before Jamiel returned to his house, he noticed the light on in Gus's kitchen window. He briefly saw a shadow, but it disappeared, and he slipped back quietly through his front door.

"Is that you, Jamiel?" called out his mother.

"Just wanted to get some fresh air on the porch before going to bed. I'm exhausted," said Jamiel as he sauntered over to where his mother was working to kiss her goodnight. Right there in that kiss, he understood he had more than Trig had ever experienced. Trig was running from a danger that was real, but Jamiel was also running from an emptiness that lurked deep inside him, an emptiness that Jamiel was afraid dwelled at his own core as well. It was a feeling that created an unconscious bond that he shared with his neighborhood friends, a bond that helped them get through one more day, not a string of days that made a life.

Despite his tired body, Jamiel had trouble falling asleep. He had let down a friend desperately crying out. It was rare for anyone from the neighborhood to reveal their fears and anxieties since it could be perceived as a sign of weakness and vulnerability, both of which could be deadly to a young man's protective exterior and his very existence. It wasn't the first time he revealed to Jamiel a glimpse of the human vulnerability that might lie underneath that thick layer of armor, but that level of raw honesty hadn't come from Trig's lips for many years now. Jamiel thought about how much fear must've been creeping into Trig's thoughts, ones he couldn't manage to push away tonight.

Jamiel tried to breathe in deeply and exhale slowly, but sleep wouldn't come. He felt as if he were drifting at sea with no mooring to give him a safe harbor, a feeling of belonging, or a sense of his own worth and identity as a man. His mother had been his rock, keeping him safe within her protection and guidance, but he had outgrown her protection without any solid ground to stand on, or an identity for the world to recognize him. He had no father. He had no nationality to give him a sense of roots or an origin for his existence. Russell was probably a name given to the family from a slave owner, so that was probably not his either. He had no sense of what being a man was really all about. Being tough, feared, respected, and aggressively taking what you wanted seemed like the only model he had known to emulate, but he'd always recognized that there was nothing real or satisfying at the heart of that persona.

Chapter 17

After a night of tossing and turning, Jamiel had finally fallen into a deep sleep, but a faint voice calling his name woke him. He jumped out of his bed. He raced to wash the sleep out of his eyes, dressed and headed downstairs as if everything was normal. He was nervous this morning and feeling different lately, something his mom could pick up on and worry about. While she displayed a look of concern, he was glad she didn't overreact and ask him about it. He ate breakfast quickly and was off to school on time.

In between classes, he ran into Father Tom in the hallway. "You're looking like your old self. How's it going this week?"

Jamiel responded, "It's goin' fine. Feeling pretty much a hundred percent. Oh, and I'm making my overdue payment on my debt."

A broad smile came to Tom's face. "Good to hear. How's that going?"

"Good. Mike is great, and Busbi's been fine but quiet. Still not sure if he likes me or not. I think he just tolerates me to get some free labor hauling those shingles up and down the ladder for a couple of old geezers."

Tom chuckled. "Maybe, but those old geezers could probably still run circles around the two of us. Are you up for working on basketball like we discussed a few weeks back?"

"I probably have two more days helping out on the roof, but Friday's good."

"Great. The gym will be open. See you then."

Jamiel found working on Gus's roof with the angles and hard-to-get-to places tougher than the previous days. Having three people on the roof made it easier to move materials, roof jacks, tar paper, and shingles around and to finish off sections quickly. His only frustration with the job was when he dropped his hammer and watched it slide down the roof and onto the ground.

"Except for holding onto that hammer, you're getting to be a pro at this roofing stuff. I don't think we could've done this without you," quipped

Mike with a grin.

Jamiel glanced at Mike and then over at Gus, who was starting to remove some of the roof jacks and seal the holes. "It's not easy work, but I learned a ton from you guys. I haven't had a chance to do something like this before."

Laughing out loud, Mike quipped, "Oh, we can take care of that. This old house always needs something done, so you'll have plenty of chances."

Jamiel noticed Gus looking down and slightly shaking his head. He probably was thinking—*we don't need any more help from that one!*

Mike asked, "How about the three of us going over to Dempsey's for a burger and a tall, cool drink?" It was an appealing offer, but Jamiel turned it down and thanked Mike, saying he was tired and needed to finish some homework. What he really felt was frustration with Gus. He got four days of hard work out of him and the man barely said, "Thank you." He enjoyed working and learning something new, but in the end, he felt as cold toward Gus as that beer Mike was looking forward to. No recognition from "the man," made him feel more rejected than before Gus had a chance to see how hard he worked and that he wasn't such a bad apple after all.

On Friday afternoon, Jamiel sauntered into the gym with the enthusiasm of someone on death row.

Tom said, "Whatever it is, I'm sure it can be worked out."

"What? Whatever *what* is?"

"Do you want to talk about it or just play?" asked Tom.

He grabbed the basketball from Tom and shot at the basket but hit the front of the rim.

"See, I knew something was up."

Jamiel rolled his eyes. "Let's just play."

Jamiel took the ball. Tom guarded him as he tried to drive hard to his right, stop short, and take a jump shot over him, but Tom was right there to jump with Jamiel and tip his shot just as it left his shooting hand. "How did you do that?" asked Jamiel with more curiosity than frustration.

"Jamiel, you have some of the smoothest and most natural moves I've seen from a high school student in some time. You love the game, and it shows. You have an awareness of the flow of the game and have some great ball-handling and shooting fundamentals to build on. If you want to play at the next level, and I believe you can, there's much more to add to your game that will help you get there. If you think the game is great now, wait until you add some more skills."

Excitement raced through Jamiel as Tom talked about his potential with conviction. He felt as if Father Tom actually believed in him. He was lucky to have a mother who did this every day, but there was something different about a man he respected and admired who validated that he was good at something—that he had value. "Like what? What kind of skills?"

"The game has come naturally to you, and you have worked hard on your own game. I'd say you are pretty coachable."

"What do you mean, '*pretty* coachable'?"

"Let's see how you do if you have to hear some criticism and need to work hard on the parts of your game that don't come as naturally to you. I also think you have great potential for leadership, but that demands a positive attitude, character, integrity, and not letting tough people or situations get you down. I'm thinking of asking you to be the team captain next year, and that has little to do with you being a good or even great player. It demands the same qualities that mature you from a boy to a man."

He was only expecting Tom to ask him to practice dribbling to his left a little more, but this vote of confidence took him by complete surprise. "Coach, are you serious?"

"Only if you are. You asked how I knew what your move was going to be, how that prediction allowed me to be right there to defend it. Do I have that right?"

Jamiel nodded with some embarrassment.

"And that move works almost every time at the park, right?"

He nodded again.

"Footwork."

"Footwork?"

"Sure. I could tell from your feet which way you were going, plus I know your preferred dribbling hand. Good footwork helps you to keep your options open as you watch your defender's feet. Once he commits to an angle, leading with the right or left, you can quickly use the footwork you've developed to fake or switch direction. Working on your strength to dribble with either hand will help you take advantage of those opportunities." Tom handed Jamiel the ball again and told him to watch his feet, moving the position of his right and left foot and asking what the best offensive adjustment would be in each situation. Jamiel was able to do the same basic move he had done earlier, but with concentration, he created separation and a position of advantage that allowed him to open up room for his shot. They worked on jumpers, fallaways, and drives to the basket that put Jamiel in the position of advantage on each possession.

After another cross-over, fake, and jump shot, he got Tom leaning backward instead of into his move, and Jamiel watched the ball make that satisfying swish through the basket before he landed back on the ground.

"How did that feel?" asked Tom.

"It felt good," answered Jamiel as he worked to catch his breath.

"What felt good about it?"

"It felt like I was in command of my game and the results. I feel like the knowledge that was invisible to me before is so clear now."

"That's good. You're a quick learner. I told you what my mother always used to say, 'The more you know —"

Jamiel jumped in, "'The more you know, you don't know.' I get it now."

"'And the less you know, the more you think you know,'" finished Tom. "Work on your footwork and what we talked about. We can practice them more next time, and there are more fundamentals we can work on too. Lots of good stuff—and the game becomes more satisfying to play."

"I appreciate it. It's good to have a day off from roofing—and from Busbi," said Jamiel as he picked up the ball and tossed it to Tom.

"You know what we were just talking about?" asked Tom. "It goes for people as well."

Jamiel nodded as Tom put the ball into the bag. They were both "gym rats" at heart, and both loved spending as much time as possible soaking in the sounds, look, feel, and even the smell of this wooden-floored cathedral. When they turned to give it one last look before flicking off the lights, Jamiel smiled, knowing that, in this area, he and Tom were definitely kindred spirits.

He said goodbye to Father Tom. Jamiel reached the sidewalk in front of his house and gazed up with a sense of pride at the new roof that he helped to lay. He also gazed at the curtained window upstairs and wondered if Gus was staring down at him, wishing he and his mother would just move back to where they belonged. He remembered what Tom had said about people and wondered what things he would be surprised to know about Busbi. It didn't seem likely that there would be many.

Chapter 18

Willie "Sure Thing" Bennet sat on the paper-thin mattress supported by the hard metal bed frame surrounded by the close confines of three white cinderblock walls and heavy bars on the fourth. The bed barely accommodated his six-foot-three-inch frame, but he didn't have to worry about food, clothes, or shelter as they had all been provided by the State of Massachusetts since 1986 when he entered as an angry and dangerous man. Since this was a maximum-security prison, that description fit many of the six-hundred-and-eighty inmates that had been sentenced to serve out their time at MCI Cedar Junction in Walpole. The level of inmate violence and suicides was higher than any other prison, and the brutal treatment of prisoners by several of the guards only helped to build a powder keg situation.

While Willie waited, he remembered the first day of his sentence, when he had arrived in handcuffs and leg irons. He had been stripped of everything and physically searched in every cavity of his body for hidden objects. It was the most humiliating thing he had experienced in a life that had always felt unfair and hopeless. At the time, he thought he could identify with how his ancestors felt as slaves, stripped of all their freedom, dignity, self-respect, and families. Today he couldn't fully understand how they felt because they had done nothing wrong to deserve their loss of freedom. They hadn't killed a seventeen-year-old boy in cold blood.

Willie's anger and temper led to constant fights with other inmates and with one of the prison guards, which had caused him to be moved to the infamous Ten Block DSU, or Departmental Segregation Unit, where solitary confinement in sound-proof sensory deprivation cells for twenty-three hours a day was often accompanied by brutal abuse from the prison guards. Punishment only hardened Willie's feelings for everyone on either side of the bars of the prison surrounded by twenty-foot walls, eight observation towers, and five strands of electrical wires. The DSU unit he was assigned to was the same one in which a man had burned to death the year prior when he set his mattress on fire and stuffed toilet paper under the door and in the lock to keep the smoke in the cell. Some questions were never resolved about why the guards didn't have alternative means of opening the door. Willie was just the next occupant to tolerate this inhumane punishment for his inhumane behavior.

But that was years ago, and Willie had made a long journey inside these prison walls to a type of freedom that he wouldn't find through his eventual physical release. A guard came to escort him from his small cell that he shared with a lifer named Sam, who he now considered his closest friend. They trudged down the hard, lifeless corridors, through several electronically controlled heavy-barred sliding doors before reaching the familiar room where he would meet his weekly and only visitor. The guard brought Willie to the visiting booth, where thick plexiglass would separate him from the man who smiled at Willie as he sat down.

"It's good to see you, Willie. How've you been this week?"

"I think I'm getting the routine down now," joked Willie. "How 'bout yourself, preacher?"

In the beginning, Willie rejected his offers to visit. He swore at him when he came and refused to see him most weeks, but Reverend Rich still came, calling each week to get approval and taking the train out to Walpole, a small town thirty miles outside of Boston. After several years, when Willie realized that Reverend Rich wasn't going to give up on this seemingly irredeemable black gang leader from Lenox Street, he thought he could use him, someday, to advance his parole chances. He had to act as if he was becoming a remorseful and reformed man and meeting with a Christian preacher on a weekly basis couldn't hurt, but something happened along the way—Willie began to bond, to trust, and to open up for the first time in his life with another human being.

Reverend Rich had come from the same neighborhood as Willie, with the same hopeless and fatherless experience, and had served time as a juvenile in a program that focused more on mentoring, skills development, and education than detention. He told Willie that he was fortunate enough to meet someone who changed the course of his own life and then, afterward, the lives of everyone Reverend Rich touched when he started his new life with conviction, purpose, and faith. This mentor changed how Reverend Rich saw himself and the world. He was called to make a positive difference. When he saw Willie, he didn't see what others saw—a soulless, selfish, evil black gangster. He saw a son of God created with worth, love, and purpose that got suffocated before he had a chance to know it and, more importantly, believe it. Willie knew this because Reverend Rich let him know it over and over again.

"Nothing to complain about and everything to be thankful for. I'm doin' well," responded Reverend Rich.

"How's he doing?" asked Willie as if it were the only thing he really wanted to know.

Hesitating, Reverend Rich then exhaled through his pressed lips. "He's doin' okay. Just a bit worried about a few things lately. Don't you think we should let him know about you?"

Willie snapped back, "I don't want to be answerin' that question every week. You swore you wouldn't tell him anything. I don't want him knowing I'm in here."

Reverend Rich shook his head and then nodded to acknowledge his promise. It was a promise he made early on, and the only reason Willie agreed to continue seeing him. It was only after years of talking and building some level of trust with Reverend Rich did he begin to have real discussions with him about his life. Willie believed faith and belief in God were soft and appealed more to women. He was strong and completely independent with no need for anyone, especially someone who didn't exist. Personal testimony meant little to Willie, and Reverend Rich tried to appeal to hard logic and even science to open up the possibilities for him.

During one of those early visits, Reverend Rich had brought some books with him. "I ain't goin' to school. What's up with the books?" asked Willie with a suspicious glare.

"Just good hard facts and science for us real men."

"What're you talkin' bout?"

"Just read about the First and Second Law of Thermodynamics."

"Thermo-what?" said Willie, as if it was the last thing he wanted to know about.

"Thermodynamics. Just two simple concepts. Hard, objective facts for non-emotional, hard objective guys," answered Reverend Rich with a broad smile.

Willie wouldn't let him know it, but he was coming to respect Reverend Rich and appreciated his persistence to see him despite the often unfriendly and distant responses Willie usually gave him. When Reverend Rich returned the following week, Willie was ready for his exam, but not the reason for it.

"So, did you have a chance to read your science homework?" asked

Reverend Rich.

Willie was academically smarter than he often let on and read more books than anyone was aware of. He was curious but never discussed many areas of life because there was no one to open up to safely. "I think I got it. First Law is about matter and energy; it's all here and can't be created or destroyed. The second one had something to do with entropy. I never heard the word before, but it made sense. Things run down and wear out over time. The energy isn't lost but becomes less available. Hey, cars, houses, even people break down and wear out over time, so I guess everything does."

Putting his right thumb up, Reverend Rich smiled. "So, what does that mean about the universe?"

Willie pulled back with a wrinkled brow. "How would I know? Don't they have people study that?"

"Sure, and the overwhelming consensus is that the universe and everything in it had to have had a beginning. It couldn't have been around forever because it would have burned out by now. Some call the beginning the 'Big Bang.'"

Willie grinned back. "I actually read about that in one of the later chapters. Sounds like if you believe in science, there has to be a beginning to everything."

"So, what existed before that beginning?

"I guess nothing," answered Willie.

"Nothing at all. No matter. No energy. No time. No space. No thing."

He tilted his head, curious. "Okay. So how could everything create itself from nothing? It couldn't. You're saying that the universe can't be the cause of itself because it didn't exist to do it and couldn't."

"Right. For anything to exist, move, or change, there had to be a cause outside of the natural material world because it wouldn't have existed. That's why they use the term, 'supernatural.' That first cause would have to be incredibly intelligent, all-powerful—"

Willie interrupted, "I get it. This was my 'God really exists' talk. Well, I don't want to hear it. No God would create or allow all the misery in the world. And if he did, he must hate black folks 'cause I'm not seeing God's loving hands in thousands of years of slavery, poverty, and hatred. If he exists, he must be one mean old bastard."

"Willie, I can understand the depths of your anger about what you've seen and experienced. For next time, read the chapter on how incredibly fine-tuned the universe is that allows us to exist, and then, just for a moment, separate your opinion of God from the idea that he must exist. Think logically and honestly about the only explanation for everything that exists. Think about the existence of right and wrong, good and evil. Those aren't material things."

"I don't know."

Reverend Rich peered at Willie in the eyes with an expression that cared. "Ask yourself one question. If it were true, would you want to know?"

When the guard came to bring Willie back to his cell, Willie turned and answered, "I don't know if I would." But he thought about it a lot over the next seven days before the next Wednesday visit from Reverend Rich.

Wednesday came, and before Reverend Rich sat down to say hello, Willie said, "Okay. Okay. There is no other reasonable way everything and everyone could have come from nothing without God. I don't know if I like him, though!"

That was the beginning, the opening for many Wednesday discussions about life that would change everything for Willie. Knowing there had to be a God was much easier than coming to believe he was a personal and unconditionally loving God who never gave up on anyone. The idea that our essential free will can cause evil and that suffering can have purpose and meaning seemed so unimaginable to him before, but now seemed to make sense. This new lens opened up the possibility of seeing Jesus through a whole new light. Jesus was now someone who entered into human suffering, experienced rejection, abandonment, betrayal, mocking, humiliation, and even scourging and death for something he did not do. Willie felt as if he could identify with Christ's suffering and soon came to see Christ's life and ultimate self-giving sacrificial love as the real example of what being a man was all about. The more he learned, the more he opened up those thick protective walls and challenged his false sense of self-absorbed masculinity, and realized how damaging his attitude and behavior had been.

Up until that point, everything he learned was more of an intellectual awakening, but, after several years, Willie felt moved to pray for the first time in his life, not a formal prayer, but more like an awkward first conversation with the Father, Son, and Holy Spirit. He remembered imagining himself alone in his cell with all three, so he spoke to all three at once and found it less intimidating than one-on-one. Before he even started to utter his first words, he began to cry the tears he had held in for so many years. In Willie's world, men didn't cry, and he had constantly repressed any type of emotion that might cause the hint of a tear.

He surprised himself as he tried to get the words out, "I'm so sorry—for taking so long—to talk to you. I've lived such a wasted and bad life. I don't deserve it, but I'm asking for—I'm asking for—I'm so sorry." He spent the entire time sobbing while feeling surrounded by these three persons, not ideas or intellectual concepts, but three real persons in one God. He didn't have to think through it as he felt a rush of peace and a release of so many years of anger, bitterness, and hate. He didn't need to talk any more as he was moved to simply be in their presence for the entire time.

The largest hurdles for Willie came next as he and Reverend Rich continued to work over the years believing in his self-worth, the real purpose of life, and forgiveness. Despite his now-unwavering belief and commitment to follow Christ, Willie hadn't been able to forgive the world, and more importantly, he couldn't forgive himself. The grace was there, but he didn't feel worthy enough to let it in.

On this visit, Willie found himself drifting off for a moment, but then he heard Reverend Rich respond, "I won't break my promise. I just think he needs you now."

Willie ran his fingers along his hairline and felt his throat tighten, "I know."

Reverend Rich asked, "When did you say the next parole hearing was scheduled?"

"Next month. I'm hopin' you can make it."

"Nothing matters more to me or would keep me from being there for my friend."

If Willie was a crying man, he would have let go of a few tears, but he just nodded with gratitude. "It means a lot. How is CeCe doin'?"

"She is a remarkable woman. She comes with a smile and a spirit every week that gives me a boost. She's really something, but I think she is worried as well."

Willie thought of CeCe every day and hated to think of her as just another casualty of his reckless and misguided youth. She deserved so much more than he had given her, which was one of the three main things that he couldn't forgive himself for until he had made it right — something he didn't believe was possible.

"I know we've discussed one of my favorite parables many times, but I brought a book that I thought might be good to read." Reverend Rich held up the paperback book with a picture of a painting of an old man with his arms on the shoulders of a young man on his knees. The title read *The Return of the Prodigal Son* by Henri Nouwen.

"More insights for a stubborn brother?"

"Maybe. I think it has some good food for thought. I'll leave it with the guard if you're interested."

"Sure, maybe you can bring some copies for the guards as well. I think they could use some of your attitude adjustment techniques," Willie said with a slight smile.

"Not a bad idea. I'll see you next week and let you know how things are going."

"I'd appreciate that."

Chapter 19

That Wednesday night, Jamiel lay in bed methodically making two-handed chest passes with his basketball to see how close he could get to the ceiling without hitting it. The ball rotated in slow motion until it came within a half-inch of the repaired plaster. Some people meditate with prayer, rosaries, or yoga breathing, but this repetitive motion and the ease with which he came so close made the rest of the world and all its demands disappear for a few moments. Then he heard a muffled thump on the wall from Busbi's apartment, breaking the spell. He thought, *What's that old man doing over there now?* Then he recalled what his mother said a few days ago, "Mr. Busbi came and sat with me the first day and then the next and then the next." *Why the heck would Busbi visit him in the hospital every day? How did he even know or care about what happened to him?*

For the moment, there were no answers to be had, and he fell fast asleep with his clothes on. When he finally woke and stood by the window, rubbing the sleep out of his eyes, he heard the sound of a door closing and noticed Busbi walking down the street. Jamiel had seen him leaving early on other days, but he never knew or cared where he went, until this morning.

* * * *

Every Monday and Thursday morning, Gus made his way several blocks to the Eastside Café. As he approached the café, he spotted Mike patiently holding the door open for him until he was about two steps from it and then let it shut. Years ago, Gus would have laughed and found a quick way to get even with Mike, but he simply took it in stride, opened the door himself, and found his place at the table next to Mike, who kiddingly acted surprised to see him.

"Hey, Gus, you finally showed up. Any leaks yet?"

"Are you asking about my roof or your nose?" responded Gus.

Mike snorted a laugh and seemed delighted since he hadn't heard even the attempt at a joke, no matter how bad, from Gus for some time. "I think you're ready for the Comedy Connection."

"I'm sure you can cover for the lame comedian slot they have open," retorted Gus.

Mike announced to the table, "Two! Everyone. Let's hear it for two joke attempts by the amazing Giggles Busbi on Wheels!"

Everyone chuckled and then chatted about Schilling's 6–0 win against Tampa the night before and things going on in the neighborhood, including recent robberies and the shootings. The waitress, Linda, survived the usual routine banter from the guys, who took a few casualties in return.

Mike was shoulder to shoulder with Gus as he sipped his coffee. "Jamiel did a good job helping us on the roof. He seems like a good kid, don't ya think?"

"He did all right. I've been hearing some concerning things about the company he keeps," responded Gus as he held his coffee cup, rubbing the brim with his index finger.

"You said he's never had a dad around, didn't you?" asked Mike.

"Not that I'm aware of. There's two things we knew when we were young."

"What's that?"

"How babies were made and taking care of your responsibilities. I know there's a lot of things involved in each case, but something's gone off the rails when it comes to things that we knew mattered. Society seems to care less about family, responsibility, and commitment," replied Gus as he gulped his hot coffee. "It's not the kid's fault."

"Nope," agreed Mike as Linda started to deliver the plates full of eggs, toast, bacon, and hash browns.

* * * *

Meanwhile, Jamiel finished up his breakfast and headed off to school. One of the students in the hallway next to his locker mentioned that the temperature was going to hit seventy-three degrees that afternoon, and all Jamiel could think about was playing ball after school. He felt as if time was moving at a snail's pace as he continued to glance at the clock during each of his classes. Finally, the last bell rang, and he raced to his locker, where Father Tom was standing. "I figured you'd be hustling to get out of here today."

Jamiel's head pulled back. "Why? What's goin' on today?"

Father Tom pointed towards the sunlight coming in the front door. "Unexpected warm day in April," he said, then added, pointing at Jamiel, "and basketball player. Put them together, and it's game time."

He smiled and nodded. "I'd love to talk but, as you just said, it's game time."

Tom smiled back. "Shoot. I had some mopping in the school I needed your help with."

Jamiel's eyes widened until Father Tom nudged him with a grin. "Show them your new moves. Still up for working on some techniques tomorrow? Suppose to be a toasty eighty-one out."

"That'd be great. Have fun with your mopping," shouted Jamiel, racing out through the glass entrance doors as Sister Helen shook her head with a smile.

In record time, he was dressed and down at Ramsay Park, where the court was already full of players just finishing a game in front of an array of onlookers providing the sideline cheers and commentary. He greeted several of the players with various fist bumps and handshakes and then took a few shots, noticing Leonard eyeing him as he was talking with Trig and Halfway. There was something special about a spring day that felt as if summer was knocking on the door, and a higher level of energy was evident during the games. Jamiel tried to put into practice the footwork and moves he had worked on with Father Tom. He wasn't smooth with the moves yet, but he felt as if he had more weapons at his disposal and got a few vocal reactions when he faked out his defender and blew right past him with a move.

After a few games, Jamiel noticed Leonard motioning him over to the area behind the basket where he was conducting business. "A few new moves for my Jam? What's up, man?"

Jamiel gave Leonard some dap as he grabbed his outstretched hand. "Doin' all right, Cool. You good?"

"Keeping it real, man. Nice day like this makes you think about summer. Any plans to make some scratch? Colleges aren't cheap."

"Got another year of high school. No plans yet. Not a lot of jobs around to be had," said Jamiel.

"There's lots of good work here for a loyal man from the hood," said Leonard with his hand on Jamiel's shoulder. "You are thinking of going to college, right?"

"I've been getting a lot of letters from local schools and some out of state asking to visit. Mostly from the basketball programs. Some scouts came to a few games last season. It'd be great to play college ball and be on a full," answered Jamiel.

For years Leonard had been encouraging Jamiel to pursue that rare opportunity for kids from the Lenox neighborhood and to create some separation from the gang, but recently, things seemed to have changed. Trig's questions the other night and an eerie feeling that Leonard still wasn't sure why Jamiel had been at Grant Manor with Tyrell that day obviously made him feel uncomfortable. Being abandoned at such an early age had left Leonard with an intense need for absolute loyalty, and Jamiel knew that he didn't deal well when that trust was broken. Leonard would need to know if he could still trust Jamiel and that he wouldn't identify them under pressure. This was a dangerous game, and he'd need Jamiel's guaranteed loyalty, even if it was forced.

Leonard shook his head, and Jamiel asked, "What is it, Cool?"

"Nothin'. I just don't want to see you taken advantage of."

"Hey, they're giving me four years of big bucks to play ball. I couldn't make two-hundred grand in four years while goin' to school."

"Yeah. Yeah. That's how they want the poor brothers to see it. You're nothing but slave labor to them. The tuition is inflated, and you'd get a needs scholarship to most of these schools. Hardly any of the ballers they buy ever get a degree, and they could care less if you did. White Southern plantation owners made lots of money selling that cotton and needed black slaves to get it for them. Now you have white colleges making a ton of money selling tickets, TV rights, merchandise, alumni donations on sports, and they need black players to get it for them. This isn't about the school giving poor black boys an opportunity to lift themselves out of hopeless poverty. You're just raw material to feed the machine. If you tear that knee or your Achilles snaps along the way, they'll move another brother into the field to pick that cotton or dunk that ball."

Every envelope Jamiel received in the mailbox from a college gave him an emotional boost. Someone had noticed him. Someone wanted him. It gave him a renewed sense of hope about his future and a sense that he was valued somewhere. Leonard's dismantling of that structure of hope was upsetting, not so much because it was negative, but because it sounded real. He had considered those letters as a gift of hope for his hard work and intrinsic gifts, but all of a sudden, they seemed corrupted and repulsive. Leonard had touched a sensitive button that brought out familiar feelings of anger and resentment, and he sensed that Leonard knew it.

"I want the best for you, but I don't want to see you used or abused. You always have brothers here pulling for you and willing to go to the mat for you. Mal and Halfway are still facing that armed robbery charge, but I can guarantee they are keepin' you clean on that. They won't rat you out—ever. You can count on that from me."

Jamiel fidgeted. "I appreciate that, man. I do." He was uncomfortable with the conversation because Leonard had a reason for everything he said. Turning back to the court, he played two more games but was less focused and finished with a disappointing loss in the last game. He stood on the sideline, working to catch his breath as the sweat rolled down his face and back. He slung his tee-shirt over his shoulder as he noticed Trig standing next to him.

"You started off good today," said Trig.

"Anyone can start off good; it's the finish that counts," replied Jamiel as he turned toward Trig. "Things still quiet for you?"

"Mal and Halfway would never snitch. They have a hearing comin' up in a few weeks, and we need to get them out of the armed robbery charge. Convince the court that the gun was left by someone and never on them that night. We've got to make sure we stay tight on our stories. We picked you up, and you had nothing to do with anything. We picked some other guy up, and we don't know who he was."

"Random hitchhikers don't usually get to ride shotgun," said Jamiel.

"That's the story. We need your help on something to keep you clean. They're probably going to call you back in to go over your story again and again. Keep it simple and the same. Don't offer any details, names, descriptions, anything they can get us with a conflicting story. They're going to try to trip you up, so stay cool."

"No problem. That's it?" asked Jamiel.

"That's the easy part. We need to pay for the lawyer for Mal and Half. It's no small change. So, I need your help with a delivery."

"What kind of delivery?" asked Jamiel, sure that his sweat-covered face showed concern.

"You don't need to know. I just need a co-pilot for a few hours. This is for you as much as it's for them. Remember, they're coverin' for you."

"I know. I know. When do you need me?"

"Right now. Wheels are right there." Trig pointed to a car Jamiel hadn't seen before.

Jamiel's mind was racing, thinking, *Great. Package—I don't know what's in it, but it doesn't take a genius to know what makes a lot of money quickly. Car—probably stolen. Driver—a fugitive. What the heck am I getting myself into?*

Jamiel could feel his heart pounding as they drove down the Southeast Expressway and then through some side streets in Quincy until they reached an abandoned shipyard. There was an eerie quality to the empty lot with overgrown ragweeds coming out of the cracked pavement, broken-down storage bins, old damaged boats, and several large rusted metal warehouses. He expected a tumbleweed to roll by as the ocean breeze offset the warmth of the unfiltered sun. The minutes dragged by before a black Lincoln Town Car pulled into the shipyard and slowly approached their vehicle. There was a rush of panic as wild possibilities raced through Jamiel's imagination. Trig reached into the back seat and retrieved a black canvas bag that clearly bulged with something heavy. "Jam, walk this bag over to the back window on the driver's side and wait until the window rolls down and someone hands you a package. Once you have the package, you hand this over—not before. Don't look anyone straight in the face. Got it?"

Not feeling ready for this, Jamiel replied, "Trig, you don't want me screwing this up, whatever '*this*' is."

"Don't worry about it. They know that I have you covered. I'd be a sitting duck if I walked over to the car unprotected. We won't have any trouble. Just a precaution. Trust me."

Jamiel wanted to trust Trig, but when it came to his own life, there were few people on the planet he trusted. Maybe only one. He leaned back his head. "I don't want to get involved in this stuff."

"Hey, man, you're already involved. Mal and Half are coverin' for us. The least we can do is help them the best we can. It could make the difference of ten to fifteen years in prison and you having a record. Do you want that?" chided Trig.

The pounding of his heart only grew as he felt his chest tighten. His legs felt like jelly. The salty sweat from playing basketball had dried, but there were new beads of sweat coming from his brow that stung as a drop rolled into his left eye. He wiped his forehead as Trig reached over and opened his door by the handle. Standing with the canvas bag in hand, he finally began walking slowly toward the Town Car. With each step, he could hear himself yelling inside his head, "*Don't do this. Get out of here!*" But, instead, he made his way to the darkened back window that remained closed for several seconds. The sun reflected off of the window, blinding Jamiel's sight as he waited. Finally, the power window began to wind down, making that whirring sound until it reached the bottom. Jamiel started to hand him the bag and then remembered to wait until he received the package first. He kept imagining a gun coming out of the dark interior to blow a hole through his chest, but instead, a bulky manila envelope appeared. He started to reach for the package, but it was pulled back a little until Jamiel remembered to raise the bag to the open window. The whole exchange couldn't have taken longer than a few moments, but to Jamiel, it seemed like the longest moments of his life. He never saw the man's face or heard a voice.

Jamiel returned to the car, and Trig took the envelope and tore open the end with the flap to see two stacks of bills before waving to the Town Car that drove away. Trig obviously didn't want to be here any longer than he had to and quickly drove off onto the expressway and back in the neighborhood in a half hour. As they sat in the parked car, Trig dropped a roll of bills on Jamiel's lap.

"What's this?" asked Jamiel.

"Couple of dimes for helpin' out," replied Trig. "Don't worry about it."

Jamiel shook his head and tried to hand back what looked like two thousand dollars. "Trig, I agreed to help out. I don't need this."

"We want you to have it."

He noticed that Trig's tone didn't sound like "We would like you to have it," but more like, 'We need you to take this." He couldn't put his finger on the feeling that he was getting trapped. He wanted to keep the peace but didn't want to take the money. "Really, I don't want to take it."

Trig reached over and pulled the door handle to open Jamiel's door. "It's a college donation. I don't think Cool would be too happy if you refused dough you earned. I've got to get rid of this car."

Jamiel stood by the curb and watched Trig drive off while holding onto the one hundred twenty-dollar bills that he stuffed into the deep pockets of his shorts. All he had wanted to do was to play some basketball on a perfect weather day, but now he wished he had mopped the floors at St. Francis instead.

Chapter 20

It took Jamiel twice as long to walk home as it did for him to get to the basketball court that afternoon. He approached his home and heard a muffled yell from the yard. He trekked down the driveway towards the garage and stopped. It was a familiar voice calling, "Son of a gun!" Gus held his right hand that was dripping red with blood.

Jamiel rushed to him. "Are you all right?"

"Fine. Fine. Just lost my footing on the ladder and smashed my hand on a limb on the way down," responded Gus as he stood up, looking more embarrassed than injured.

"You should get that cleaned and bandaged. Maybe some ice."

"I'm okay. I just wanted to get this thing trimmed before the buds started."

"If you take care of that hand, I'll help you finish."

"I can do it." Gus reached down to pick up the saw with a grimace.

"Sure you can, and I can play like Michael Jordon with one hand tied behind my back," said Jamiel sarcastically. "Come on, let me help you." Jamiel picked up the handsaw and walked with Gus over to the side door to help him up the stairs. Without hesitation, Jamiel went into Gus's bathroom and called out, "Where're your bandages?"

"Second shelf of the linen closet, on the right."

Back in the kitchen, Jamiel turned on the faucet and ran the warm water gently over the gash in Gus's hand to clean it out, then dabbed it with a dry towel. "Let's sit and take care of that."

They sat down at Gus's kitchen table as the lowering sunlight came in through the window showing the gash and the bruised swelling beginning to appear. As Jamiel examined his hand, Gus's eyes started to well up. He carefully dabbed the wound dry and put some antibacterial ointment over the cut before laying on a gauze pad and wrapping it with bandages. "Do you feel like it's broken?"

"Just a little pain. It'll heal fine. Thanks for wrapping it."

"You might want to see a doctor tomorrow if it feels broken at all," said

104

Jamiel as he made sure the bandages adhered.

"Okay, now your part," said Gus.

"My part?"

"You said you would help finish trimming that tree."

"Oh. You want to do that now? Don't you want to hold that up—" Gus held his arm up at the elbow.

Jamiel followed him down to the scene of the crime—or, in this case, the fall.

Gus pointed with his left hand. "This is an apple tree. I did most of the pruning last month, but I noticed a few branches that are diseased and should come off. There are also some branches competing with each other that will reduce fruit production." He showed Jamiel how to cut above the collar near the base of the branch and why pruning and spraying were so important to make sure the tree had the best chance of bearing healthy fruit. "If we let the bad branches and the parasites have too much influence, they will choke off the tree's strength and ability to bear good fruit. Make sense?"

Jamiel smiled to himself as Gus imparted his wisdom gained over the years. Gus showed him the peach tree and the grapes growing over a trellis next to the garage. They inspected each and took care of the cancerous branches to ready each for a good growing season.

At one point, Jamiel asked, "Mr. Busbi, what's in the garage? I've never seen it open."

Gus immediately became quiet. "I think we're losing the sunlight for today. Thanks for your medical and pruning help." He started toward the house, leaving Jamiel standing there, holding a pair of Gus's pruners.

Gus's abrupt departure made him more curious about what secrets had been sealed in that garage. The doors were padlocked and the windows covered on the inside with thick packing paper cut out for each pane. He folded the ladder and placed the saw and pruners inside Gus's door at the bottom of the stairs before heading in to see his mother. He was starting to worry about how easily he could compartmentalize and act in these different worlds in which he lived. *Am I my real self in any of them? How many people are totally different in each of these seemingly unconnected compartments in our lives?*

Chapter 21

Tom was right about Friday being even warmer and nicer than the day before. When the last class finished and he headed to the gym to change, he heard his name. "Jamiel, how are you doing, young man?" It was Angelo working on a broken light fixture. "I heard you've been expanding your roofing service."

Jamiel smiled. "Hey, Mr. Salvato. Thanks to you. It almost seemed like I knew what I was doing."

"You're a fast learner and a good worker. Unfortunately, it's not easy to find kids willing to work hard these days. Looks like you're going to play ball?"

"Ya, I was going to work on a few things with Father Tom," replied Jamiel.

"He said to tell you that he would be at the Fens waiting for you. Do you know what that is?"

Jamiel smiled, "Yup. Basketball courts in the Back Bay Fens. Thanks for telling me." The walk to the Fens courts was only ten minutes, closer than to Ramsay, but Jamiel rarely played there. Approaching the courts, he spotted Father Tom talking with some players. Once Jamiel reached the court, he noticed how smooth and evenly painted it was, compared to the courts at Ramsay. Tom turned and beamed with a smile waving him over, "Jamiel, glad you could make it. Trev, Big Russ, meet Jamiel."

Big Russ, a quiet, six-foot-seven young man, shook Jamiel's hand as the more outgoing Trevon said, "Hey Tom, you given up on the other old geezer you normally play with? Now you're pickin' on little middle school kids?"

While Jamiel's instincts were to give Trevon some of his own trash talk back, he knew, from Tom's coaching, that the best revenge was a surprise win, so instead, he gave Tom a wink and a nod.

Tom said, "Maybe you're willing to play for that ball you beat me out of a few years ago?"

Trev laughed. "That old thing didn't last more than a few games, but I'll play you for that new ball you got!"

"An old geezer and a baby against the two pros from the Fens? We'll see if we can avoid being shut out," kidded Tom as he took the ball from Trev, shot from beyond the three-point arc, and promptly nailed the shot.

Tom huddled with Jamiel for a second and then handed the ball to Trev to take it out first.

Trev gladly took the ball and dribbled to his right behind a screen from Big Russ for a path to the basket and a quick layup, or so he thought until the ball was tipped at the last second by Jamiel.

Trevon smiled and quipped, "Woooo woooo. What do we have here? A baby ringer in the house?"

Jamiel retrieved the ball and dribbled to the top of the key, passing the ball quickly to Tom, who immediately lobbed it up towards the basket just as the darting Jamiel jumped, caught the high pass, and dunked the ball with authority.

Trevon shook his head in frustration, "Big Russ, you gotta seal that basket. The kid's not even shaving yet!"

Big Russ nodded as he moved to cover Tom under the basket while Jamiel dribbled and made a nice bounce passed to Tom. Tom immediately sent a two-handed chest pass back to Jamiel, who swished the outside shot, making the score two to nothing. This was Trevon's court, and he didn't seem happy about the start of this game.

Trevon and Big Russ got more aggressive and were able to take an eight-to-six lead at one point, but Tom and Jamiel fought back to a ten-to-ten tie. Jamiel was impressed with the shape Tom was in for someone more than twice his age, but even more, taken by his obvious love for the game. Trevon dribbled up top while Big Russ fought for a low post position against Tom. Trevon passed the ball into Big Russ to take advantage of the size difference, but Jamiel was able to sneak behind him at the last second and strip the ball before he was ready to go in for a power move. He passed to Tom, who shot out to the top of the key and sunk it with no hesitation.

One more shot and the old man and the baby would win the rights to be Kings of the Fens for the day.

Trevon covered Jamiel and taunted, "This is where the cocky youth loses his confidence when the real shots are on the line." Trevon handed Jamiel the ball.

Jamiel watched the position of Trevon's front and back foot and noticed his tendency to put his right foot forward to cover Jamiel's drive or shot from the right side. He started to go right but quickly crossed over with his dribble and drove, stopped on a dime and floated a pretty fadeaway jumper before Trevon could recover. The ball seemed to rotate in slow motion as everyone watched it float underneath the clear blue sky until it dropped through the net like a feather—or more like a dagger.

Tom high-fived Jamiel. "Great game."

Big Russ scratched his head and congratulated Tom and Jamiel, while Trevon stared at the basket in apparent disbelief. "You got game, kid. Sorry you had to carry this old man on your back."

Jamiel slapped Trevon's hand. "I think you owe this old man a ball."

Tom laughed. "It's okay. Don't worry about it. He plays pretty good for a baby, huh, Trev?"

Trevon responded, "But can he do it again?"

They played two more tough games, and Tom and Jamiel took the last one in overtime to maintain their crown. If they felt anything like Jamiel, all four players were exhausted, and they shook hands before heading home. Tom and Jamiel ambled back as Jamiel bounced his newly won basketball. "You played really well today, Jamiel."

"It's all in the footwork," laughed Jamiel. "It's all in the footwork."

"You were poised, moved well without the ball, aggressive, and played smart. Your footwork was good, but I think you'll see it keep getting better as you practice."

"Thanks to you. Father Tom, I have a couple of questions I was thinking about."

"Shoot."

"I've been getting a lot of letters from colleges that say they are interested in me. I think it's just because of basketball."

"Your early letters are probably because of your basketball talent, but you've got much more to offer than that," answered Tom. "What's on your mind?"

"I don't know. I heard a lot of schools are just using athletes for the money, and they could care less if you get an education, especially black players. Almost like they're buying you until you're no use to them anymore. It's all about the money, and we're just—you know. I mean, how many make it to the pros or even graduate?"

Tom stopped and motioned to the park bench by the river that ran through this greenway. "That's a legitimate question, and I don't think the answer is the same for every school. Some schools have especially horrible graduation rates for black students, but you have a lot of schools with pretty impressive rates, as well, for all athletes. I think you need to study each school you might be interested in to see if they are a meat market or actually care about your education. Stanford, Notre Dame, Gonzaga, and even BC, up the road here, have pretty solid graduation rates, but you should visit the school, talk to the student-athletes themselves and check them out."

"I guess they can't all be the same, but it sure seems like there's a lot of money involved that most of these players will never touch."

"You've got that right. I do think it offers an opportunity that a lot of kids would never have—the chance to go to schools they might not have been accepted to and to cover the crazy costs that many families are burdened with for years. Even if they hold the strings, it's a two-way street that each student-athlete has to take some ownership for his success."

"I guess so, but it seems like a lot."

"I think it's a huge challenge to balance the demands of practice, games, and traveling while still concentrating on your studies—which is hard enough on its own for many coming out of bad schools. I'll be happy to help out when you start applying."

"*If* I apply."

"I hope you do. And I hope you end up feeling you found the right place to challenge you. I know you like a challenge," Tom said, laughing.

Chapter 22

Saturdays were good. No school. No church. And no real yard work since they didn't own the house. Jamiel thought *This is the real day of rest,* as he rolled over in bed to sleep in. And then he heard a thump and then another on the side of the house. He pulled the sheets and blankets over his head to get back to the dream he was having, but he was awake now. He didn't want to look, but his curiosity got the best of him as he edged over to the window to see Busbi trying to move the long extension ladder with one hand gripped to the rung above his head and the other still bandaged. *What's that old curmudgeon trying to do now?*

He took a deep breath, changed into some old clothes, and trotted downstairs to the kitchen. "You do know it's Saturday?" asked Celia with an astonished expression on her face as her right hand rested on her hip.

"I heard that rumor, Mom. I couldn't believe it at first, but I did hear it," he kidded as he wiped pancake flour off her nose.

"I was makin' up some batter if you're interested?"

"Okay, but I've got to check out something first."

She responded by cocking an eyebrow at him.

He stepped out the side door and around to where Busbi was making all the racket. "Mr. Busbi, what're you trying to do with that bum hand of yours?"

"I'm all right. This side of the house took a beating last year and over the winter. I just want to get it painted before everything comes in," Gus said, pointing to the garden beds.

Jamiel stood there with his arms folded, staring up at the height and width of this side of the house. "There is no way an old one-armed grump is going to make that happen!"

"Who you calling old?"

"There's no one else here."

"I can run circles around you with no arms,"

"And that's all you'd be able to do—run. You need arms to paint on a ladder."

Jamiel could tell by the expression on Gus's face and his slumped shoulders that he knew he wasn't being realistic, thinking he could scrape and paint the largest side of the house. The way he held his hand made it obvious that it hurt more than he wanted to admit. They both stood there staring up, neither uttering a word until Celia came around the corner to break the awkward silence. "Looks like we've got a good project going. How about some breakfast to fuel you up?" It wasn't hard to coax them in for a stack of pancakes, sausages, and scrambled eggs. "Sit down and dig in. This should give you a good start." As they sat, Celia noticed the bandage on Gus's hand. "You all right, Mr. Busbi? That hand doesn't look too good."

"I told him that he should see a doctor when I bandaged it up yesterday," said Jamiel as he poured himself a tall glass of orange juice.

"You bandaged him up? My son, the doctor?"

Jamiel watched as Gus peered around at the kitchen where he used to live. He couldn't tell what Gus was thinking or feeling, but at one point, Gus shook his head as if he were feeling dizzy.

"I hope you're okay, Mr. Busbi. Dig in while they're still hot," said Celia.

He sat there motionless, and when he glanced up, Jamiel was staring into his eyes to see if he was okay. The visceral reaction seemed to disorient Gus, who stood up and suddenly blurted, "I'm sorry, but I can't—" and left by the side kitchen door.

"More pancakes for me," said Jamiel as he started to reach over toward Gus's plate.

Celia made a weak attempt to swat his hand. "Something was really bothering him."

"Yeah, he finally realized he was about to eat with black folks."

"I don't think it's time for joking," said Celia.

"Who's jokin'?" said Jamiel.

Chapter 23

On Sunday morning, Jamiel didn't see Marnie at church, which made him wonder even more what she may be thinking of him now, with the range of possibilities consuming his thoughts during the service. Reverend Rich came over to where he was standing at the social gathering afterward. "Jamiel. Did you know that I can actually see all of you when I'm preaching?" Jamiel froze, searching for a response as the reverend continued. "You seemed as if you had a lot on your mind."

"Probably more than I'm aware of. I'm okay, Reverend."

"I don't know if you know this or not, but a lot of people are thinking about you and praying for you every day. Even people you don't know yet."

How would someone be praying for him if they didn't know him yet?
"That's good to know."

"And a lot of people who care for you are praying that you are heading in a healthy direction in your life. Some of these neighborhoods can drag you down and shut the door on your dreams and potential. I don't know if they need to be, but some people are a bit worried about you these days."

What does he know about me?

"I'll bet that young lady you're probably thinking about today is one of the people rooting for you. You know who I mean."

Jamiel glanced at Reverend Rich. *How does he know?*

"I know from personal experience that it's rough to grow up without a father around."

"I have a father?" asked Jamiel sarcastically.

"We all have a father, even if he's not around."

"You mean like Jesus's dad wasn't around?"

"Jesus's dad is always around. For Him and for you. But He did have a man stand in to be His dad—Joseph. He had someone around to physically talk to about things growing up. Neither you nor I had that, and it's important to have mentors as you are charting some rough seas transitioning to being a man."

"You want to be my dad?"

"I wish I could, but I am here for you. To talk things through or just listen."

"Reverend Rich, you always have been there. Nothing personal, but it still seems like something is missing."

"I know—and I mourn that hole in your heart with you. I used to use it as an excuse when I was your age, and that wasn't the answer."

"Thanks," said Jamiel as he shook Reverend Rich's hand and then helped clean up before leaving. When he got home, he peered around the back and noticed the ladder was still where Busbi put it the day before. On the ground, he spotted a bucket with scrapers, sanding blocks, and rags. The clapboard siding was not in bad shape but had some peeling and fading from the south side sun. There was also some rot developing in the corners of the molding and loosening of glazing around the windows. Jamiel reached out and pulled some of the peeling paint from the siding, and a larger section of paint than he expected started to separate from the wood. He grabbed a scraper and held the handle as he worked it back and forth to scrape off the loose paint.

The scraping sound against the side of the house must have caught Gus's attention as Jamiel saw some movement from his kitchen window.

Within seconds he was out in the backyard. "What are you doing?"

"I think they call it scraping. You've got a lot of loose paint here."

"I know, but why are you doing this?"

"Because you've got a lot of loose paint here," said Jamiel as he continued to scrape.

Gus winced and stared. "So, you're saying—"

"I'm saying you better make sure I know what I'm doing or your house ain't gonna look too good, boss."

Gus stood there. "You know, you are one stubborn son of a gun."

"I guess that makes two of us," said Jamiel as he continued to scrape.

"I guess it does." Gus grabbed another scraper from the bucket with his left hand and started to work on the peeling paint on another clapboard.

"How much of this do we need to scrape?" asked Jamiel.

"When you have a house, one of the most important things to avoid is rot. Water on wood causes rot if it cannot dry quickly, and water that sits behind the paint won't dry. So you get—"

"Rot."

"Right. It's a lot of work that no one will ever see because you are going to paint over it, but the prep work, scraping all the paint, sanding down the board, and priming it before you brush on the actual paint is huge. Otherwise, you'll be doing this all over again next year."

"Aren't we doing it again now?"

"Sure," replied Gus, "but it's been almost ten years since I did this last. And that was almost ten years since—" Gus's voice tightened as he appeared to drift off again.

"It's going to take some time to do this right then," said Jamiel.

"Are you sure you are up to it?" asked Gus. "I can pay you for your time."

"Hey, I live here too. My mom says, 'It's your home. You don't get paid to take care of your own home.'"

Gus nodded and smiled slightly. "Okay, let's get going."

Jamiel was surprised by how much progress they were making as they worked together, something he was still having a hard time believing he was doing. For some reason, he wasn't feeling uncomfortable with Gus today, even in this almost intimate setting. He seemed human and not bitter, angry, or hateful. "How long have you been in this house, Mr. Busbi?"

"A long time."

"Mom told me you lost your wife before you rented to us? How long had you been married?"

"Forty-three years."

"Wow. I hope I can be married to someone that loves me for that long. When did you meet her?"

"You know Mike. Mike and I served in the war together."

"You were in the war? Which war?"

"The War of 1812."

"Wow. I knew you were old," chuckled Jamiel.

"We were in the Korean War from '51 to '53 when it ended."

"How old were you when you went in?"

"How old are you?" asked Gus.

"Seventeen, but I'll be eighteen in the fall," answered Jamiel.

"I was your age when I enlisted."

"Seventeen? Man, I'd be shakin' in my boots if I was going to war right now," said Jamiel as he scraped and shook his head. "Did you see actual action? Did you get shot at?"

Gus seemed amused by Jamiel's curiosity. Jamiel had heard that most of the older generation men didn't usually talk about the war. "Mike and I were both on the ground and saw a lot of the action. We did plenty of shaking in our boots too, as we took a lot of gunfire and bombing. Watching boys you spent that much time with dying before your eyes is not something you like to think about, never mind experience."

They were both quiet for several minutes as they scraped and sanded.

"So, how did you meet her?"

"Mike took me to a dance that he knew his kid sister would be at. Before he could introduce me to her, I spotted this girl across the room. There was just something about her that mesmerized me."

Jamiel was almost taken more with the look in Gus's eyes than the story itself. It was as if he were a young man again seeing his bride for the first time.

"I left Mike and went over to meet her, and we talked for over an hour before I remembered Mike and that I was supposed to meet his sister. When I finally spotted Mike alone, I excused myself and walked over to explain that I met this girl named Julia and that I thought she was the one I had been looking for."

Mike laughed and said, 'That's funny. I have a sister named Julia, too. What a coincidence!' I turned around to see Julia standing behind me and laughing along with her brother. So, I kept a good friend and found the best one I've ever had."

As Jamiel watched Gus speak with misty eyes, he thought of his mother being alone all these years, and he thought about finding someone he would feel that way about someday. "I wish I could've met her. How long before you married?"

"It was four years. I was working to save up enough money to give us a good start, and Julia had to take care of her mother, who was sick, for a few years, but we had a fun courtship and finally got hitched in 1958, right up the street at St. Francis."

"Huh. Where I go to school. That's something to be together all those years. I know many kids who don't have parents together."

"Responsibility. Commitment. Sacrifice. Honesty. Those are parts of love that we seemed to have lost in relationships. Too many people seem more self-focused and have lost sight of the real beauty of friendship and marriage." Gus put his sanding block into the bucket and stepped back to look at what they had accomplished together.

"You know, we take all these classes in math, history, and English, but we never hear much about relationships. Seems like an important subject on its own," replied Jamiel as he stepped back with Gus.

Gus said, "That was some impressive work on the ladder there. You seem okay with heights."

"I'm scared to death, but I like doing this. I like working with you."

"I do too, and you're right about relationships. That's what life is all about. Not sure if a classroom is the place to learn about it, but I know the street corner won't help. You do good work. I think you deserve some compensation if you are going to do this."

"I think I got some," said Jamiel as he brought down the ladder for the evening. "Take care of that hand, Mr. Busbi." For the first time, Jamiel felt as if Gus saw him differently as he waved to Jamiel on his way into the house for the evening.

Celia said, "Where in the world have you been?

"Just hanging around with someone." Jamiel put his arm around his mom's shoulder and pulled her close to him. "Are we eating soon? I'm starvin'."

"You think a little huggin' is gonna get you some food, Mister? I guess you're right." His mother laughed as she gazed up at him.

Chapter 24

On Monday, Jamiel hustled out of school after his class as if he were heading to a basketball game. On the way down the hall, he heard his name.

"Mr. Russell. I see we've got our energy back."

Stopping short, he turned and replied, "Healthy and all healed, Sister."

"I'm thinking we'll be seeing you at the SAT college prep then."

"Sure thing. When is it?"

"We start in five minutes," she said, pointing to the large classroom down the hall.

Jamiel's heart sunk as he headed in the direction of her finger. Sister Helen glanced at him every time he peered at the clock during the prep class. Finally, it was over, and he was out of his seat and running down the street toward his house. When he reached the backyard, he saw Gus up on the ladder, trying to scrape with one hand and keeping his balance using his wrist. "Mr. Busbi! I'll be right there. You shouldn't be on that ladder!" he shouted up.

"Only so much daylight this time of year, and I need to beat the rain coming later in the week."

"We'll get there," Jamiel called, scooting around the corner and into the house to grab a cookie from a plate his mother left with a note, *Something to keep you going until I get home.*

Gus chuckled at how quickly he changed and was under the ladder.

"Let me hold the ladder while you come down."

Gus smiled as he carefully made his way down. "You're right. I just wasn't sure if you were coming today, and I don't want the bare wood getting wet before we can sand, prime, and hopefully paint before it rains."

"Thanks. I had a surprise SAT prep class. A surprise to me, anyway."

"Ah, that's a priority."

"Maybe. I'm not sure about college."

"I never went, but those were different times. You seem like someone who should think about it. It gives you perspective and more options in life if you take advantage of it."

"Do you regret not going?" asked Jamiel as he started climbing the ladder with his scraper, rag, and sanding block in his back pocket and a bucket of bleach and water to clean shadowed areas covered with green and black mold.

"Sometimes. I've done a lot of reading and taken night classes to catch up a bit, but part of me wishes I could've gone."

"Nothing stopping you now. We can share a dorm room," Jamiel laughed.

"Maybe I could get a basketball scholarship?" Gus pointed to a spot for Jamiel to clean.

"Did you play?"

"A little bit."

Huh, Jamiel thought. While they were working, they talked about the South End of Boston, working at Dennis, the Red Sox's heartbreaking season last year, the last Celtics championship team in 1986 when Jamiel was born, the Patriots, and how much Jamiel loved playing ball. It was harder to have a more personal conversation when one of the parties was fifteen to twenty feet in the air, but it was enjoyable. Jamiel thought about how much he missed these types of conversations with a dad. They managed four straight hours of work before the light of the day was lost. Luckily, they had finished all the scraping, sanding, and much of the priming. The work was tedious and hard, but there was a sense of accomplishment as they stepped back together to see that stage finished.

Jamiel planned to get home as early as possible the next day, as they were going to actually paint. There was no SAT prep class, but as he approached his house, he could see a car with darkened windows sitting out front. His shoulders sunk several inches and he stopped. He feared that it could be gang members from Grant Manor planning to finally get their revenge, something he thought about every day. As the car window rolled down, he could see Trig in the driver's seat, motioning to him to come over.

"What did you think, I was here to gun you down or something?" laughed Trigg.

"I didn't know who you were. Where did you get this sled?" responded Jamiel.

"Birthday present."

"Trig, it's not your birthday."

"I didn't say it was *my* birthday present," said Trig with a smirk.

Jamiel was trying to figure out how many stolen cars he had ridden in over the years. Trig stole his first car at eleven and drove around the South End and Roxbury until he finally hit a car and ran before anyone knew what happened. Plenty of people saw this little kid, who could barely see over the dashboard, driving by in this big car, but no one bothered to do anything. "What's up? I've got to get to work,' said Jamiel.

"You gotta job? Doin' what? How much do you make?"

"Painting a house. Doesn't pay anything," responded Jamiel, who was starting to worry that Trig was not just dropping by to say hello or show off his new car of the day.

"I can beat that. Hop in."

"I really can't, Trig."

"I'm thinkin' you can. Get on some other digs before we go, though."

Jamiel glanced down at his dress pants and penny loafers and went into the house to change into some baggy jeans, basketball sneakers, and a black hooded sweatshirt. He looked in the mirror and thought, *You wouldn't even know it was the same kid.* He considered not going back out, but Trig wouldn't leave until he did. He leaned on the outside of the open passenger side window. "Trig, I really can't go with you."

"I don't know about that. Cool wouldn't be too damn happy with either one of us. Come on," said Trig as he leaned over and opened the door. Before Jamiel could figure out how to stay on the curb, he was sitting in the car and driving away from his home.

"Hey, man. Good to see ya," came a voice from the back. It was Halfway.

"What's up, Half? Your lawyer takin' care of things?" asked Jamiel.

"I hope so. For all our sakes, I hope so," replied Halfway.

Jamiel got the message as they rode the back streets and then down a pothole-filled road to an old warehouse building that appeared abandoned. Trig pulled the car up next to the side of the building and then behind an old dumpster before he and Halfway got out of the car. He leaned in to look through the window. "Come on, man." As they walked to the warehouse, Jamiel could tell that Trig was armed when he reached under his jacket to adjust the piece. Halfway did the same just before making his way through the metal door and closing it after Jamiel. The building was dark, damp, and echoed as they trudged down the open passageway and up some metal-grated stairs to another door. A white dude with a collared shirt, jacket, dress pants, and shoes stood outside with his arms folded. The man squinted as he inspected Trig, then Jamiel, and back to Trig. With a slight movement, he cocked his head to the left.

"Cool can vouch for him. He's all right," said Trig.

The man turned back to Jamiel, trying to make eye contact, but Jamiel looked away, which felt safer.

Inside was a large operation of people working at folding tables, cutting up drugs, and creating smaller packages for sale. An unshaven man with combed-back gray hair, a Hawaiian shirt, loose khaki pants, and canvas shoes who seemed to be managing the operation, glanced up at the Lenox Street team walking into his world. He seemed particularly interested in Jamiel since he hadn't seen him before and couldn't risk what may have been a multi-million dollar operation to a loose-lipped kid. As Trig approached him, he leaned towards his right ear. "What's with the surprise guest? He looks like a schoolgirl."

Cuffing Jamiel's arm around his shoulder, Trig said, "Joey, this young man and I are like brothers. You can trust Jam as much as Cool does, and Cool wanted him along."

Trig had told Jamiel about Joey Caporale and this operation before, but seeing it in person was a whole other thing. Joey was born and still lived in the North End of Boston. He was a soldier who was able to make his local caporegime a lot of money every week dealing in the eastern part of Massachusetts and Rhode Island. They dealt in crack, heroin, meth, salts, cocaine, amphetamines, Benz, ecstasy, and pot. Each was packaged for specific dealers and markets. Leonard was dealing with the addicted poor in the local neighborhoods but also helping with drop-offs to distributors on the South Shore and the Cape. Others specialized in rich professionals now addicted to opioids, cocaine, and anything else they wanted. Some dealers worked the college campuses through a network of students looking for a part-time job and had the connections for those looking for 'weed, speed, and anything they need.'

Jamiel was working hard to hide how uncomfortable and nervous he felt standing in the middle of this operation. Nothing was good about it. He felt himself getting sucked deeper into a dark pit with no escape and felt that Joey could see it in his eyes.

"You okay, kid?"

Jamiel nodded as Trig handed him several black canvas bags to carry, and then Trig handed Joey a large envelope he had brought in. Joey motioned to a guy wearing all black who took the envelope and quickly counted the contents before nodding that it was all there. Joey fidgeted, making it obvious that he wanted these transactions to happen quickly.

Trig, Halfway, and Jamiel were back in the abandoned parking lot, blinking in the bright sun, to make several drop-offs around town, including the old shipyard in Quincy where they had gone the last time.

When Halfway got out of the car to make one of the drops, Jamiel turned to Trig, "Trig, I can't be involved in this stuff."

Trig continued to stare straight through the windshield in front of him. "You already are, Jam. Just stay cool."

Jamiel thought about the boy from across the hall he had grown up with, but now Trig wasn't that little boy any longer. His life was slipping out of control, and he didn't know how to handle it. Complaining or panicking right now wouldn't help. They made six drops, and each one of them handled two deliveries, despite Jamiel's internal resistance. When they dropped him in front of his house, he felt dazed. He stumbled around to the back of the house only to see Gus back up on the ladder painting under the eaves.

Jamiel called up, "Hey, Mr. Busbi. I know this is going to sound like another lame excuse, but I *was* planning on being here right after school."

Gus glanced down from the top of the ladder, "You okay?"

"I'm okay."

When Gus reached the bottom, he asked, "So it *is* a lame excuse?"

"Not really."

"What happened?"

Jamiel ran his hand across his cheek, "I can't tell you."

Gus didn't change his expression. "Well, if you want to help out, I'd put on some old clothes you don't mind getting paint on, or I have some painter's pants in the house if you don't have anything." Jamiel didn't usually do any painting and took advantage of Gus's spare clothes.

Before he climbed up to where Gus was working on the ladder, Gus showed him how to work the brush under the clapboard lip, to start in one direction, and then finish to make sure there would be a good seal and cover of paint on each section. He started slowly to get the technique and then moved along more quickly, covering broad sections before they moved the ladder to the next section, painting from the top down.

Jamiel was there immediately after school the following day, and they were able to work together on the lower sections. "No problems today?" asked Gus.

"No. No problems today. I'm sorry I couldn't tell you why, but things are okay," replied Jamiel, unable to look Gus directly in the eye.

"Just as long as you're okay. Some of those boys I saw you with a few weeks back didn't look like the best company."

Jamiel was defensive in response. "Oh, because they were black, you assume they can only be a gang of thugs?"

Gus's shoulders dropped. "Jamiel, I don't assume young blacks are hoodlums and gangsters."

"No, just poor ones that can't dress like the good white boys," said Jamiel as he dropped his brush in the paint can and stomped off to the house in the old paint clothes he had on. He passed his mom as he rushed up to his room, closing his door with a slam.

Chapter 25

Jamiel lay on his bed, trying to sort out what had just happened. Why did he get upset so quickly lately? Was he the one being judgmental or was Gus? His life was closing in on him from all sides and would crush him. School and maybe getting into college seemed as if they were enough to think about. Why was he unsure about wanting to go to school? Was he afraid he couldn't handle it? Maybe he wasn't smart enough and would get exposed?

Then he started thinking about his old neighborhood. Something was definitely different since the shooting. Why was Leonard, who was always trying to put some distance between Jamiel and the shady side of what they did, now pulling him in without a choice? There was nothing on that path that was going to end well.

Is that going to be my destination in life? I mean, how many guys from the hood have a choice anyway?

He was too restless to stay in his room, so he trotted downstairs and out the door until he reached the front of St. Francis. He didn't know why he was there, but he ambled down the driveway and stood in front of the rectory door, hesitating to knock.

Angelo stood at the kitchen window, and Jamiel had already spotted him.

Tom peeked out the window and opened the door. "Jamiel. What's going on? Are you coming from paintball or something?"

Jamiel glanced down at his clothes. He still had on Gus's paint pants and shirt with various paint colors splattered here and there. "I forgot what I was wearing. No wonder no one talked to me on the way over."

"I'm glad this wasn't your idea for new basketball uniforms for the team this year," chuckled Tom. "What do you think, Angelo? Maybe these would be so distracting to the other team that they'd lose their focus?"

"I like them, and you don't have to worry about getting them dirty. Less laundry," joked Angelo. "Do you want some *pasta fagioli* with us? There's plenty."

"No, thanks. My mom's making dinner. Probably wondering where I am."

"And where are you?" asked Tom.

"I wish I knew. I can't figure the Busbi guy out. At first, he's grouchy, rude, and like a porcupine to be around, and then he's not. Sometimes he says things that make me wonder if he's a racist white guy—no offense—and then, I don't know. Sometimes he looks at me as if he likes me, then other times he eyes me as if I am his enemy."

Tom motioned him into the room. "You seem a little on-edge yourself lately. Anything else going on?"

"Not much." Jamiel thought, *Well, not much I can talk about.*

"Okay. I'll act as if I believe you. Gus is an interesting individual. You're right to think he has been a crank who doesn't want to be around anyone. It's not you, and I can tell you he's no racist."

"Do you know him?"

"I coached with him," replied Tom.

"What? Coached what?"

"Nothing you'd be interested in. He coached the high school basketball team at St. Francis for a long time. He even brought one of the teams to the state championship game to only lose on the last play, which is pretty good for a small school like ours. If I told you he was funny, loved kids, and was a great player in his day, would you believe me?"

"I don't believe you," replied Jamiel, waiting for a sign that Tom was kidding.

"He's a great, great guy. Loving husband. Incredible father—"

"Wait. I know his wife died just before Mom and I moved in, but you said he had a kid?" asked Jamiel with interest in his voice.

"He had a son. Julia and Gus had always wanted kids, but after nine years, they had resigned themselves to the fact that it wasn't in the cards. They loved each other and were very involved with the Church and the community. Gus used to go over to Ramsay Park, where you play, and hold clinics to teach the younger kids how to play. He was an impressive player on that court from what I hear."

"You guys have got to be pullin' my leg or something," interrupted Jamiel.

"Hand on the Bible that this is true. Well, just when they figured their life would be without children, Julia became pregnant, and they had a boy in 1968 and named him Danny. Julia told me that Gus was in seventh heaven the moment he knew he was going to be a father. He loved being Danny's dad, and I hear the love was mutual. They were almost like best friends. Danny played here and was as good as you, and that's a compliment to both of you. He loved the game as much as you do."

"So, what happened?" Jamiel leaned forward.

"When he was your age, seventeen, he was gunned down on the street right in front of the porch of your house."

"What? What are you saying? Gunned down by who?" Jamiel suddenly had a sick feeling.

"It was someone from a gang," replied Tom.

Jamiel sat open-mouthed, staring at Tom.

He hesitated for several seconds, watching Angelo stir the beans and pasta soup, and then asked, "Was he black? Was the shooter black?"

Tom nodded several times. "It crushed Gus and broke his heart, but he continued to coach, and he and Julia stayed active to honor his memory. He was different, though, for those fourteen years. Then Julia died, and Gus seemed to fall into a black pit. Life had lost its meaning when Danny died, and then it lost its soul when Julia was gone. I've talked to Gus, and I've talked to his brother-in-law, Mike, many, many times, but he has given up. Well, it's more like life seemed to give up on him. Love, purpose, a reason to get up in the morning all seemed to vanish with Julia's death. It's been three very painful years for him."

Jamiel sat there in silence for a full minute and then suddenly got up to leave.

"Where are you going?" Tom asked.

His eyes welled up as he turned to Tom. "I have a house to paint," he said, then opened the door to sprint home. When he got there, Gus was on a step ladder painting a section of the house, and then he peered down to see Jamiel stirring a can of paint and holding a brush in his hand. Without a word, Jamiel started painting the section next to Gus.

"I thought I lost you," said Gus.

"You can't get rid of me that easily," replied Jamiel as he continued to brush with the strokes Gus had taught him.

"Jamiel," said Gus.

Jamiel stared at Gus.

"I'm sorry I acted the way I did when I saw your friends on the porch and the times you came up to offer help. I—"

"It's okay," interrupted Jamiel. "I think we can make some good headway if we get moving."

Gus smiled and worked on the next row.

By the time it was dusk, they were standing side by side, admiring the completed section. "Looks pretty good if I have to say so myself, Mr. Busbi."

"More than pretty good. That's a professional job, Mr. Russell."

They seemed surprised when a voice behind them blurted out, "Now that the mutual admiration society is done patting themselves on the back, are you hungry for some roasted chicken and raspberry pie for dessert?"

Gus and Jamiel turned to each other and then back to Celia, nodding in unison with big smiles.

"All right, but only after you clean up this mess and wash up before you sit at my dinner table," exclaimed Celia as she returned to the house.

Seated at the table, Gus thanked Celia for the invite and the plate of green beans she was passing him. "You've done a nice job making this a home. It deserves a good family." Gus's eyes misted.

"Thank you, Mr. Busbi. This does feel like home to Jamiel and me, and we have you to thank for that. I don't know what we would've done."

Gus asked Celia about her job, about the colleges that were sending letters to Jamiel, and talked about the history of the house. He left little time for questions about himself, and by the time the raspberry pie was polished off, they all sat back with full stomachs and groaned, followed by laughter. Gus said it was the nicest dinner he had eaten in quite some time.

Chapter 26

Jamiel was surprised to find himself looking forward to working with Mr. Busbi after school. He shot out of his last class when the bell rang and started for home at a fast pace. As he approached his house, his mood sank when he spotted another black car parked in front for the second time this week. He stopped in his tracks. He thought for a second and then backed up and made his way down a small alley and across a few neighbor's backyards until he was able to squeeze through the opening in the fence near Gus's garage. He quickly changed and reached the side of the garage where Gus was working without being seen by anyone except for Gus, who was scratching his head.

"Don't ask," said Jamiel as he used the scraper edge to open the can of paint and to stir it before painting the next section.

As he painted, he asked, "Mr. Busbi, were the neighborhoods around here always like this?"

"What do you mean by 'like this'?"

"Crime. Shootings. Drugs. People scared to let their kids play outside. You know—it kind of sucks to think about raising a family in some of these neighborhoods."

"You sure you don't want to talk about more complicated subjects—like why the Sox can't win the World Series?"

"Maybe some other time, but you've seen these neighborhoods firsthand for a long time."

"You mean, I'm old."

"You're looking younger every day."

"Well, it's gotten pretty bad over the last several decades. If you do some reading, there have been lots of neighborhoods that have gone from being nice to a ghetto and back again."

"Where did that happen?"

"Have you ever been to the North End?"

"Only when Mom and I walked the red brick thing when I was ten."

"You mean, The Freedom Trail?"

"Yeah, that's it. It was pretty neighborhoody, and the food was good. What's that thing with the cream in it?"

"A cannoli?"

"Yeah, those are good. What's Busbi for a name?"

"It's Italian."

"Mom thought so. Why don't you live in the North End? There are lots of Italians there, aren't there? They've probably been there since Columbus."

"Not exactly. The Italians didn't come until much later. There's a lot of history in that neighborhood from Paul Revere, John Adams, and the start of America to this day. Did you know that there were small communities of free African American families around Cobb Hill from the 1600s through the 1800s?"

"What? Are you sure they were free?"

"Yup. There were a lot of people in Boston, especially the North End and Beacon Hill, who were abolitionists. There was a Baptist Church that blacks belonged to in the North End, and the first African meeting house that you can still see on the 'red brick thing' is in Beacon Hill."

Jamiel wanted to smile at that last comment but was surprised to hear for the first time about this community. "How do you know all this?"

"I read someone's report project on it once. The North End was the fashionable place to be and one of the most important parts of town in the 1800s, with rich British living there. But by the time it was abandoned by all but the poorest, it was full of crime, prostitution, murders—you name it."

"Is that when the Italians moved in?"

"Nope. There was a massive wave of poor Irish that moved into these ghettos. They faced very harsh treatment, job discrimination, illness, and hatred from other groups. They lived in extreme poverty with large families in a single room. Much of the resentment was because they were so poor, Irish, and Catholic."

"Seems like they run the town now. How bad could it have been for them?" asked Jamiel.

"It was really bad, but they were eventually able to work railroads, construction, housekeeping, and such to finally make a go of it. Soon, they were joined by Jewish immigrants who faced their own history of discrimination and hatred. Then the Italians started coming over in the late 1800s into unbearable conditions. Most of the immigrants were unskilled and uneducated and were treated with very strong discrimination."

"So the North End was Irish, Jewish, and Italian?"

"Most of the Jewish and Irish residents moved to another section of town. Guess where that was?" asked Gus.

Jamiel shrugged, painting a little slower as Gus talked.

"Right around here. Roxbury, Dorchester, Mattapan, South Boston, and around these neighborhoods. The Italians struggled to be accepted as they were treated poorly and described as dishonest, violent, uneducated, criminal slime—even in the newspapers. More like animals than human beings. Sound familiar?"

"You're not trying to say Italians were treated as bad as black slaves, are you?"

Gus replied, shaking his head noticeably. "No, I would never say that. Freedom is the most fundamental and important gift we receive from God as humans. Even in the worst conditions, having freedom is better than being someone's slave, no matter what your conditions are.

"Poverty and starvation were so bad in parts of Italy that four million came over for the hope of a better life, but these uneducated, unskilled men often lived fifteen to a cellar pit and couldn't make enough to get out of the poverty and rise above the discrimination. Down South, many were farmers who worked on the plantations after the Civil War freed the slaves. They were sharecroppers with a debt to pay off that often took all their earnings, so they were stuck working that plantation. The Italians would work side by side with Negroes, who continued to work the plantations, and they were hated because of that too. They were lynched, imprisoned, and executed on false charges. It was so bad that two million of the four million that came over went back to the poverty and harsh life they had left for the promise of American roads that they had heard were paved with gold."

Gus turned to Jamiel, "Sorry, I got sidetracked. My point is that neighborhoods are often the people that share a heritage and common experience. Many groups experienced unlivable conditions and prejudice for a long time before they were able to push forward. Italians were shunned for many reasons, but sometimes because their skin was dark and they looked different than others. I think blacks face the toughest battle to be accepted because that difference and their history are so distinct. Prejudice and hate come from fear and ignorance. I know there can be an overwhelming feeling of hopelessness and despair with no chance to get out, but I think young men such as yourself can break that cycle and be that hope for others."

Jamiel had stopped painting and felt frozen in place. He didn't know whether to feel an incredible sense of elation that Gus saw potential and strength in him or anger at the arrogance that Gus could even pretend to know what it's like to be a black man. No matter how hard any other group felt they had it, they weren't forced like over-stuffed cargo in the bowels of a ship in chains, separated from their families, their homes, their dignity, and their freedom as a human being. Instead of lashing back, he remained quiet, thinking about all Gus had said until he finished the final sections and stepped down beside Gus to admire their work.

Gus turned toward Jamiel, who didn't return the eye contact. "Jamiel, I'm sorry if I said anything that upset you. I've been watching how hard you work and how quickly you pick up on things. I see how your mother is raising you with character and depth. I've often heard other people talk with admiration about your gifts. I just don't want to see any fears or excuses get in the way of you becoming the man you were created to be. No matter what anyone else thinks of us, they can't take that gift of who we were made to be away from us. When it comes down to it, we are all human beings made by the same God with the same dignity and worth. Heck, we even have the same parents!" laughed Gus.

Jamiel finally made eye contact with Gus, "What are you talking about, the same parents?"

"I was reading about it. They've been making a lot of discoveries with the breakthroughs in DNA and studies of our chromosomes. Studies now show that the DNA of every human being on earth can be traced back to a single male and a single female parent—the same ones. So, you might not like it, but we are related, and both parents come from Africa. How's that for dispelling the myth that there are different races?" asked Gus as he painted the end of Jamiel's nose with his brush.

Jamiel was so stunned that he instinctively reacted and painted a blue line down Gus's face with his still-wet brush. Once he realized what he had just done, he waited for Gus to yell, but instead, Gus bent over, picked up his can of paint that was still a quarter filled, and held it over Jamiel's head for a second. For a second, Jamiel thought he was actually going to tip the can over his head—and then he did. A second later, Jamiel was dumping his can of paint down Gus's shirt. Celia came outside and started to raise her index finger until it was obvious that they were laughing—and covered with paint. When Jamiel and Gus glanced at each other and then at her, she turned, said, "Oh, no!" and quickly ran back in the house.

Jamiel heard the kitchen window being cranked open and his mother yelling, "If you two boys ever get cleaned up, and if you promise not to include me in your human art experiment, maybe I'll have some dinner and homemade lemon cake waiting for you! Those are my non-negotiable conditions!" She then cranked the window closed.

It took a while to scrub up and finally change, with a few remnants of battle paint still visible before they could enter the kitchen for inspection and permission to sit down at the table. They sat and laughed at their ridiculous antics and how much better the house looked than either of them did a half-hour ago.

At the end of dessert, Gus thanked Celia for another tasty home-cooked meal after a long day at work. "This was nice. Your son is more than a good work partner. I couldn't have finished this job without him. I've offered to pay him for his work several times, but he won't accept it. Is there anything I can offer the two of you?"

"You already have, Mr. Busbi. You already have," said Celia with tears in her eyes.

At the door, Jamiel stepped out into the chilly evening air with Gus. "I can help put away the ladders and stuff tomorrow."

"Take tomorrow off. You've earned some rest and fun this week."

"Well, have a good night, Mr. Busbi. Maybe we can talk more about what we were discussing earlier. I don't know exactly how I feel about everything you were saying."

"Anytime," said Gus. "I never want to say anything that would disrespect you or have any misunderstandings."

Jamiel tilted his head up toward the sky to see the bright moonlight on the clouds, "It looks like rain."

"Hopefully, not tonight! Sleep well."

"You too."

He went inside but noticed that Gus stayed out for a few minutes to gaze at the sky and the accomplishment of the newly painted back of the house. He wondered how he was feeling after their time together today.

Chapter 27

No different from any other Thursday, Gus woke up early to get ready for breakfast at the Eastside. What *was* different was that he wasn't fighting an overwhelming feeling of despondency and malaise in facing the day and people in general. He still felt a profound sense of sadness and loss, but the loneliness that pervaded his very being seemed less dark this morning.

When he sat next to Mike at the Eastside and struck up a conversation with a few of the other guys at the table, Mike gave him a look as if he could tell that something was different. Gus wasn't his old self, but he wasn't his new self either—the loner new self that Mike worried about so often.

"Gus, let me know when you need help with painting that back side of your house," said Mike.

"All set on the painting front," replied Gus with a little smirk on his face.

"What do you mean you're all set, and what happened to your hand?" asked Mike, staring at the bandage wrapped around his right hand.

"Hey, show some respect for our beautiful waitress. Good morning, Linda," said Gus as she approached the table.

Linda jutted out one hip and held out her ordering pad with a definite air of playful short-temperedness as she rolled her eyes. "Who put happy pills in your coffee this morning?"

"Not you, since I haven't gotten my coffee yet," joked Gus, bringing a round of laughter at the table.

"Keep that up, and you won't be getting any either," quipped Linda.

Mike leaned closer to Gus. "You seem good this morning. Anything going on?"

"Nope. Just enjoying your company."

"Sure. Sure. Now, what's this about your house painting being all set?"

"Jamiel and I took care of it this week while you were out of town."

"Jamiel and you? You two couldn't seem to do anything but lock horns most of the time! He's a great kid, but I'm surprised you two could do that size of a job without a referee."

"It's odd. I'm working with him, talking, or teaching him things, and it feels comfortable. I like him, but other times I look at his face and get a bad feeling inside. I almost feel angry about everything. It's more emotion than I've felt for a while, but it's confusing as hell."

"Huh. You've worked with a ton of boys that were black since Danny and not said anything like that. Did you ever feel that same way?"

"I don't think so," said Gus as Linda brought their coffees and took their orders.

After breakfast, Gus strolled the familiar blocks to his house, thinking about Jamiel's question on how the neighborhood had changed. Many neighbors' houses had been torn down and replaced with larger brick apartments and office buildings. Protestant churches and Jewish temples had come and gone, as had different small businesses that had tried to give it an enthusiastic go over the years. A lot of the people he and Julia knew when they first moved into the neighborhood sold their homes to developers and joined the exodus to the suburbs. The influx of new ethnicities of people and cultures was not new to Boston but changed what was familiar and created a less-connected neighborhood. It wasn't as if they weren't friendly, hard-working, good-hearted family people, but the cultural bonds that made it a more open and connected neighborhood had disappeared. Instead of an American culture with different ethnic groups making up the fabric of that culture, the neighborhood felt more like many separate cultures that happened to share the same physical location. Or maybe Gus was just getting old and had no family and less involvement to still foster those connections.

When Gus got home, he cleaned up the area where they had been painting for the past four days, carefully folding the tarps, putting away the ladders, and organizing the paint, brushes, rags, and scrapers for the next side to be tackled in the fall. In the entryway mudroom where he hung his jackets and hats and kept his boots, he noticed a rolled-up pair of jeans and a black hooded sweatshirt. He remembered that Jamiel had changed into the paint clothes he had given him and must have left these behind. He picked up the bundled clothes to fold them, and a roll of bills dropped to the hallway floor. He gazed down at the sizable roll, held together with a green elastic wound tightly around it. If these were all twenties, this was at least a thousand dollars. As he held the money, he could think of few good reasons Jamiel would be carrying a roll of bills like this. He wanted to give Jamiel the benefit of the doubt, but this, coupled with the late arrivals that Jamiel didn't want to talk about, didn't look good. He put the money back into the pocket, rolled the clothes back up, and stuffed them back in the corner where Jamiel had left them.

* * * *

Jamiel sat in English class, listening to one of the students reading from the Dickens novel they were studying. With the mention of money in the story, Jamiel suddenly remembered that Trig gave him another wad of cash after the latest drops, stuffing it in his pocket and not allowing any argument. He panicked, thinking about Gus finding the money in the rolled-up clothes.

Sister Helen was substituting for the regular English teacher and glanced at Jamiel several times before finally addressing him. "Mr. Russell, when you're back from the mental excursion you seem to be on, could you let us know what you think about Eliot's poem?"

He could tell by the tone of her voice that she knew something was wrong.

At lunch, he sat down with his lunch tray to the buzz of a full cafeteria, but he wasn't eating or listening to the conversation at his table. Suddenly, he got up and made his way through the cafe and out a side door to see if he could retrieve the bundle of clothes.

When Jamiel reached his house, he quietly crept down the driveway and around the house to see Gus with paint supplies in his hand. Jamiel moved his back along the side of the house and remained undercover behind a large holly bush. He was feeling almost more nervous than he had meeting Joey Caporale because this was more personal. When Gus entered the side door to the cellar, Jamiel sprinted by the entrance and reached the door to the hallway mudroom. The door was open. He breathed a deep sigh of relief when he saw the clothes just as he had left them. Quickly, he grabbed them and ran around the other side of the house until he safely reached the front porch—except that Sister Helen was surprisingly sitting on one of the rockers looking up at him. If he thought his heart was going to pound through his ribs before, he was in full panic mode now. *What was she doing here?*

"Would we be planning on another excursion during school time, Mr. Russell?"

Holding the change of clothes, he tried desperately to think of a response."Ahhh, Sister Helen. I, um—"

"That's exactly what I thought you were going to say," said Sister Helen, appearing half-upset and half-concerned. "Did you get to finish your lunch? It would serve you right to be a little hungry, but I'd not be wantin' your stomach growling while the other students are trying to concentrate."

"I had my sandwich. I just wanted to get something I forgot before my next class started. I was planning on going right back. Really, I was."

Sister Helen peered down at the rolled bundle of clothes in Jamiel's arms and raised one eyebrow. "I can see why this was so urgent."

Jamiel tightened his grip on the bundle and stuttered, "I'll just put this in the house and be right there!" He left Sister Helen standing on the porch, and Jamiel's heart stopped as he heard voices when he got back downstairs.

"Mr. Busbi," said Sister Helen.

"Sister Helen. What are you doing here?" asked Gus.

"Rounding up lost sheep," she replied with half a smile.

When Jamiel opened the screen door, Gus asked, "Is everything all right?"

"I'm thinkin' a level five emergency," said Sister Helen as she walked down the stairs and toward the school.

Jamiel shrugged as if to excuse himself and quickly followed her.

"So, Mr. Russell, are you really okay?"

"I'm working on it, Sister. You don't have to worry," replied Jamiel, although he imagined himself being dragged back from a jailbreak by the warden and her bloodhounds.

"I don't know if you knew this or not, Jamiel, but religious sisters are women, and worrying about people we care about is what we do."

Jamiel suddenly felt a sensation run from the back of his neck to the front of his scalp with the realization that she may actually care and worry about him. They strolled the last block quietly until they reached the driveway to the school.

Angelo was on a step ladder, trimming some shrubs. "You two out for a nice stroll on a spring day?"

Jamiel gave Angelo a half-smile.

Sister Helen quipped, "Maybe if you concentrate on your own work, you'll have time for a stroll as well, Mr. Salvato."

****

Back at home, Gus had been left scratching his head by what had just happened. Why was Jamiel home from school in the middle of the day? And why was Sister Helen on his front porch? By the time he went into the backdoor mudroom and saw the bundle of clothes gone, his curiosity was piqued. Jamiel must have remembered the clothes and snuck out to grab them before Gus noticed them—which only proved that he was well aware of the large sum of money being there and that he didn't want anyone to know about it. *Where did he get that kind of money, and what was the panic to leave school when he would be home in a few more hours? And how the heck did he manage to sneak in and out without me seeing him?*

Gus was too restless to let the questions roll around in this head, so he decided to go for a walk. Without intentionally thinking of where he was heading, he found himself in front of St. Francis, the church in which he and Julia had been active parishioners for many years until her death. This was the place where they had developed close friendships, including a dear friendship with the wonderful pastor, Father Mike Coleman. This was the place where they deepened their faith, taught students, coached basketball, did mission work, honored Easter and Chrismas seasons, and celebrated Danny's baptism, first communion, and confirmation. This was also the place where they were supported after the loss of Danny, during and after his funeral. By the time it came to Julia's funeral Mass and burial, Gus was numb and empty. His grief clung to him like a thick, dark fog. The pain and emptiness were the only way to hang on to Julia. Moving on and having fun seemed wrong. He stopped attending Mass, social events, and coaching the basketball team. He just stopped living.

Father Tom had come to the parish a few years before Julia's death and developed a deep respect and love for both of them. He'd never met Danny but spent many hours talking with each of them about their son and their continued struggles to ease the pain of the violent loss of their only child. After years of marriage with no children, it was such an unexpected gift to them when Julia became pregnant and more of a gift as they raised him with love and admiration of the man he was becoming.

All that ended on a September afternoon in 1986 when a bullet from the shotgun of an angry gang leader tore a hole through his chest. There hadn't been a night since that Gus hadn't relived his son dying in his arms as he held his bloody body, waiting for the ambulance to arrive. Julia would be startled on many occasions when Gus was jolted awake by his nightmare, with Julia screaming, "No! No!" from the porch, followed by a loud gunshot and then watching Danny fall to his knees and collapse. The shooter brazenly stared at Gus with no emotion except the anger he came with and then jumped into the old black Cadillac that rounded the corner to get him out of the situation. There was no remorse shown by the shooter at the agonizing trial Gus and Julia attended, and he gave the same look again to Gus as he was led out of the courtroom after having been convicted of first-degree murder. Gus could never forgive him.

It was the first time in three years he made his way down this driveway between the church and the rectory, with the school and basketball gym in front of him. He turned around after a handful of steps to go back, but he felt a tug to go through the large wooden doors into the church. As he opened the door, the sunlight streamed in where his first steps landed on the stone-tiled floor. He looked up at the majestic height of the ceiling, and instantly all of his senses were awakened to the beauty of this church, the feel of the marble, the sounds of his footsteps echoing, and the faint smell of incense and burning candles.

Each step brought a memory to mind, and a more profound sense in his soul that longed to be in the presence of Christ, here in the Church that Jesus promised would live forever. He hadn't expected to feel this rush of emotion after so many years of not feeling anything at all, and he was humbled by it as he walked down the center aisle and sat in one of the middle pews where the sunlight through the rose window above the entrance landed on the marble floor. He sat and prayed, asking forgiveness for abandoning his relationship with God, for being angry at Him when He took away everything he lived for. After several minutes of just being still, he finally asked, *God, I have no business asking for favors, but I'm asking you to take care of Jamiel and make sure he's on the right path.*

Just as he asked again, Gus sensed a presence behind him. Someone had managed to make his way down the aisle quietly and slip into the pew behind Gus. It was several minutes before Gus heard a voice.

"You've always got a friend here."

Without turning around to confirm the owner of the familiar voice, Gus replied, "You've always been a good friend."

Tom got up and sat next to Gus. "Thanks, but I wasn't talking about me. What brings you back?"

"Just passing by."

"And I'm Mother Teresa."

"I wanted to talk to you about something, or more accurately, someone."

"He wouldn't happen to go to school here and live downstairs from you, would he?"

Gus turned toward Tom. "And how did you know that?"

"Sister Helen mentioned that she spoke to you when she fetched him from your house."

Gus ran his hand along the top of the smoothly worn wooden pew in front of him. "I didn't know if anything was going on with Jamiel that you were aware of."

"Like what?" Tom didn't want to break his confidentiality with Jamiel about the night he picked him up at the police station.

"I don't know. I think he's a good kid, but I get a feeling he's being pulled in a bad direction. I didn't know if you knew of anything."

"We've all got things pulling us in different directions, away from our purpose. He has grown up in a tough neighborhood, and I'm not sure if some of those friends have his best interests at heart. It's tough enough being a teenager these days, and he hasn't had it easy in a lot of ways. Celia is a great mom and person, so he's lucky there, but he's never had a father around or a male mentor at home to guide him."

"You're right on that. I'm just not sure about things," said Gus.

"I think you're doing the right thing by praying on it. You might be surprised at how much better His plans are than ours." Tom smiled.

"I know, trust the Big Guy. Right?"

"Something like that. Well, exactly like that," Tom said with a smile.

Gus nodded.

"What about you, Gus? I haven't talked to you for far too long. I miss having you around, and I know the boys do as well," said Tom.

"I'm sure they're in good hands," replied Gus.

Tom smiled. "It's a two-way street. Kids are good for the coach as well."

Putting his hand on the bench to help himself up, Gus muttered, "They are, indeed, but there's a time to move on."

Tom stood up with Gus and stepped into the aisle. "And a time to live. You've got a lot of giving left in you, Coach." They ambled to the back, and Tom genuflected toward the altar before continuing outside with Gus. "Jamiel's got a good chance to be the man we all see in him. I'm glad he has your influence to offset those who want to drag him down."

Gus returned home thinking about retreating into his self-imposed routine of solitary confinement, but the door wouldn't shut as easy as it had for the past three years. As much he wanted to pull it shut, something was keeping it open these days.

Chapter 28

The final bell on a Friday afternoon always brought a smile to Jamiel. He was looking forward to a relaxing night without homework, and he left school in a good mood. When he reached the end of the school driveway, he noticed a car that didn't look like it belonged to a parent. The window rolled down, and he could see Trig in the front passenger seat. Trig waved him over, and he could see Mal driving and Ricky in the back with Halfway. "Jam, school's out for the weekend. We've got some tickets to the Sox game tonight. You up for it?"

Jamiel wanted to say no, but his mouth said, "Cool. I'd be up for that."

"Good to hear it, man. We'll come by around seven and park on the other side of the Fens courts," said Mal.

As they took off, Jamiel tried to put his finger on what he was feeling. He should be excited to be going out to a game on Friday night with his friends, but he wasn't. He could feel how much he craved acceptance from his old neighborhood brothers, a male affirmation that all the hugs, compliments, and loving looks from his mom couldn't fill. He knew she loved him more than herself, but she was his mother and saw him through a different lens. He needed to transition from being a boy to a man with value and respect, but he also knew the acceptance and affirmation from his Lenox Street brothers never seemed to satisfy that need for very long.

At dinner, Jamiel and his mom talked about their days. "I'm really proud of you, Jamiel. Replacing the roof and all the time you put into painting the house with Mr. Busbi was impressive. I hope you're learnin' a lot and that things are going better with Mr. Busbi. They seem to be."

"Yeah, he's all right once he sorta lets you in from time to time. I did learn a lot from him and Mike. Maybe when I buy you a house someday, I'll know how to take care of it."

"Wouldn't that be something, to own your own home with a nice girl?"

"Yeah, and what's your idea of a 'nice' girl for your son?" smiled Jamiel as he took a bite of dinner.

This might have been a loaded question since she had gotten pregnant without being married. He certainly saw her differently from all the girls he knew from the old neighborhood that got "knocked up" and either had abortions at the local clinic or stayed at home with their moms to raise another baby in this cycle of poverty and hopelessness. Somehow Celia was able to push past her lack of confidence and skills to fight for Jamiel. She attended school at night while working her way up at a local company and consciously maturing and improving herself. None of this came easily for a young girl with the demands of being a caring and present mother and working to break through her own personal challenges. She didn't do it alone as her mother, sisters, and members of her church pitched in to make things possible and encouraged her to take the risks that she would have resisted if Jamiel wasn't in the picture. She wanted him to be proud of her when he was old enough to think of that—and he was. He thought often about how much he admired his mom, and now he wanted her to be proud of him.

"That's a good question. I guess someone who cares. Cares about God. Cares about her family. Cares about herself. And will care about you. There are a lot of girls out there looking to feel better about themselves by catching a boy like you. There are a lot of boys out there wanting to use girls for their own pleasure—they're players with no real desire to do what's best for a girl. To respect her and honor her dignity. To treat her the way you would want someone treating your own daughter. A girl should respect herself, be honest with herself, and think about more than only herself. Hopefully, she'll be strong and love you with more than feelings and want what is best for you. She should be someone who wants you to get to heaven. Without a strong faith, your relationship won't have a real foundation."

"She sounds like you, Mama," laughed Jamiel.

"Yeah. And you're going to have to be a real man to deserve someone like me," Celia laughed back as she rubbed her hand in his hair. "Hopefully, even better."

"Hey, Mom. Some guys from school wanted to go to the Red Sox game tonight. Someone's dad got tickets and asked if I'd like to come along."

"What boys?"

"No one you know. Father Tom asked me to be captain of the basketball team next year, and I think it would be good to get more connected with the guys. I don't even know everyone that's going," said Jamiel as he scooped up the last of his beans.

He always knew when worried thoughts ran through his mom's mind, but he could sense she wanted to trust him. "Okay. Please be safe and have fun."

Jamiel replied, "I'm planning on it." He grabbed a piece of bread and kissed her on the cheek before heading out the door with his jacket and hat.

He jumped in the back of the car as the crew headed over to a spot where they could park for free and walk the remaining quarter mile to Fenway Park. Halfway pulled out a cold six-pack of Budweiser and handed one to each of the boys as he pulled them off of the plastic rings.

"Cheaper than in the park," said Trig as he guzzled the frosty amber brew.

"We'll make up for that," said Mal.

Jamiel took a sip and asked, "Mal, how's the case going? I haven't heard back from anyone."

Mal replied, "Still working with my lawyer, but I copped to stealin' the car just before we got picked up. I said I didn't know the gun was there until we noticed it sliding out from under the seat, explaining our prints being on it. We didn't know that the stuff was in the back, and I picked you up a block away. Your story ties and our stories tie."

Jamiel asked, "How do they tie it if you didn't tell them you stole the car that night when they pulled us in?"

"All we said was, 'We didn't know anything about the gun,' and, 'we didn't know anything about the stolen goods.' And, 'We picked you up later,'" said Trig. "So we didn't fess up about stealing the car at first—understandable, but no conflict."

Mal added, "Somehow, I'm going to have to pay for borrowing the car, but there are no witnesses that can I.D. us and no proof that I did it. Highly suspicious—sure. Can they win in court? Maybe, but they are stacked up with cases, so I pleaded down."

"Huh," said Jamiel as they got out of the car and walked down Jersey Street to the buzz of the crowd closer to Fenway Park.

Ricky motioned them to an entrance on Lansdowne Street, which sat behind centerfield and the infamous left-field wall. Ricky had a friend at the ticket booth who had 'passes,' which allowed them to sneak in. In return, the ticket guy would get his drugs next time at a good price. As they showed their passes to the ticket taker, they handed him a fifty-dollar bill and were in. Jamiel said, "I thought you said you had tickets?"

"I just asked if you wanted to go to the game," smiled Trig.

Jamiel half-smiled and followed them through the crowds to make their way from the right-field grandstands to the standing area above the Red Sox dugout and first base. "We can stay here until we see open seats for people who didn't show. In the meantime, we can enjoy the game and make some money." With all the people bumping into one another, picking people's pockets and bags was easy as the other guys worked in pairs. Trig and Halfway worked the beer line as they stood behind the better-dressed fans who were focused on not spilling their beers from thin plastic cups. Once they paid and stuffed their wallet in their back pocket, Halfway would drop something and bump the fan before they grabbed their beers. This gave Trig an opening to lift the wallet as he bent down to help. The fan wouldn't realize his wallet was missing until several innings had passed, and Trig and the team had moved on to another concession stand on the third-base side. Few white fans ever made eye contact with them, and they didn't try to engage.

Mal and Ricky spent more time working the fans crisscrossing the open spaces and constantly stopping or bumping into each other. Open bags, purses, and large wallets were easy game. Their pickpocket clothes were bulky, with pockets sewn in to hold the easy pickings. Jamiel just stood behind the last row and tried to watch the game itself as the Sox tied the score in the third against the Royals on a home run from Damon and then a double from Millar that scored Bellhorn. Jamiel admired the skill of the players' games and enjoyed the excitement of plays that brought fans to their feet, but his companions only saw these moments as opportunities to take advantage of preoccupied victims.

By the eighth inning, the crew was ready to leave, having filled up on opportunities and emptied the wallets of any valuable content in bathrooms stalls before tossing them in the trash can.

The Red Sox were down by two runs, by a score of 6–4, so Jamiel was disappointed to leave early and give up on the game. Outside the park, they returned to the car, and Jamiel could hear the loud cheers as he later found out that Bellhorn hit a two-run homer to tie the game, and Varitek doubled with two outs in the bottom of the ninth to score Ramirez for the walk-off win.

In the car, the guys started pouring a surprising number of bills of different denominations into a black canvas bag. Jamiel couldn't believe how much cash they were able to lift without being caught. He wanted no part of it, and he was more disappointed about leaving the game early than they were excited about the profitable evening. Halfway lit up a joint as they drove home, and Jamiel passed as it made its rounds. As they got closer to Jamiel's house, Ricky tried to entice him to hang out with them, which might be until very early morning. "Don't be a wimp, Jam. The night is young, and we've got spending money to enjoy it."

"I think I'm going to call it a night," said Jamiel as they pulled in front of his house and dropped him off before their tires made a squealing sound as they sped off down the street. Jamiel shook his head and decided to walk a few blocks to get the smell of pot out of his clothes. It would make it a little later too, increasing the chances that his mother might have gone to bed after a long week of work and taking care of the house at night. He was struck by what a remarkable woman she was, but was he becoming a remarkable man for her to admire?

The church was quiet as he passed by. He noticed the light on in the back of the rectory where Father Tom lived. After a few more blocks, with the light of the waning moon above, he noticed someone walking ahead of him. If he slowed down, he could create some distance between them, or if he sped up, he could simply pass without really having to talk, but then he recognized the silhouette and walk. "Mr. Busbi?"

Gus turned around, "Is that you, Jamiel?"

"I know, it's hard to see us black boys at night."

"I was thinking that it was hard to make out anyone in the shadows of the tree you were under."

Jamiel felt a little embarrassed with his knee-jerk sarcasm. "Oh, yeah."

"What are you doin' walkin' around alone on a Friday night?" asked Gus.

"I could ask you the same question, but I get only one wiseguy question a night. I went to the Sox game with some friends tonight. I just got home and felt like walking."

"Good game to take in. Must have been an exciting finish to see in person," said Gus.

"I'm sure it was."

"I thought you said you were at the game."

"I was. The guys I was with wanted to leave early," replied Jamiel.

"Ah. Never give up on a game. That's the beauty of sports!"

"I know," said Jamiel. "Gus, the Sox have never won the Series in your lifetime, right?"

"1918 was a little before my time," said Gus.

"You were around in '46, '67, '75, and '86, right?"

"Yup. They lost in the seventh game in all four series, torture you haven't had to experience."

"Must have been something to watch. Tell you what. If they make it to the Series this year, I'll take you," said Jamiel. "I'd like to see them win it once for you."

Gus seemed touched but said, "You mean, before I kick off, right?"

"Before we both kick-off," laughed Jamiel. "Oh, by the way, Mom said there is a leak in the kitchen faucet. I don't know exactly what's going on."

As they approached the house, Gus replied, "Jamiel, I don't want to take advantage of your valuable help, but do you want to check it out with me in the morning?"

"As long as it's not too early. Mom's going to be workin' at the church most of the day. I don't know anything about plumbing, though," answered Jamiel.

"Just the man I'm looking for!" said Gus. "I'll be over at 6 a.m.." After obviously enjoying the shock on Jamiel's face, Gus said, "Shoot. I'm sorry. I can't do six. Do you mind if we do 9:30?"

A relieved Jamiel answered, "I think I can make that one." Going inside, he quickly changed before saying goodnight at his mother's bedroom door. He imagined her smiling with relief to know he was home safe.

Chapter 29

Jamiel ran down the sideline for a pass, but instead of a basketball, he ducked as a blast of bullets shot in his direction. He sprinted and jumped the high fence, spraining his ankle as he landed, but he kept running to keep ahead from those who continued to chase him. With each stride, his legs were getting heavier and heavier, and time seemed to slow down. He made it a block before another group appeared in front of him, aiming guns as he stood in front of the Grant Manor projects on Washington Street. He could hardly make out any faces except for Marnie, who was pointing at him while Tyrell aimed a shotgun right at him. He turned around, and there was Leonard, Ricky, Trig, and Mal running in slow motion at him. He thought they might save him from certain death, but then he realized they were shooting at him too. He could feel himself turning back to see Tyrell a few steps ahead, pulling the trigger. And then he woke with a gasp. The doorbell rang several times.

He looked at the clock—9:31 a.m, and he remembered. Gus had saved him from a very bad ending to his nightmare. He wiped the sleep out of his eyes as he pulled on his jeans and a sweatshirt and quickly sprinted down the stairs to answer the door.

Gus stood with a cardboard box holding what appeared to be and smelled like a welcoming breakfast. "Did I wake you?" asked Gus.

"No. No," he said as he continued to rub his eyes. "Come on in. I think Mom is already gone."

"That's why I brought us some fuel to start the day. Do you like breakfast sandwiches? English muffin, with egg, cheese and bacon, and some fresh-squeezed orange juice to get you going." Gus placed everything on the sunlit kitchen table.

"No complaints here," said a barefoot Jamiel. "Want any coffee?"

"I'm good. Thanks. Sit down and eat up. So, you saw the Sox firsthand last night. What do you think their chances are this year, Jamiel?"

"I love Pedro, Manny, Popi, and Pokey," replied Jamiel.

"That leaves all the white guys for me," smiled Gus.

Jamiel raised his eyebrows. "I wasn't even thinking about that."

"I was only kidding. There's no reason to apologize for rooting for players you can identify with. It's natural to be excited about players you have an instinctive bond with. It gives you a feeling that you might be able to be good at something too. When I was a kid, I loved watching Dom Dimaggio and later Frank Malzone. The '67 Sox had Tony Conigliaro and Rico Petrocelli. But I also loved Reggie Smith, Tommy Harper, and my two all-time favorites have to be Louis Tiant and, if you are willing to share, Pedro."

"I'm glad you have your Italian buds to cheer for, but the Sox don't have a great history with black ballplayers, so I think my rooting is more than cheerin' for people that look like me," replied Jamiel with some feelings of discomfort trying to explain that this was deeper for him.

"You're right. The Yawkeys resisted ending segregation for far too long. They were the last team to integrate when they finally signed Pumpsie Green. Not a history to be proud of and not one that helps connect blacks to the team without some reservations."

"Thirty-five thousand fans at the game and not a lot of brothers there. When did they finally sign Green?" asked Jamiel.

"Let's see. I think it was the year after I got married, so 1959."

"Isn't that twelve years after Jackie Robinson broke in?" questioned Jamiel.

"You know your history, and that's important. Jackie was a class act all the way. I remember thinking about how much courage he had risking his life to play the game he loved. Even at thirteen, I knew it was about a lot more than playing baseball. That season changed the world in many ways."

Jamiel was taken back by the impression Jackie Robinson had made on Gus as he continued.

"He said something that stuck with me always: 'A life is not important except in the impact it has on other lives.' That is a real man in my eyes. Not just a great ballplayer."

Jamiel nodded, wishing he had seen Robinson play and wishing more that he had met him.

Gus said, "Oscar Charleson. Josh Gibson. Pop Lloyd. Buck Leonard. Turnkey Stearnes. Mule Suttles. Rube Foster, Ray Dandridge. Cool Papa Bell. Willie Wells. Smokey Joe Williams."

"Who are they?" asked a confused Jamiel.

"They are your homework. Some of the greatest ballplayers that never got to play in Major League Baseball. Some got to play, but great baseball was being enjoyed by mostly black fans in the Negro Leagues. You might enjoy reading about them, and you might get pissed thinking about them being shut out for so long, but it's important to know your history—the good, the bad, and the ugly. The important thing is to do what Jackie said. Find a way to make a positive mark on others."

"But there is still a lot of prejudice and injustice going on. Many of those thugs have no choice," said Jamiel, knowing too well how so many people were stuck with the bad hand they were dealt.

"I don't disagree. Fight it where you can, but don't use it as an excuse to say you don't have a choice. We all have choices; choices to live with honesty and treat others with dignity. There is no real difference between you and me, but there are very different challenges and seemingly insurmountable obstacles to overcome. You are fortunate to have people who care about you, and you have a bag full of integrity and talents to make a difference in this world."

Jamiel ate the rest of his breakfast as he tried to process what Gus was telling him. How could Gus have so much confidence in him? He didn't really even know him. Gus certainly didn't know the guys he was hanging around with and the things he'd been involved with lately. Where was the honesty and dignity in that? How much would Gus and his mother admire him if they knew what he'd been doing?

After breakfast, Gus worked with Jamiel to troubleshoot the leaky faucet.

When they realized that it needed to be replaced, they walked to the neighborhood hardware store to pick up a new faucet and some replacement shut-off valves that were rusting out. Jamiel spent the rest of the morning learning how the plumbing in the house worked, how to turn off the water, how to cut, replace, and solder new pipe, and how to remove and replace the shutoffs and the faucet.

When Celia arrived home, she was surprised by a brand new faucet with a high arch. All the mess in the kitchen that morning was cleaned up, and the kitchen looked immaculate. She glimpsed Jamiel, who was exuding a visible sense of accomplishment.

"What's been going on here this morning, boys?" she asked.

"Just getting a little plumbing class from the master plumber," laughed Jamiel, patting Gus on the back.

"I see we have two master plumbers in the house now," said Celia as Gus smiled and nodded.

Gus turned to Jamiel. "That's enough admiring your own work. Let's get these old rusty pipes out of this clean kitchen."

They carried out the corroded metal parts and put them in the barrel. Jamiel glanced up at the old rusty basketball hoop attached to the wooden garage and asked, "Mr. Busbi, why do you keep the hoop up if you don't use it anymore?"

Gus peered at the hoop, his lips pursed as if seeming to recall memories. "I guess you're right. I hear you aren't too bad a player yourself," said Gus.

"Working on it."

Gus went into the side door of the garage and came out with an old worn leather basketball that he pumped up and tossed to Jamiel. Jamiel rotated the ball in his hands, noting the texture of the old leather and the general feel of the ball before backing up to take a shot at the old rim. He felt the pressure of showing Gus that he could shoot but hit the front of the rim. Gus retrieved the ball and passed it back to Jamiel, who took aim and hit the back of the rim. The ball bounced back to him, so he handed Gus the ball. "It throws me off with no net and that warped backboard." Gus bounced the ball out to a spot near the house. His right hand was still bandaged, so he took the ball in his left and let go of the long shot, and it sailed right through the hoop without touching iron.

Jamiel glanced at the basket and then at Gus. "I thought you were right-handed?"

"Only when it works," said Gus, smiling as he picked up the ball and brought it to Jamiel. "I probably can't take you on in a game, but I can challenge you to a game of Horse."

Grabbing the ball, Jamiel quipped, "This will be over pretty quick. A right-hand hook off the backboard." He promptly made two dribbles to the right of the basket and took a right-handed hook shot off the backboard that rimmed in and out of the basket. Jamiel never missed that shot. "Shoot! This old backboard isn't even straight."

Gus took the ball for his shot. Since Jamiel missed, Gus could take any shot he wanted. If he made it, Jamiel would have to make the same shot, or he would get the first letter in "HORSE." The first player to end up with all five letters would lose. Instead, he took the ball in his injured hand and shot the exact same hook shot that Jamiel had attempted and banked it off the tattered backboard into the basket. "Remember, a winner makes no excuses for any conditions. Work with what you have and find a way to make it work for you."

Jamiel picked up the ball and repeated the two steps and hook shot, concentrating on the best spot to hit this uneven backboard and nailed a perfect shot, avoiding getting the first letter. They ended up playing five games as Gus showed Jamiel shots and moves he hadn't seen before, and Jamiel showed Gus a few of his own. Gus won the first two games, and Jamiel finally took him in the third and fourth by a letter. Gus gave him some pointers on slight adjustments on how he held the ball, how he aligned his elbow with his shooting hand, and how he used his legs in making his shot. They were small changes that felt awkward at first but were effective. In the last game, they were both "H-O-R-S" when Jamiel jokingly went up to dunk the basketball, something Gus couldn't do at his age, and pulled on one of the bolts holding the rim to the wooden backboard. It snapped, leaving the rim hanging by the remaining bolt. Jamiel felt a panic that he broke something that had meaning to Gus, but Gus said, "I concede and take my 'E.' I don't think I could do what you just did."

"I'm really sorry, Mr. Busbi. I was only making a joke and didn't mean to do that."

"As you said, this hoop has seen its day and is old like me. It wasn't your fault. Don't worry about it." Gus shook Jamiel's hand to congratulate him on the win, even if it was questionable in Jamiel's eyes.

Just when he thought he knew Gus, Jamiel was surprised again. The hoop was one of his last pieces of Danny. Jamiel would have felt angry, but here Gus was giving him grace so that Jamiel wouldn't feel guilty. "Old ain't so bad, and you surprised me. I don't know if I could've beaten you today. You can't tell anyone!"

Gus smiled. "I bet you one thing; I'll be sorer than you tonight. I think I'll go in now and shower." As he walked towards the back door entrance, Gus turned and said, "You're a pretty good player. If you work at it, you could be exceptional."

He stared at Gus. His words had touched something deep inside him. "Maybe I'll be able to beat you one-handed someday." He glanced up at the old rim that was now dangling over the entrance to the mystery garage. What did Gus keep in that garage? He thought *It's probably full of years of junk.*

When Jamiel came into the kitchen, Celia was turning the new faucet on and off. "You like that, don't you, Mom? And you don't have to turn it so tight to get the drip to stop anymore."

"I can't say that I don't, and it will make washing my hair a lot easier. Did you help with this?"

"Busbi showed me what to do and let me do most of it myself. He said that you can learn more by doing than just hearing."

"My, my. It looks like you had some competition out there!" said Celia with a broad grin. "Better than when I used to take you down to play as a toddler."

"He's pretty good for an old man. How old do you think he is, anyway?"

"I don't know. Sixty-something?"

"Wait a minute. He said that he was twenty-four when he got married. I think it was in 1958."

"That would make him seventy. I hope you won!" laughed Celia.

Seventy! Huh, thought Jamiel. *That old bugger knows his stuff.* Jamiel had gained respect for Gus in ways that surprised him. That night in bed, he kept going over in his mind some of the tips Gus gave him to try to make them his own.

He found himself even thinking about them during Reverend Rich's sermon on Sunday.

Gus's pointers weren't all he thought about. He also noticed Marnie was absent for the second week in a row, and it troubled him.

Chapter 30

When Jamiel returned home from morning church services, he poured himself a tall glass of water from the new kitchen faucet. As he gulped it down, he suddenly stopped. Through the bottom of his empty glass out of the window, he could see the garage and a new backboard and hoop with a white mesh net hanging from it. He stared silently until his mother called from the other room. "Are you all right?"

Jamiel waved her over. "Come here and take a look out the window."

"Yup, it's a window and a yard. What're we looking at?"

He pointed her line of vision to above the garage door. "Where did that come from?"

"I don't know. Maybe Mr. Busbi is going to start playing basketball again?"

Jamiel shook his head and went outside. As he stood inspecting the new backboard and basket, a new ball rolled to his feet.

"It works better with a ball," said the familiar voice.

Jamiel glanced over.

Gus's smile radiated how much he was enjoying the stunned expression on Jamiel's face.

"What's this?" asked Jamiel as he picked up the ball.

"Well, it's a new thing that I'm thinking of calling a 'basketball hoop.' What do you think?"

"I think you're crazy. Why did you do this? When did you do this? You had to have spent your entire evening making this."

"Try it out."

Jamiel bounced the new ball and stepped back to take a shot. It sailed right through the net, making a perfect swish sound. "See, I told you it was the hoop yesterday!"

"You're going to have to prove that." Gus laughed.

Appearing from the side door, Celia's eyes locked on Jamiel's suit coat, tie, and dress shoes from church. "No one's provin' anything in those Sunday clothes!"

"Okay, Ma. Don't worry."

He turned to Gus to say something, but Gus jumped in first, "Why don't you change, and then test it out when you come back?"

He plucked his shirt, embarrassed. "Okay. This is just what they wear at church. I only go for my mom."

"Well, I hope you won't be going just for your mom for long," replied Gus.

"Hopefully not. It would be nice to sleep in on Sundays."

"What I meant, Jamiel, is that I hope you start going for yourself. There's nothing more important than your faith."

"Yeah? Do you go?"

"I did. Every Sunday."

"Well, why don't you still go? I heard that there's nothing more important than your faith," said Jamiel with a smirk.

Gus became more somber and quiet as he seemed to search for an answer. "I'm going to have to think on that one."

Jamiel grabbed a bite, changed, and was back outside within ten minutes. He liked the feel of the new ball and the basket as he moved around the perimeter of the driveway and hit one shot after another.

"That's a nice stroke you have. You can pick up a big advantage in the game if you can improve your release time."

Gus worked with Jamiel on the quickness of his catch and release and also off his dribble. It became quickly evident that Gus wasn't only a student of the game but an effective teacher.

Jamiel was surprised at how well Gus moved at seventy but didn't want to treat him as if he were seventeen either.

When they had finished, Jamiel had sweat streaming from his brow and down his chest and back.

Gus tossed him a towel. "Your love for the game really shows. Not a lot of players are so open to being coached to get better at things we cannot always see in ourselves."

"Kind of like life, huh?" replied Jamiel, wiping the sweat off the back of his neck. "Do you mind if I use your ball for a little while to practice my foul shots?"

"It's not my ball. It's yours. So is the hoop, so don't hesitate to play here anytime. I think I'm going to go in to rest a bit and watch the ballgame," said Gus as he inched his way to the door to his apartment.

Jamiel shot for another few hours, working on some of the things Gus had just shown him, as well as some of the moves Father Tom taught him. From time to time, he found his mother peering out the kitchen window and smiling. By the time he was done, he was exhausted and collapsed on the couch, a tall glass of lemonade in hand. He could never count all the things his mother had done to sacrifice for him, but he couldn't remember anyone else doing something for him as Gus had just done. Why would he spend all that time cutting out a backboard, painting it just right, buying a new hoop and net, getting that old rotted backboard down, and putting this one up? Why would he put up a hoop for him? Why would he take time out to coach him? And why did he come to the hospital all those days and sit with his mother?

* * * *

Upstairs in his apartment, Gus sat in the same leather chair he had sat in since first buying the house. Julia had never sat in Gus's chair unless he playfully pulled her to sit on his lap. The Red Sox game was on in the background, but he was thinking about Jamiel's question. "Why don't you still go?" Three years is a long time when you attended Mass every week for your entire life. He was devastated when Julia died, and part of her had been missing for so many years before. He didn't hate God, but he wasn't too happy with Him. He hadn't given up on God, nor did he want to get back at Him by not going. He closed his eyes and tried to let the thoughts come to him without analyzing them. He believed God was as Jesus described Him in the parable of the Prodigal Son, an unconditionally loving and forgiving Father who never gives up on anyone. He struggled with an honest answer to Jamiel's thoughtful question. He couldn't say exactly why he had abandoned the Church that he had loved for so many years.

Gus made his way over to the rectory to see if Tom was available. He knocked on the side door, but there was no answer. He walked around to the back of the rectory to the garden where Tom sometimes prayed. Angelo was there, taking care of the roses.

"Angelo, how are you doing?"

"Pretty good. How about yourself?" asked Angelo.

"Not too bad. Is Father Tom here?"

"I think he may be taking care of a few things in the church."

"Thanks. Hey, if you ever need any help on jobs around here, Jamiel Russell is getting to be very handy," said Gus as he watched Angelo pruning some dead branches off the rose bush.

"I believe you. He helped me with some repairs to the roof. He was a fast learner and hard worker too, which isn't always easy to find these days."

"You should hire him," smiled Gus.

"It's a great place to work, but he might not like the pay—a cot in the shed and three square meals."

"Sounds like a prison to me," said Gus.

"We can make our own prisons anywhere. To me, this is peace and freedom, and I have a great friend in Father Tom."

Gus patted Angelo on the back. "Very wise words. I'll go in to see if I can find him. Have a good rest of your day, Angelo."

Gus walked around to the front of the church and opened the wooden door. The church was quiet as all the parishioners, the choir, the altar servers, and ushers were now long gone from the morning Masses.

A different kind of peace descended over the church when it was empty and quiet. Gus stared up at the crucifix, then stopped at the baptismal font and felt the desire this time to dip his fingers into the holy water and bless himself—asking for forgiveness for his very long absence.

Tom came out from the sacristy as Gus was standing at the back of the church. He waved and made his way down the aisle to shake hands with Gus. "Gus, good to see you in church on Sunday."

Gus nodded. "I know, I'm a little late. Well, a lot late. I was struggling with something and didn't know if you had a few minutes."

Tom grinned. "How do you know it will only take a few minutes?"

"Well, I don't, but I didn't want to bother you if you're trying to get a break."

"You're not bothering me at all. I'm glad to see you. I was praying it wouldn't take another three years." Tom laughed and waved him toward the front pew. "Come and sit down."

They sat in silence for quite a while. Gus was having a hard time figuring out why he came. Tom was a good listener and was obviously letting the Holy Spirit guide Gus to the root of his struggle.

Finally, Gus shifted in his seat and said, "You know Jamiel."

"I think I've heard of him."

"Well, he asked me a question that I couldn't answer. I hadn't thought about why I stopped coming to church, why I stopped living."

"Those are great questions, and the answers are important ones. Smart kid," replied Tom.

"I was angry for a very long time after Danny died, but I don't think I ever blamed God. Free will is a great gift, and people do bad things with it. I think I held things together for Julia during all those years. She was heartbroken enough losing her son, but, in many ways, she lost her husband as well. I just held it together and coped, but it all came back when Julia died," said Gus as his throat tightened, and his voice broke.

"One thing I know is that you loved them both with everything you had to give. I've never had a son or a wife, so I can't imagine what it's like to lose the two biggest parts of who you've been—even if you cherish the gift of the time you had."

"I do. I couldn't have been a luckier guy," said Gus with a long pause, "but I miss them so much."

"It's in that pain that we know we had something special. Some people wouldn't take that chance, but you were never 'some people,' and you still aren't."

"Yeah, well, um—I still can't answer that question. This relationship here with the Church means a lot to me, but I feel resistant to coming back."

"Most people would say it's because they're angry and hurt by the injustice of what God could have stopped—and didn't," said Tom.

"I've thought about that over and over, but that doesn't feel right."

"Many times, our subconscious hides sensitive things to protect us. It's a pretty sophisticated protection mechanism but not always a healthy one. Kind of like when our bodies overreact to an ankle sprain, and the swelling won't let us heal until we ice it down," said Tom. "The man that killed your son—"

Gus got very uncomfortable with Tom's last words and snapped back, "What about him?"

"I'm sorry if I'm going places that you don't feel comfortable going," said Tom.

Gus did not respond but just sat staring ahead.

"Have you ever contacted him?"

"Why would I do that?! What good could possibly come from contacting that— What does that have to do with why I came?"

"I don't know. I was just curious. Do you mind if we pray together, instead?" asked Tom.

Relieved that Tom moved away from talking about his son's killer, something Gus hadn't dealt with and didn't want to deal with. Gus nodded.

Tom spoke slowly and clearly. "Our Father, who art in heaven, hallowed be thy name, thy kingdom come, thy will be done, on earth as it is in heaven. Give us this day, our daily bread—and forgive *us* our trespasses, *as we forgive* those who have trespassed against us—"

Gus didn't hear the rest of the prayer. It was as if he had lost his hearing, and the silence was louder. Gus had recited the prayer Christ gave His people thousands of times in his life and had never heard what he had just heard. He stood up and marched towards the back of the church and out the door.

Emotionally numb, Gus climbed the stairs to his apartment and stood frozen in front of his desk. He hesitated before opening the side drawer that contained rows of unopened letters he'd never read. He slammed the drawer shut and sat in his leather chair.

Chapter 31

Willie ran his hand through his goatee as he sat in the waiting area for the guard to get him for his weekly visit.

Reverend Rich gave him a broad smile as he sat and picked up the phone. "How's my good friend this week?"

"Couldn't ask for a nicer vacation spot," Willie replied with a half-smile.

"I thought you might be looking forward to your hearing in two weeks."

"You know, when I first stepped off that bus to start my term, I had no fear. No fear of dying and no fear of takin' care of anyone that got in my face. I didn't care about anything except bein' treated with respect, and I got that through fear. Now—now—lots of things worry me." Willie had Reverend Rich's full attention. "I care now, and I feel like there's something to lose. Before, I had nothing to lose and focused on one thing—how people respected me."

"What do you worry about most, Willie?" asked Reverend Rich.

Willie slowly exhaled and shook his head. "Oh, man. I might not get parole because of how I behaved here for years. I don't know what I'd do to survive if I got out. Everything I thought I would do is no longer on my options list—thanks to you, by the way."

"I won't apologize for that one," said Reverend Rich. "What else?"

"I think about seeing them, but I'm nervous about how they'll respond."

"I could talk with them to prep them if it would help," said Reverend Rich.

"No. No. I don't want you doin' that," replied Willie sharply. "I guess I worry 'cause I'm still angry at myself for everything."

Reverend Rich nodded. "We discussed a lot of readings where Jesus lets us know how much our Father loves us—*unconditionally*. There is *no* sin too great that he won't forgive us and welcome us back with open arms. That includes you, Willie."

"I know that in my head. I do, thanks to you. But something is in my way. I know my worth comes only from God. I know he has a plan for me. I know that I can be the person he made me to be if I believe what Christ taught, but I can't seem to get there—down here. "Willie pointed to his chest.

"Ah, the longest journey in life—from your head to your heart," replied Reverend Rich. "I have a feeling you know God can forgive you, but maybe you haven't forgiven yourself? I think this may be keeping you from being free and trusting fully in God's forgiveness and in the man he made."

"Forgive myself? How can I forgive myself for the things I have done? I've killed two human beings that people cared about. I've lived an unforgivable life. No amount of retribution can make up for it."

"Because you're special?"

"No, because two lives no longer exist because of me," responded Willie, his head lowered.

"Willie, they exist and, hopefully, they are having the time of their lives in the loving arms of God right now. Remember, we said unconditionally. You just need to repent and be truly sorry. Some awful things can happen to people while on this earth, but nothing can really kill the most important part of ourselves. We are immortal beings in God's eyes, and with Christ's sacrifice to free us from the bonds of death, Danny and Kyrie are okay."

Willie covered his eyes with the palm of his right hand as he shook his head. "Their families can't forgive me, so how can I, with all the pain that still exists?"

Chapter 32

Gus woke up early. It was May 13, and the morning light was getting bright earlier. It was time to get his raised garden beds ready for planting his tomatoes, zucchini, lettuce, peppers, basil, and parsley. He'd always loved planting and taking care of the garden, his fruit trees, and vines, but he now did it out of habit.

Being Thursday, he dressed to head to the Eastside for breakfast. When he opened the back door and glanced up at the new basketball hoop, it made him smile.

At the restaurant, the men noticed Gus joining in the conversation more.

Even Linda remarked on it. "Well, well. We have another talker at the table, just what I needed."

As he sipped his coffee and Mike talked about his wife's good news, passing the five-year mark for being cancer-free, he noticed Father Tom sitting at another table with someone. While they were waiting for their breakfast, Gus got up and approached them to say hello.

"I didn't know you frequented high-end establishments like this."

Tom glanced up. "Hey, Gus. I was going to check in on you after our last conversation."

"Maybe afterward."

"Sounds good. Oh, do you guys know each other?" asked Tom.

"We've said hello probably a hundred times, but I don't know your name."

"Gus, this is David Kelly, a very good friend of mine. David, meet Gus Busbi." As they shook hands, Tom said, "David keeps me on my toes with basketball, although I think you could probably still take both of us. David, Gus used to coach the high school team, and I'd love to talk him out of retirement for the next season."

"Very good to finally know your name, Gus. Your breakfast club seems to be a great bunch of guys. I don't think I could handle Linda on my own," kidded David.

Linda groaned as she brought out the plates of eggs, pancakes, and

French toast to Gus's table.

Tom said, "Gus, I'll leave with you after your breakfast. Take your time." Gus nodded and rejoined the gang for the morning meal and banter.

The morning was warming up as Gus and Tom stood outside the diner and began the trip back. "So, have you known David for a long time?"

Tom replied, "Almost two years now. He's a really great guy. Awesome family and not too bad on the hardwood. He helps me coach the younger kids."

Gus stuffed his hands in his pockets. "That's great. I remember him at the Eastside from years ago. He seemed like a great guy, but one of those busy execs with his papers and one of those portable phones. Thinking about it, he does seem different these past few years—a little less preoccupied maybe?"

"He's just freer to be himself. An incredible story for someday. So, how have you been?" asked Tom.

Gus didn't respond for several moments. "I'm fine. Sorry about the other day."

"Don't worry. You wouldn't be the first person to walk out on me. Anything you want to talk about?"

"I thought I did, but it doesn't feel like the best time for me," replied Gus as he rubbed the back of his neck.

"Understood. It seemed as if you might have stumbled upon something," said Tom as he looked Gus in the eye.

"Some things are better left alone."

"That's rarely the case, even if it feels like it," said Tom. "Resistance can look like safety to our conscious feelings."

"Fine. I'm not in the mood for psychotherapy or exploration of my inner feelings right now," said Gus curtly as they approached his driveway. Gus and Julia had spent many hours with Tom trying to come to terms with Danny's death. Initially, Gus had gone at Julia's request, but he came to respect Tom's easy approach and intuitive insights.

Tom stopped, but Gus continued down the driveway. "I forgive you," yelled Tom with a hint of humor in his voice. Gus didn't turn but nodded and raised his hand as he turned the corner and was out of sight.

Gus spent the day fixing the boards on the raised bed and sifting the compost turned over during the year. Before he knew it, Jamiel was back from school, changed, and out back practicing his shooting.

"Is it okay, Mr. Busbi?" Jamiel asked as he held the ball as if to shoot it one-handed.

"You don't have to ask," answered Gus as he spread the compost over the garden beds.

"What are you working on?" asked Jamiel.

"It's time to plant the vegetable gardens. Mid-May is a safe time to avoid the risk of any nighttime frost."

"Could you use any help?" asked Jamiel.

"Sure. Fill up the wheelbarrow with that sifted compost and bring it over to these beds."

Jamiel returned with a full wheelbarrow. "Why do you build up the beds above ground like that?"

"Good question. I like your curiosity. They're called raised beds and have a lot of advantages over just digging out the ground. They give you more space to plant. Better air circulation and drainage of water to avoid soggy roots. Soil compacts less, which lets the roots spread more. Harder for tree roots to interfere, easier to work, and best of all—less weeds!"

Smirking, Jamiel responded, "I'm convinced. What are we planting this year?"

Gus pointed over to the side of the garage where he had taken out the plants he had started from seed under sun lamps. "These are tomatoes— Italian plum and Big Boy. Those there are peppers, and these are zucchini plants. I've got some herbs inside, too. Let's start with the tomatoes." Gus showed him how to wrap the base with cut newspaper to protect the plants from cutworms and to add lime and fertilizer to the soil before placing each plant into the evenly spaced holes and adding water. In another bed, Gus showed Jamiel how to mound up the dirt and plant the zucchini, and then they finished with the peppers. "We can plant the basil and Italian parsley later. How about working on some of those shots?"

Gus smiled inwardly. Jamiel clearly enjoyed learning new things and working with him. As Gus made passes, Jamiel practiced quick catch-and-shoot moves, and then made some fakes with a pivot and fade away move. Gus knew that encouraging Jamiel to work on each move over and over would help him to develop the muscle memory and confidence to add these to his game. Jamiel thanked Gus several times for his willingness to spend this time with him and the patience to practice a move over and over until he got it down.

Gus saw Jamiel panic when one of his shots bounced off the rim and almost landed in the newly planted bed of tomato plants. "I'll try to shoot from the other side from now on."

"I crushed a lot of my father's plants growing up practicing my shots. I appreciate your being careful about the garden, but don't overreact if it happens. I have some extras just in case." Gus smiled and winked.

Jamiel sighed in relief. "I have a bad feeling we may need them. Mr. Busbi, I've never seen the inside of your garage. Why are the windows all papered over?"

Gus was slow to answer. "There's nothing of interest in there."

"So, you just have an empty garage?"

He seemed agitated by Jamiel's insistence not to drop the subject. "I just said, there's nothing of interest to you in there."

"I—"

"I mean it!" snapped Gus as he picked up his shovel and headed to his apartment.

* * * *

Jamiel felt the tension and underlying anger that seemed to come from nowhere. Why was Gus so sensitive? The joy of practicing went out of him. He headed up the driveway toward the house with his ball when he saw Tom and a boy he did not recognize coming toward him.

"Hey, Jamiel. Glad to see you practicing. I wanted you to meet someone," said Tom. Next to Tom was a teenager about Jamiel's age, except he was white as he could be and stood a few inches taller. There was something about him he instantly didn't like. "This is Bradley. He's transferring to St. Francis next week."

"And?" said Jamiel. *Does he want me to babysit him? Show him around all the cool spots in town?*

"And I wanted you to meet him. I thought that you two might be good co-captains for next year's team," said the smiling Tom.

I thought I was the captain. What's with this lily-white hick, who probably can't play a lick, waltzing in and being named captain with no dues paid? Jamiel glared at Tom as the boy reached his hand out to Jamiel.

"I hear you're pretty good," said the boy, waiting for Jamiel's hand that never came.

Jamiel knew he was being rude, but felt angry about the situation. "Bradley?" Jamiel said with a little bit of a mocking tone. "Sounds like a rich boy's name."

"Bradley John Croop, but call me BJ," he replied.

"BJ Croop. BJ Croop? Now that sounds like a white baby's ailment."

"Be nice. BJ's from Texas and just arrived in town today," said Tom.

The boys looked at each other like a stare down at a heavyweight boxers weigh-in, except Jamiel was the only one who seemed angry.

"Um, maybe you two could play a little to get acquainted?"

"I don't think Busbi would be in the mood for us shooting around here today," said Jamiel, who quickly noticed Tom's eyebrows lift.

"Jamiel, how about taking BJ over to the Fens courts?" asked Tom in a way that seemed less like an offer and more like a directive.

Jamiel's shoulders drop a little as his eyes rolled. "All right, Bradley. Let's make Father Tom happy." They strode in silence for most of the way to the courts. "You're from Texas?"

"Yup. Y'all should see it sometime."

"I know—it's big!" replied Jamiel with an exaggerated tone. When they crossed the stream and reached the Back Bay Fens courts, they saw one game going on and the other court empty. "So, what're you good at besides being sorta tall?"

"I like passing," said BJ as Jamiel handed him the ball.

"Well, this is one-on-one, so good luck with the passing," quipped Jamiel.

BJ suddenly tossed the ball up for a bounce off the backboard and promptly slammed it through the basket. "Oh, yeah. I like dunking too," responded BJ with a broad smile.

Jamiel thought he probably deserved it with the attitude he was giving BJ. He was surprised that BJ's skills didn't align with the slow white guy he assumed he would be. BJ obviously loved the game as much as he did and had as much of a competitive spirit as they fought and scrapped through five games of one-on-one until they collapsed to the pavement to rest. Each had won two hard-fought matches, and the fifth and deciding game went back and forth, each gaining respect for the other's game with every basket. BJ hit the final two shots, a reverse drive layup, followed by a long-range dagger to take the match. Breathing heavier than he had in a while, Jamiel said, "I just gave you that one as a welcoming present on your first day."

Sweat was pouring off of BJ's forehead as he caught his breath. "I felt that warm welcome from the first moment." He smiled as he wiped his brow with the sleeve of his tee-shirt.

Jamiel laughed back to himself, thankful that the physical game had worked off his bad mood.

* * * *

Meanwhile, Tom knocked on Gus's door.

Gus's head popped out from the window above. "Whatever you're selling, I'm not interested," Gus barked.

"Peace and love, brother," quipped Tom.

"You might get a bucket of water on your head instead!"

"As long as it's just the water and not the bucket too," replied Tom with a smile.

"Right now, I wouldn't test your luck," Gus snapped back.

"Hey, I can't forgive you if I'm dead. I'll just hang out in your garden where it's safe," said Tom as he strolled over to examine the newly planted beds.

Gus peered out a few times and realized Tom wasn't going to quietly leave, so he grudgingly made his way down the steps to the garden.

"You're going to be waiting there a long time if you are expecting some free vegetables," said Gus as Tom turned towards him. "You're as stubborn a priest as I've ever met."

"Just trying to model myself after you, Gus."

"Hmmm. Come back in August, and I'll have some nice tomatoes for you."

"I will. I'll get hungry between now and then, though. So, what's been happening?"

Gus was in no mood to get into anything heavy. "Nothing's happening, as usual."

"You're very bad at lying, but you know that, don't you?" asked Tom.

"Why are you so interested in my life? Don't you have enough sad cases to handle at that parish of yours, with no assistant?"

"There are many, but I love you too much to watch you fall back into that hole you have recently shown signs of climbing out of."

"My hole is just fine. You don't have to worry about me."

"Sometimes what you call worry might just be caring. You know where I am if you ever want to talk," said Tom as he started making his way home.

"And, unfortunately, you know where I am, too," called out Gus as he stood in the middle of his now-empty yard. He climbed the stairs and stood in front of his desk again, thinking about all the letters he had refused to open over those years. They meant nothing to him because he couldn't trust their sincerity or forgive the transgression. A few days ago, when Tom recited the Our Father, he'd known why he couldn't return to Mass. We asked God to *"forgive our trespasses as we forgive those who trespass against us."* He couldn't forgive Danny's killer for what he had done and for the defiant lack of remorse each day of the trial. Gus knew he couldn't be a hypocrite and couldn't go to Mass to receive the actual body and blood of Christ, who died to forgive all of our sins if he, himself, refused to forgive.

Chapter 33

On Friday, Tom told Jamiel it would be a good idea to include BJ in his daily workout. Despite their awkward start, he said it was important that they bond during the summer months before the school year, ready to be teammates.

Jamiel decided that BJ should see some real basketball and took him down to Ramsay Park. On the way, Jamiel asked, "What's a rich boy like you movin' up to this part of Boston, anyway?"

"Job opportunity for my mom. My dad was in the Navy and then worked the shipyards in Corpus Christi but didn't hang around too long. I don't remember him much."

"Sorry to hear that. I never heard of Corpa—what?"

"Corpus Christi. It's on the Gulf near the border. I liked it. My mom had to scrape to keep us going while she went to school'n'all at night. Took about ten years to get her degree in nursing, and then she met a woman from up here who recommended she apply to some Boston hospitals. Y'all got a lot of them. She got an offer, but we had to come up pretty quick to get it. She felt bad about pulling me out of school so late in the year, but I couldn't whine after all she's gone through for me."

"You played at school?"

"Yeah. We had a good team too. I think we had a chance for States next year," replied BJ. "How's the team at St. Francis? Father Tom said you're pretty good."

"Don't listen to him. Well, he's a good guy to listen to on and off the court. Just don't listen to anything he says about me," replied Jamiel as they reached the courts, and everyone stared at Jamiel's companion. "How many brothers you got down at Corpus Christi?"

"Not too many. Not like this," said BJ with a smile.

One game had just finished, and the guys waiting needed one more to play. "Hey, Jamiel. We could use ya, man! Warm up."

"I'll switch off with BJ here if you don't mind," responded Jamiel.

Leonard waved him over to the fenced area near the baseline. "Hey, man.

166

What's with the wigga?" asked Leonard in a serious tone.

"His name's BJ. He's all right."

"Man, that white boy is reflecting so much light, I don't know if I can watch this. What's up with bringin' him down here?"

"I don't know, Cool. Just wanted to show him some real ball," said Jamiel as he watched the other teams trying to figure out what to do with the situation.

"I don't need to play," said BJ as he approached Jamiel.

"You don't need to be here, period, boy," growled one of the players.

"How about this?" asked Jamiel. "Me and BJ and any three players will take on any five. If we lose, he's gone."

By challenging their honor and manhood, none of them could refuse to accept. Jamiel and BJ watched the others huddle. Reluctant players who were lower on the talent scale, compared to the top players, were sent over to Jamiel's team.

Jamiel huddled with BJ, Popcorn, Lewis, and Raz. "Okay, I know you guys might have mixed feelings about playing hard here, but none of those guys think we have a team that can play, never mind win. You're here to earn some respect, so don't worry about playin' with this redneck hick. Play hard and show 'em what you got."

The game didn't start out well for the underdogs. The other team was tough and played rough, especially with BJ, who they banged into and hacked him at every opportunity.

Jamiel noticed that BJ didn't let it get under his skin as he continued to play hard. The other players on Jamiel's team noticed as well and started picking up their effort. Jamiel and BJ proved to be a good tandem on both defense and offense, working together to smother the player with the ball off a steal or rebound, and building a rhythm on fast breaks to pass and score impressively. The frustration started to mount as the underdogs pulled ahead, 13-11 in a game to fifteen.

The opposing team, made up of a lot of guys that were much older than Jamiel and BJ, took a timeout to figure out what to do to avoid the loss.

Jamiel and the team used the time to catch their breath and get ready for anything. Jamiel peered over beyond the baseline where Trig, Fish, Ricky, and Leonard stood. Jamiel could sense Leonard glaring back at him. His message was clear: *Do not win this game.*

The other team scored the next two baskets, tying the game and bringing a nod from Leonard. On the next play, Jamiel brought the ball down the sideline and made a quick cross-over dribble before driving to the basket and making a beautiful behind-the-back pass to BJ under the basket. As BJ went up for the shot, two of the defenders came down hard on him, almost bringing him to the ground. He gathered himself quickly, keeping his cool as one of the players tried to stare him down. *Enough of this crap!* thought Jamiel.

He pointed to BJ as he took the ball out and passed to one of his teammates while another set a baseline pick for Jamiel to loop back around to the top of the key for a return pass. It was becoming natural to put into practice some of the techniques Tom and Gus had taught him. He got the defender leaning one way, and he cut the other way, stopped, and went up for a fake jump shot before firing a pass to BJ for a hard, decisive dunk. On the next defensive play, Jamiel reached behind their best player and poked the ball out of his control to BJ, who grabbed the loose ball and rifled it back to a streaking Jamiel for an elevated layup over the only guy that got back to defend the final nail in the coffin.

Jamiel's winning team congratulated each other as the opposing squad stood pointing fingers at each other and arguing about whose fault the loss was.

The loss didn't reflect well on the neighborhood team, even though only one player on the winning team wasn't from the neighborhood. BJ played remarkably well for the first time on their courts and deserved some acknowledgment, but none was forthcoming. Leonard waved Jamiel over again. "What's up with that?"

"We played a competitive game and won. It's just a game, Cool."

"It's more than a game, and you know that! We've got enough working against us, so we've gotta stick together. Where's this cracka from?"

Jamiel was getting anxious about where Cool was going with the conversation. "He's from Texas and might be playin' ball at school."

"Texas? Man, he *is* a cracka. Tell your boy to hop on his horse and ride back to Texas. I want to talk to you about somethin'," demanded Leonard.

Jamiel explained to BJ that he had to stay and pointed to the streets that would take him home. BJ didn't argue. "Jamiel, you're the captain as far as I'm concerned, and you showed it today. Nice playing."

As BJ walked away, Jamiel called out, "Croop, not bad yourself."

Leonard walked Jamiel to an area of the park where they could talk alone. "Look, you played a good game, but next time keep it in the neighborhood. Loyalty is king in the hood for a good reason. This ain't just a game, either."

Jamiel listened and nodded. "I wanted to ask you about that girl, Marnie."

Jamiel acted confused with the change in the subject. "What about her?"

"How much do you like her?" asked Leonard.

"I don't know. I haven't seen her in a long time."

"So you don't know if you like her, but you went over that day to take her out?" pressed Leonard.

"I thought she might like to go out, and I just dropped by to ask her," replied Jamiel, getting fidgety.

"Don't you usually call a girl up or ask her at school? You just happened to drop by out of the blue on that particular day?" asked Leonard.

"Yeah. I don't know. I've never asked a girl out before, and she doesn't go to my school. I guess I don't know what I'm doin'."

Leonard laughed out loud. "You've never been out with a girl before?"

Jamiel shook his head as he looked around to see who might be close enough to hear.

"Does that mean you've never done it with any girl before? Never?"

Jamiel didn't answer, which was clearly an answer on its own to Leonard.

Under Leonard's breath, he said, "Well, it's time for some growing up tonight."

"What?" asked Jamiel. "I think I'm goin' to head home, Cool."

"Jamiel. Come here," said Leonard putting his arm around him. "You know I love you like a little brother, don't you? Go on home, have dinner with your mom, but tell her you're goin' out tonight and be back around eight. Okay?"

Jamiel nodded as he started for home.

"It's Friday night!" yelled Leonard as he joined his crew for some plans.

When Jamiel showed up at Lenox Street around eight-o'clock, the guys gave him an enthusiastic greeting and talked about the upcoming summer. He felt as if he was among male friends that knew him, accepted him, and wanted him to be there. He felt almost like one of them, but then he didn't, which was confusing. For the moment, he enjoyed the comradery. He sat on the steps joking and telling stories with the others as Terri walked by, and silence fell upon their conversations. All heads turned to enjoy one of the prettiest and sexiest girls in the neighborhood. Her long legs were covered by a pair of tight jeans, and she wore a fur-collared leather jacket that her dark brown curly hair bounced upon. She slowed down and stopped in front of the group, staring right at Jamiel. "Hey, Jamiel. I heard you were in the hospital, but you're doing better? You sure look like you're doin' better."

There was a "woah" from the other boys as Jamiel became visibly embarrassed and tongue-tied.

She came closer to Jamiel. "I was going to say you were a handsome boy, but it looks like I should say 'man.' You're lookin' pretty fine tonight, Jamiel. Where've you been hidin'?" She sat down next to Jamiel as the other boys moved out of the way. She whispered in his ear, "I feel a little awkward talkin' with all the boys around. You want to walk so we can talk without the audience?"

Jamiel got up and gave Terri his hand to assist her. No one gave him a hard time as they strolled down the dark sidewalk.

Terri asked, "Are you feelin' better now? I heard you were shot up bad."

"It wasn't so bad," replied Jamiel.

"Are there scars?" asked Terri as she put her hand on his chest.

"Small ones. Like I said, they're not so bad."

"Can I see them?" asked Terri, who had inched closer to Jamiel with the curve of her body almost touching his. "I have my car right here. Maybe we can sit inside and talk easier and be warmer?"

Jamiel didn't respond as she opened the door locks and then the back door to let him in. They sat next to each other on the leather bench seat in the back, and Jamiel could feel tingles in his chest as the air was thick with sensuality.

Terri inched closer to him. Her ebony skin was smooth, and the expression in her eyes was hard to resist being pulled into. "I hope this is okay. It just seems more comfortable and easier to talk."

"Sure," Jamiel said.

"I was just curious about what they looked like. Is that okay?"

"Sure. Like I said, they are no big deal," answered Jamiel.

Terri opened up the first button on Jamiel's shirt and asked, "Is it okay?"

He nodded, so she continued, opening up his shirt to see two of the small scars he had received from the buckshot. Her eyes widened with sympathy as she placed the palm of her hand on his chest. "Does it hurt?" she asked.

Jamiel shook his head, feeling a sudden flush at the ease with which he was ready to be seduced.

Terri leaned over and brushed her lips against his, and then pressed herself against him as her lips caressed his, kissing him. He was awkward, but she didn't let on as she kissed him more deeply. Her lips moved to his ear, kissing it and saying, "I want you. I want you, Jamiel."

He didn't want her to stop, but he felt a rush of fear that was greater than all the other sensations he was experiencing. He started to pull back a bit, but she only leaned in closer as his back pressed against the door. "Jamiel, don't you think I'm attractive?"

"I do. I do. You're the prettiest girl I know. I just think I should go," replied Jamiel as his hand fumbled nervously for the door handle.

"Don't you want me?"

Jamiel stopped. "Terri, you don't know how much I do, but—" The door suddenly opened as he pushed the latch, and he climbed out of the car. "I think I should go. Are you going to be all right getting home?"

Terri peered up at the brick building they were parked beside and said, "Don't worry about me, my gentleman." As he darted off, she yelled out, "Button up before you get home, boy!"

Chapter 34

Without Tyrell's leadership, the Grant Manor gang had been rudderless for several weeks. His second in command, Stanley "Tookie" Walker, didn't have the composure or presence of Tyrell, but his energy and focus were fueled by constant anger about never getting the respect he felt he deserved.

As a boy, Tookie had dreamed of being a baseball player, but once that dream ended, his life of crime began. He was known to be a hothead at times but also showed the ability to gain his revenge in time. He was close to Tyrell and knew his family, dropping by to see Bette and Marnie to let them know he would take care of things. Both of them made it clear that they wanted no part of his concept of "taking care of things."

Tookie and his right-hand man, "Fat Fingers" Williams, stood on the stone pavement where Tyrell had drawn his last breath in a pool of blood. The blood had been scrubbed off and flushed down the drain as if it were nothing more than any other liquid stain that needed to be cleaned. Life was over in an instant, and now, just a few weeks later, a replacement was standing on that spot. Tookie waited for Marnie to return home from her Saturday music lesson. When she tried to avoid him, he called out, "Marnie!"

Marnie waved hello, but he motioned her over. "How you been doin'?"

"Fine. Just trying to get home to do some homework."

Tookie noticed how quickly she was maturing from the little girl that he had watched weave her way through the minefields of growing up in this neighborhood.

"I never asked you somethin'."

"What?"

"What was that boy from Lenox doin' here that day?"

"Jamiel? He's nobody to worry about," replied Marnie.

"Then what was he doin' here? Been talkin' to people that were there, and some thought they saw him grab Tyrell's arm so he couldn't defend hisself," said Tookie with an ominous tone to his voice.

"I don't know anything about that," Marnie quickly replied.

"I heard he just happened to be here minutes before the Lenox Cardinals' drive-by. Guaranteed it was them. That's too much of a coincidence. Are you two dating?"

"No."

"Are you two best friends or somethin'?" asked Tookie.

"Not exactly. We just know each other from church," replied Marnie.

"So, you aren't that close, but he just drops by enemy territory and leaves you just when Tyrell is trying to defend himself. Now your brother's dead, and we don't see Jamiel anymore. Sound just a little odd to you?"

Fat Fingers nodded in agreement.

"Well—I—I—I don't know. Please stop asking me. I don't know!" said Marnie as she turned to go into her apartment building entrance.

Tookie yelled out, "He used you and killed your brother. Don't that bother you?"

Marnie dropped her water bottle and shook her head as she rushed up the one flight of stairs to her apartment. She seemed confused and conflicted, but Tookie was not.

Chapter 35

Jamiel had a hard time falling asleep Friday night and slept late. As he washed his cereal bowl in the sink, he noticed Gus working in the garden. It was hard to figure Busbi out with his moods swinging back and forth and his closed world that would open and then close again in an instant.

Suddenly, Gus entered the house only to return minutes later, clothes changed. He headed down the driveway.

Jamiel was curious enough to dress quickly and catch up to see where Gus was going. He tailed Gus to St. Francis, where Gus stopped and seemed to hesitate before knocking on the door to the rectory. Jamiel's curiosity was piqued when Tom answered the door, letting him in.

* * * *

Inside, Gus was quiet as Tom asked him how he was doing.

"I've been feeling restless," said Gus.

"That may not be a bad thing," responded Tom. "There are often a lot of insights to be found in our restlessness."

"Yeah. Yeah. So far, it's just meant less sleep," grumbled Gus.

"If you need a place to take a nap, I have a spare room that's empty," said Tom, smiling.

"I can get bad jokes every Monday and Thursday at the Eastside," quipped Gus. "I've been thinking about how I've been reacting to a few things lately. The conversation we were having in the church and then another with Jamiel. Maybe, I'm just getting too sensitive about things."

"Probably means you're starting to live again but with some deep wounds that haven't been allowed to heal. We often hold on to our pain because we believe the ones we've lost stay with us in that pain," said Tom.

"Maybe. I do know why I haven't been able to come to church."

"Something to do with forgiveness?" asked Tom.

Gus lifted his eyes toward Tom. "Maybe. When we got to that part of the 'Our Father' where we ask God to forgive us as we forgive others, it struck me that I'd never heard it so clearly before. I feel like I'm willing for God not to forgive me and go to hell because I just can't forgive that—" Gus's face turned red as his eyes welled with tears.

"*To forgive or not to forgive? That is the question.* I know you can," said Tom with compassion.

"I cannot! How can I? He doesn't even have any remorse!" said Gus as his eyes bore into Tom's.

"Gus, I think this is a good thing to talk about, but I want it to be the right time for you. The problem is that there may not be a right time for you, if you don't push through it."

"Push through it? Make believe Danny never died the way he did? At the hands of that no-good hood?" snapped Gus.

"Forgiveness isn't saying what happened didn't matter or doesn't hurt anymore. Showing an act of love to someone is hoping the best for them—hoping they see the light in what God wants for them and that they do repent for what they have done to find their way back to Him. No, it's not easy, and it doesn't mean we now like them and are okay with what they did. It means we're not holding onto hate, only love. I don't mean love like the feeling of love, but the act of love. Jesus forgave the murderous thief who was crucified beside Him because he surrendered to belief. He found his way, even then, at the final moments of his life."

"I'm supposed to want the best for him when he ended my son's life and broke Julia's heart?" questioned Gus.

"Not just for him, but for you as well. When we hold onto our resentment, it robs us of life and peace. There's not a part of Danny that would want you to live that way, and there's not a part of Danny or his memory that is kept alive by that resentment. His only wish, right now, is for you to be with him and Julia someday in heaven. Gus, Jesus didn't say to love our enemies and to do good to those that hate us because it is easy but because it was the right thing to do. It's easy to love people we like or who treat us right, but not easy to love someone who has done us wrong—especially something so painful as this, but love is the only path to God. Forgiveness is what He asks of us, even when it doesn't feel right."

"I can't do it. What he did is *not* forgivable," said Gus.

"Man has turned his back on God throughout history, but God keeps coming back with love and forgiveness. Jesus withstood betrayal, mocking, scourging, and the most brutal form of execution known to man, and he said, '*Forgive them for they know not what they do.*' He asks us to love unconditionally and without expectation for anything in return—even in the face of the worst of all transgressions."

"Father Tom, I just don't think I can," Gus said in a strained voice.

"I understand. Really, I do. It's something we can work on, but remember that it's not your giving mercy to this man but allowing God's mercy to flow through you to him. You may have a great deal of resentment holding you back, but we need to trust God's plan to let this happen. Some things God asks of us make absolutely no sense to us until we trust Him and do it." Tom put his hand on Gus's shoulder. "If you think you are willing to take him to hell with you, you won't be the one to decide if he's going with you or not. Let God be his judge, and you listen to Jesus to take care of your soul."

He wanted to reject Tom's words, but he knew deep down he was right.

"I can't do this on my own."

"I don't think we were ever meant to do any of this on our own, Gus. We weren't meant to be alone in this world, no matter how hard we try sometimes," replied Tom. "You are a good friend of mine, and I want to be there for you—and for Julia and Danny."

"Maybe. I'm not sure this is a good time for me. I've been short-tempered lately. Jamiel asked a simple question the other day, and I snapped and walked away from him," said Gus.

Tom smiled.

Gus said, "Yes. Just like I walked off on you."

"Do you mind my asking what Jamiel asked you about?" Tom inquired.

Gus stared at Tom for a few seconds and then tipped the brim of his cap and walked out the door.

When he was back in his living room, he reflected on his conversation with Tom for a long time.

Finally, he went back downstairs and stood in the backyard outside of Celia and Jamiel's kitchen window.

It was several minutes before Jamiel came into the kitchen to pour a glass of water and noticed Gus.

Gus didn't motion or look away; he just stood there until Jamiel came out. "What did I do wrong now?" asked Jamiel. "I haven't played hoop or been near your garden."

"I wanted to apologize for snapping at you the other day and walking off—and for the way I treated you earlier on. I was too wrapped up in myself to notice how I was treating people," said Gus as he peered directly at Jamiel.

"Don't worry about it," said Jamiel.

"I should. It's not what you deserve. You asked a perfectly reasonable question out of curiosity. You did it respectfully, and I didn't give you respect back. Just because—just because—" A lump formed in Gus's throat, making it difficult to finish his sentence. Without saying a word, he unlocked the large wooden garage door and reached down to pull the bottom latch up. The wooden door creaked as it slowly made its way open for the first time in seventeen years.

Jamiel's eyes widened, taking in every inch of the old wooden garage.

Besides the dust, the garage was organized with built-in work tables on either side, tools hanging, and a Red Sox calendar on the wall from August 1986. Overhead lights dangled, and in the middle of the cement garage floor was a tan cloth tarp covering a large object.

He watched Jamiel marveling at this world of its own inside the old wood structure and maybe imagining the hours Gus had spent working there, a place where men hung out to work, to make things, to fix things, or to just get away. There were wheels, hubcaps, tires, and jacks on one wall. His eyes then became fixed on the large covered object in front of them. "This is something. Why don't you use this? What's under the cloth?"

Gus had thought he was ready to show Jamiel, but he suddenly could not respond. Gus took a deep breath and silently, slowly, let it out with a long exhale.

"What is it, Mr. Busbi? Did I say something wrong?"

Instantly, a rush of tears filled Gus's eyes. "I'm sorry. For some reason, I thought I could do this."

Jamiel's eyes widened, and his mouth fell open by the sudden and probably unexpected emotion from Gus.

Seemingly out of character, the stoic Gus was letting his emotions pour out in front of Jamiel, holding his hand over his face to wipe the tears that still seemed raw to him.

Gus shook his head and took several deep breaths again to collect himself.

Jamiel was patient and remained silent.

Gus undid two ties and then slowly pulled off the large, beige cloth to reveal the hood of an old car. Under the years of dust, the hood was blue with two large black stripes. They could see the chrome "*Chevelle 396 SS*" above the driver's side headlights and "SS 396" on the front grill. Gus pulled the cloth off of the rest of the car that was on cinder blocks and in need of work.

"Wow! What is this?!" asked Jamiel, moving around front to admire the sports car.

"That's what they call a *muscle car*," Mike responded as he approached from behind. "I dropped over to inspect this professional paint job I've heard about—and now you two are onto something more ambitious?"

Gus nodded and continued to gaze silently at the car that had been covered for too many years.

Jamiel kept circling the car with his right hand on his head. "This could be such a cool ride. What's a muscle car?"

Mike smiled at his enthusiasm. "Well, you've got your pony cars, like the Mustangs, and then you have your large block V8 engines like this one that they call a muscle car because of its engine power. What year was this again, Gus?"

"Sixty-nine, as you well know."

"That's cool. 1969! Would it be okay to see the engine?" asked Jamiel as he looked inside the windows at the worn leather bench seats and an all-black interior.

Gus pointed over to a thick bench with another tarp covered object.

Jamiel untied the straps and pulled off the tarp to find a bare engine block sitting on the bench. "I've never seen one of these out from under the hood. Why is everything sitting here collecting dust?"

Gus searched for the words and the strength to respond, but no words passed his lips as Jamiel leaned forward, waiting for an answer. Gus closed his eyes and pressed his lips together as he took a long breath. He shook his head. He excused himself and left the garage to head to his apartment.

* * * *

Jamiel turned to Mike for some clue for what had just happened.

Mike said, "When I showed up today, I was surprised to see this garage door opened for the first time in seventeen years."

"Why all that time?"

"Gus and I were always working on cars, and as Danny grew up, he fell in love with engines and cars. Danny was Gus's only son, and my nephew and godson. He was such a great kid. You remind me of him in many ways."

Jamiel listened intently.

"On Danny's sixteenth birthday, Gus and I gave Danny this car to restore. Part of the present was the sports car itself, but more importantly, was the time working together on it. We spent evening after evening and weekend after weekend, taking this thing out, sanding and fixing what we could, and hunting down replacement parts to make this a beauty. Most of the body has been refurbished, and that engine block has been rebuilt, but everything stopped when—"

Mike's voice shook, and a tear made its way to the corner of his eye. He choked up unable to go on.

Quietly, Jamiel said, "Father Tom told me that he was shot to death."

Mike nodded and hesitated for several seconds before replying, "In cold blood right in front of the house. Nothing he ever did deserved that."

"I'm really sorry for your loss. I wish I had known him. Now, I can understand why Mr. Busbi didn't want to see this Chevy, but why do you think he showed it to me if he's still hurting so much?"

"I don't know, Jamiel, but I think it's a good sign, and I think he likes and respects you more than you might know." Mike gave Jamiel a half-smile as they helped each other cover the car and engine and close up the garage.

From the driveway, Jamiel peered up at the window. He wondered what Gus was feeling and why he had shown him the car. He pondered why Gus was so good to him at times and then seemed full of disdain at other times. He doubted that he would ever find the answers to those mysteries.

Chapter 36

As usual, Celia and Jamiel headed to the Hope Baptist Church on Sunday morning. What was unusual was that Gus dressed and walked to Mass at St. Francis for the first time in three years. The morning sun broke through scattered clouds as parishioners climbed the stairs to be greeted by Father Tom.

Gus entered through a side door and sat in the back.

After the Gospel reading, Tom raised his head to give his homily and always took the time to gaze at the parishioners. His eyes smiled as they caught Gus, and Gus knew he'd been spotted. Gus didn't go up to receive Communion, but he stayed to sit in the church after Mass. At one point, he was the only one remaining until someone sat down next to him without a word.

"Why does he test us so much?"

"Real love isn't easy, but it leads us to the life God has planned for us."

"*Love your enemies? Pray for those who persecute you?* What kind of plan is that?"

"That's one we'll have to trust Him on."

"I want to trust Him, but I just don't know if I can do this one particular thing. I can't be perfect."

"He's not asking you to be perfect by yourself. Alone, that's not possible, but being transformed in Christ makes it interesting, and makes everything possible."

"Yeah, yeah. Forgiving, praying, blessing, and loving those who hate just seems like too much to expect—even for the best of people."

"Gus, you were a Marine, weren't you?"

"Yes. Why?"

"What do Marines never do?"

Gus hesitated. "Never leave another Marine behind."

"Never?"

"Never. Not on the battlefield. Not ever."

"What if you didn't like them or had a beef with them?"

"It wouldn't matter, but that is different than an enemy."

"Jesus said that it was easy to love people that loved us, but the test of love is to love your enemy. We're not talking about liking them or a feeling of love, but an act of the will. It's not being passive or weak to turn the other cheek, but an act of courage and love to follow Christ's example—to be the man that He was, even with His enemies."

Gus sat silently, feeling more anger and resentment in his heart than love.

"Gus, why would you risk your life to carry someone off the battlefield?"

"To get them home."

"And you would risk your own life to do that?"

"Yes."

"That is what Christ is asking of us. We are all Marines, and in Christ's eyes, we are all children of God, all in the same unit. No matter how far off of the path one of our soldiers gets, we want to get them home, to come back to God. People do horrible things, often because they are lost and far away from God. We are called to love or will the good for another without regard for any return to us. Christ is asking us to try to win that person back, to bring that soul to heaven, to get them home—even our enemies. God is the judge and will make sure justice is done, not us."

Gus stood up. "Not if they have no remorse. Not for what he did!" Gus stomped out the door and left Tom sitting on the bench. Gus was too ramped up to go straight home, so he took a longer route to let his heightened negative emotions work their way out of his system. As he calmed, more and more of what Tom said felt like the hard truth that he had been resisting. *When people go bad, do you want them to finally get it and to turn back to God, or do you want them to stay bad?* In his mind, he could say yes, but in his heart, the answer felt very different. Was he wishing that Danny's killer never found his way to God? Was he hoping the man would go to hell without any hope of redemption?

Without realizing the streets he had taken, Gus found himself approaching Ramsay Park. Not the safest place these days to be walking, but it was quiet on Sunday morning. He stood by the fence and watched two young boys trying to reach the basket with an old ball. He remembered coming to this court with Danny and working with many of the predominantly black players that came here. Two of the boys were on his team at St. Francis and friends with Danny, so he was vouched for and accepted as he helped work with anyone that wanted to develop their skills.

When they realized how much he knew about the game and gave them tips they had never heard of before, he gained their respect because he respected them.

Danny became especially friendly with a boy named Anthony, the brother of the Lenox Street Cardinals gang leader. Anthony was one of the best basketball players at Boston English High and kept himself apart from his brother's criminal dealings. Despite coming from the same background and challenges, Anthony had the intellectual and athletic talents to escape his hopeless prison that was the neighborhood reality in which these young men and women were born. Anthony loved spending time at Danny's house, playing one-on-one in the back, and hanging out. It was much more than a temporary escape from his life at Lenox Street as it was more about a close friendship and mutual respect with Danny. Gus and Julia enjoyed having Anthony to dinner, and the four became close.

As Gus stood by the rusty chainlink fence, he could picture Danny and Anthony playing at a different level than the other players, using the techniques and games skills he had practiced with them. Their love for the game made him happy as he watched them work skillfully and unselfishly as a team.

Gus stepped onto the court and showed the boys how to hold the ball and use their legs to shoot with more power. They were tentative at first, but as the ball reached closer and closer to the basket, they got more engaged. Finally, one of the boys made a basket, and their elation seemed transcendent as they jumped up and gave each other high-fives.

On the way home, Gus felt bad about punishing Jamiel for his own anger toward Danny's killer. Danny would have liked Jamiel and most likely would have befriended him. He would have wanted his father to be welcoming as a friend and a mentor to Jamiel.

When Jamiel and Celia arrived home from Sunday services, Gus made sure he left the garage door open and the cloth cover off of the blue Chevelle.

Eventually, Jamiel peeked into the garage to see Gus standing next to the car. "Mr. Busbi, are you okay?"

"Yes and no. I want to apologize for my erratic behavior—again. I've been struggling lately with a lot of mixed emotions that I've buried for some time."

"You don't have to apologize to me, Mr. Busbi."

"I want to apologize, especially to you. I like you, Jamiel. I think my son would have liked you too. But I need to apologize for not always giving you the benefit of the doubt. I think I've been unfairly dumping my resentment and anger on you."

"You mean because I happen to be black?"

"I've wondered about that, but I don't think that's it. I can't tell you exactly what it is, but I don't think that's it."

"Sorry to ask you that, but I've been wondering. I'm also sorry about your son—and your wife. It must be lonely without them."

Instead of brushing this reality off, Gus uttered, "Sometimes, very."

Jamiel put his hand on Gus's shoulder.

Gus fought back the tears as he reached up and put his hand over Jamiel's. "I have a proposition for you."

"More scraping and painting?"

"Yup, but not the house. If you're interested and willing to put in the work, and there will be a lot, we can refurbish this baby, and it will be yours."

"No, Mr. Busbi. This is your son's car."

"And I can't think of a better man to have it—that's if you can drive."

"I never bothered to get a license because we couldn't afford a car."

"Well, we can do something about that too."

Chapter 37

"Mom!" Jamiel yelled up the stairs as he came back into the house to change. "Mom!"

"Are you okay?" called Celia from her bedroom.

Jamiel stood, leaning against her doorway. "Oh, nothing," he replied with a smile he couldn't stop.

"What is it? I can tell something's up."

"Mr. Busbi offered me a car."

"No! We can't allow him to buy a car for you. That's too much."

"He's not buying a car. There's a car in his garage that needs to be fixed up, and he offered me the car if I work with him on it. What do you think?"

Celia beamed at Jamiel. "I think you need to learn how to drive first, young man."

Jamiel changed his clothes and raced back out to the garage, grinning at Gus. "Where do we start?"

Gus smiled at his enthusiasm and youthful energy.

As they scrubbed and cleaned the car of years of dust build-up, Jamiel became more excited about how special this '69 Chevy SS could be.

Gus taught him about the basics of how a car system is designed and how each part worked together. "It'll take some time to get the electrical wiring and hoses ready before we can put that engine in place."

"Are we going to be able to lift that thing? It looks pretty heavy."

"Mike knows someone with an engine hoist that will help—when we're ready. Are *you* ready for all of this?"

"Sure!" They started working together to install the parts that would connect to the engine, and Jamiel thought about all the weekends he lived without spending time working with a dad, someone that could have taught him how to be a man.

Jamiel lay on the ground as Gus worked with him from above to position and attach parts with the right size ratchet or wrench. Jamiel asked, "Mr. Busbi?"

"Everything okay down there?"

"Yeah. I was just wonderin' something. How do you know when you're really a man?"

"What were you thinking about?"

"You were joining the Marines and fighting for our country at about my age, but I know guys a lot older than me that still act like boys."

"I'm glad you ask easy questions," said Gus with a broad grin as he held the part while Jamiel tightened the bolt. "It's not necessarily an age thing. Sure, you mature physically as a man as you get older, but the real measure of a man is found inside."

"Inside, like how?"

"You have to learn to transition from a boy to a man. Many of those boys you know may never have had other men to teach and mentor them. They may be afraid to live life as a real man."

"Afraid? Afraid of what?"

"What it means to be a man with honor, integrity, courage, honesty—and love that is more about giving than taking. Most boys today never hear about virtues, never mind learning about them and practicing them. It takes courage to be truly honest with yourself. Most people are more comfortable deceiving themselves and avoiding the uncomfortable truths about their weaknesses."

"You mean really seeing yourself in the mirror?"

"Something like that. Every decision we make, every action we take, is something we need to be honest about and responsible for. When we have relationships, we need to ask if we are there for what we are getting or what we are giving. Do we have the courage to be honest and to do the right thing?"

"Are we supposed to be perfect and never afraid?"

"Courage comes when you're afraid and still do the right thing. Most young people are consumed with fitting in when you are called to stand out."

"That's harder than you think."

"It's always been hard, but today there's more indifference."

"What's indifference have to do with it?"

"Indifference is probably the biggest problem going on today, especially with men. It's not caring enough to make a difference. It's thinking things don't matter. The biggest thing Christ asked us to do was to make a choice in life and not be lukewarm. He doesn't want us sitting on the sidelines and being indifferent. Most people would choose the right thing if they *had* to make a choice, instead of not bothering to choose."

"How much of a difference can one person really make?"

"If everyone was indifferent, we might still have slavery."

This caught Jamiel's attention as he tried to process this. "What do you mean?"

"Well, there was a huge benefit brought to the country on the backs of African labor. Who were the people in the North to tell those in the South what they can and cannot do? But it was individuals who stood up, abolitionists, who spoke out. Read about Lincoln. Read about Frederick Douglass. Two million soldiers from the North fought in the Civil War, and over three hundred thousand men gave their lives, including thousands of black soldiers who fought and were willing to pay the ultimate price for what was right. One by one, individual men stood up and fought against indifference."

Jamiel rolled himself from beneath the front end of the car. "Blacks were soldiers in the Civil War?"

"Have you gone on the Black Heritage Trail in Boston?"

"Never heard of it."

"You should go sometime and find out about the men and women who lived on these very streets, who had the courage and integrity to stand up and change the wrongs going on. In front of the State House, there is a great memorial to the 54th Regiment, the first African Americans to fight in the Civil War. You play ball at Ramsay Park sometimes, don't you? Do you know anything about the man it's named after?"

"Not really."

"Captain David L. Ramsay. Check him out sometime."

"How do you know all this stuff about black history?"

"Danny got very interested after becoming friends with a boy from the Lenox Street apartments. He did a lot of research and shared it with his mom and me."

"Huh."

"So, if you want to be a man you can be proud of, look at the real heroes in history. Look at the men in your life who would give their own life for someone they love. If you really want to know how to be a real man, then take the time to listen to what Christ taught and what He did as a man— and then think of how that applies to your life, with your mom, with your friends, and with yourself."

Jamiel thought about how easily he went along with things that he knew were wrong just to fit in with his friends. He felt weak and ashamed. He didn't feel like a man.

"Hey, Jamiel. Are you okay?"

"Sorry, I was just thinking about something."

"Don't be too hard on yourself. You're at an important point in your life, but that will always be the case as we make our next move. Now let's see if we can get these hoses connected and call it a day."

After cleaning up the garage and thanking Gus for spending time with him and talking, Jamiel asked, "Mr. Busbi? You said that your son, Danny, became good friends with someone from Lenox? How good of friends were they?"

"Anthony. Anthony Bennett was his best friend, and Danny was his."

"Do you ever see Anthony anymore?"

Gus became quiet as memories flooded him. He started to answer, but no words came out.

"It's okay, Mr. Busbi. I didn't mean to upset you. Can we work on the car tomorrow?"

Gus nodded as he closed the garage door for the evening and went up to his apartment.

Jamiel went into his room and pulled out the two large rolls of bills he had hidden. They didn't belong to him, but he didn't know who to give them too. Determined to find a better use for the money, he told his mom that he was going for a short walk and ended up at St. Francis. They had metal collection boxes for the poor in the back of the church. He wouldn't have to explain the donation to anyone, and it would help people in need. It sounded like the 'man' thing to do. The side door was open as he gazed up at the high arches lit only by the glow of the prayer candles. It took him a long time, but he folded each bill and slid it through the narrow slot at the top of the box until he held the last one. Just as he was ready to insert the bill, he heard a voice. "Truly generous men are those who give silently without hope of praise or reward."

With the last bill in his hand, Jamiel's heart stopped as he turned toward the familiar voice. "Father Tom. I was just walking by and the door was open."

Tom smiled broadly. "This is God's house. You can take it up with Him if you want, but the door is always open anytime you want to come in. It's nice of you to help the poor."

"Oh, yeah," he said as he slid the last bill into the slot. "I've been feeling fortunate these days. Can I ask you something?"

"Anytime—"

"'—anywhere, for any reason.' I know. I was talking to Gus about what being a man is, and he said that Jesus was the best model for being a real man. What do you think he meant?"

"Well, what do men do?"

Jamiel took a deep breath and exhaled. "Ahh—I don't know. They're respected. They're tough and unafraid. They don't back down."

Tom bobbed his head. "Well, I can see why you would say those things, but I'm not sure Jesus would agree. I think Gus was right. If you want to be a real man, Jesus is our model, but the difference is that His entire focus was on others, not Himself. He was mocked, hated, abandoned, tortured, and killed, but He kept his focus on others. To Him, the answer is self-giving or self-forgetting love that is unconditional, no matter how others treat you. You're right that He didn't back down and showed incredible courage in the face of anxiety and brutal pain—but He did it for you and me. His friendship, sacrifice, and desire for us to know God's unending love models how we should think of others in our lives."

"But, don't you get respect based on how much people fear you or how much talent you have? It always seems like you're more of a man if you are stronger and tougher than others."

"If your wife or girlfriend fears you because you beat her, are you more or less of a man?"

"Less."

"If I'm tough on the outside, but hiding who I really am, am I more or less of a man with courage?"

"Probably less."

"If I get respect out of fear or how much money I have, instead of the good I bring into the world, am I more or less of a man?"

"Okay, I get it."

"People loved and respected Jesus because He was truth and love, but others hated Him to the point of killing Him. You're right, He courageously didn't back down from his mission, but He didn't make it about Him. He made it about completely pouring Himself out and sacrificing Himself for others. *'No one has greater love than this, to lay down one's life for one's friends.'*"

On his way home, Jamiel thought about what kind of man he was going to be. It wasn't going to just happen. He was going to have to decide.

Chapter 38

After school on Monday, BJ walked home with Jamiel, and they played basketball for two straight hours before Gus came home from an appointment. "Mr. Busbi. This is BJ Croop. He moved up from the South."

Gus smiled, "Rhode Island?"

"Texas, sir," answered BJ as he extended his hand and held the ball in the other.

"That *is* south. Welcome to Boston. It looks like you play ball."

"Working on it. Hoping to play for the St. Francis team in the fall."

"He's just being modest. Father Tom wants him to be captain," said Jamiel.

"Co-captain, Captain."

Gus smiled at Jamiel with an expression of surprise and pride at the same time. "You didn't say anything about being named captain. Let me see what you two have."

"Maybe after we catch our breath. Would it be okay if BJ saw what's in the garage?"

Grinning, Gus lifted the large door and watched BJ's expression.

"Sweet! This is my dream ride. Are you restoring it?"

"Just a little project for Jamiel and me. We could use your help on Saturday to put the engine in place if you're available."

"I'll be here if Jamiel doesn't mind."

Jamiel checked out the engine block. "No problem. I'm not putting that thing in alone." Jamiel was glad that Gus told BJ it was their project. After BJ left, he and Gus spent two hours working on the remaining parts to be ready for the engine. They also put together a list of things they needed to source from dealers and junkyards. No heavy discussions, just lots of questions about how the engine, steering, brakes, cooling system, and clutch worked. He liked learning from Gus. Gus was a good teacher, who never made him feel stupid for any questions he asked.

After dinner, Celia sat down at the kitchen table to do her homework.

When Jamiel sprawled out exhausted on the couch trying to read *Hamlet* for his English class, he thought he heard a movement on the front porch. He stepped outside, but he couldn't see anyone. He turned to go back inside when he heard a muffled voice say, "Jam. Jam."

"Who's there?"

"It's me. Trig."

"You can knock on the door, you know."

"Not these days. Things are gettin' red hot."

"What's goin' on?"

"Grant Manor. Drive-by last night, and they hit Fish, O.B., and Nicky."

"How bad?"

"O.B. didn't make it, and Fish is in the City Hospital. He's not looking too good. Nicky's going to be okay."

"Jeez. This thing is never going to end, is it?"

"Not in a good way. On top of that, the blues are tightening the vice on Mal. They want him to snitch on everything that happened that night. Me, you—everything. I want to trust him, but they can play games with his term in the house. I think he may be crackin', thinkin' about a backdoor parole in a pine box if you know what I mean."

"He thinks they'll kill him in prison?"

"There are a lot of brothers in the PEN from Grant or the Dawgs who'd like nothin' better than to settle a score with new fish."

"What do you think?"

"Don't know. I think he's crackin'. We just gotta stick together."

"What do you want me to do?"

"Cool's concerned he hasn't seen much of you lately. He likes you, but you don't want to diss him—I can tell you that."

"How have I ever not respected him?"

"I'm just sayin', I wouldn't. Be there when we need ya. No snitchin' and—"

"And what?"

"And nothin'."

"Trig, and what?"

"What were you doin' there that day?"

"I've been through this with Cool. Trust goes both ways."

"I hear ya, but there's a war on, if you didn't notice. You need a better answer."

"I don't know how to give a better answer than the truth."

His conversation with Trig bothered him all week, but when he woke up on Saturday morning, he was feeling positive. He was dressed and out to the garage early, but Gus and Mike were already there with donuts and, more importantly, the engine hoist. BJ showed up five minutes later, and they were ready to get to work, lifting the engine and gently lowering it onto the motor mounts.

BJ's love for working on cars showed in his grin and enthusiasm, but he had never helped install an engine. They worked on attaching the clutch pedal, driveshaft, starter, distributor, flywheel, cables and hoses, and then the radiator. Jamiel never imagined there was so much to putting a car together. Gus and Mike explained how each subsequent part worked along the way, and three hours later, they were ready for the test—after all this—would it start?

Gus handed Jamiel the keys he had planned to give to his son.

Jamiel jumped in the driver's seat and poked his head out the window. "What do I do?"

After a laugh from the crew, Gus slid into the passenger side and took Jamiel through the steps to put the car in neutral gear and start the engine—and it did.

"Purrs like a kitten," said BJ.

To these four amateur mechanics, it was the sound of pure beauty. They checked the timing and reinstalled the hood with the two wide, black racing stripes. As they sat back to admire their work, Celia came out and smiled at the sight. "I don't want to interrupt this romantic moment but is anyone hungry for sandwiches, cold drinks, and apple pie?"

Sitting around the kitchen table, they ate and joked, and Jamiel felt as if this was one of the best days of his life. No one was black or white, old or young, just four guys enjoying the comradery of the moment and sharing something unique. It made him forget about his earlier conversation with Trig.

As happy as his mom seemed over his accomplishment, Jamiel could tell that she took particular joy in seeing the expression on Gus's face.

When Jamiel turned to Gus, he wondered if Gus wished Danny was the one to hear the engine come to life. He saw Mike glance at Gus, who nodded and returned the smile.

Chapter 39

Right after Sunday services, Jamiel rushed back home to change and work on the Chevy with Gus.

Gus asked, "Do you like going to church?"

"I don't have a choice, and I don't like getting up early on the weekend," answered Jamiel.

"I hear you, but do you like the church you go to?"

"It's all right. Well, there are some really good people there, and Reverend Rich has been a great minister, and it makes my mom happy when I go. I suppose it's the least I could do."

"So, would you go if she weren't here and you were on your own?"

"I don't know. You stopped going."

"Not for a good reason, though. I've been struggling to forgive the man who killed Danny. He showed no remorse for what he did, and I may have been angry at God for a while."

"So, you believe in God?"

"Oh, yes. Very much."

"I'm not sure if I do sometimes."

"That's okay, but He always believes in you."

As they worked to connect the exhaust pipe, Jamiel thought about the people in his life that believed in him. His mom, but that didn't count because that's what moms do. Reverend Rich and Father Tom. He didn't know if his friends from his old neighborhood believed in him—heck, they didn't even believe him. Then he thought of Marnie. She talked like someone who believed in him, but not after Tyrell's death. She may even hate him now. Then he thought about the father he never knew. Would he believe in his son? He sighed at the fact that he would probably never know the answer to that question.

Gus stopped turning the wrench. "I believe in you too."

Jamiel's eyes welled up for a second in response to the unexpected revelation. Didn't he represent those who had taken his life away, taken Danny's life away so brutally?

When they finished with the exhaust and stood face to face, Jamiel asked, "Why—why do you believe in me?"

"I don't want you to think you're a substitute for my son. In some ways, you do remind me of Danny, but I think you have something special in you—a strength, a good soul, and who you are. This car was made to be a real beauty, but it needs to be taken care of to let it show, instead of being wasted and rusting away. I'm not sure all those boys you hang around with care about letting the real Jamiel shine, but I do."

Jamiel now knew why Gus had sat in the hospital all those days that he was unconscious—he cared. Despite all the struggle and confrontation, Gus still cared about what happened to him, that he was going to be all right. Maybe it was time he started caring about himself too.

Over the next several weeks, Jamiel and Gus spent afternoons and weekends with antique car part dealers, at junkyards, car shows, and individual owners to find the right replacement pieces they needed to refurb the car: car seats, fenders, hubcaps, mirrors, and radio. Jamiel talked about all the things he might have discussed with a father if he had one, asking questions and debating ideas. They talked about sports, college, honesty, courage, religion, race, and friendship. Gus borrowed Mike's truck to pick up the parts and started teaching Jamiel how to drive.

On one drive south of Boston, Gus asked him to drive down a road that led to a sandy beach with a clam shack open for the early season. Jamiel ordered a burger and a shake, and Gus ordered fried clams and challenged Jamiel to broaden his horizons and try a clam. He was surprised that the taste wasn't as bad as he expected.

"Mr. Busbi—"

"Jamiel, you can call me Gus."

"I don't know. It feels weird now—Gus."

Gus smiled as Jamiel bit into another clam. "That wasn't so bad, and you survived."

Jamiel nodded and smiled back. "Mr.—Gus. Can I ask you about something?"

"You've asked a thousand questions already, and that's a good sign because you can't learn anything you don't wonder about. What's on your mind?"

Jamiel hesitated for several moments.

Gus asked, "Something to do with girls?"

Embarrassed, Jamiel glanced over at Gus. "Maybe. Okay, yeah. I hear so many conflicting things about what a guy's supposed to do and not supposed to do. I don't need another lecture, just to understand why one is right."

"Ahh. Few young men would care enough to ask that question. They're more than happy to turn off the brain and just go after what they want. Is there a girl you're interested in?"

Jamiel smiled, "All of them. Well, there is one girl I've been thinking about."

"I remember being totally taken with this girl when I was in high school, and I'm not sure how I got anything done. She was all I thought about. Her eyes, the way she wore her hair, her smile—she was the prettiest girl I had ever known."

"Did you ever ask her out?"

"Nope. I couldn't keep my eyes off of her during class, but I never got to know her, and she moved out of Boston the next year. When I think about it, I didn't know anything about her, just how she made me feel when I looked at her. Men are visual beings and become interested when a girl is attractive to them."

"Is it wrong for guys to be so focused on how pretty a girl is?"

"There is nothing wrong with appreciating beauty in anything God creates. The question is, do we see more than the outside of a girl, or do we use her as an object for our pleasure? Your mom is a very attractive woman, wouldn't you agree?"

"Sure. I think so."

"But you know there is so much more to her beauty than her outside appearance. Do you think she deserves more than to be seen as an object?"

"No question."

"Don't treat any girl you see with any less dignity and respect than you would want someone to treat your mom. You may not know Pope John Paul II, but he said something that I think is right. 'The dignity of every woman is the duty of every man.'"

"Huh."

"I think most young men would like to have it both ways. They would want their moms, sisters, and wives treated one way, but they would like there to be another group of women who they treat a different way—for their own pleasure. Men can compartmentalize things in life."

"I kinda know deep down that using girls for sex isn't right, no matter how much we might want to do it. The guys in the neighborhood talk about gettin' some—like the more girls you have sex with, the more of a man you are. I know they're just using them like things and discarding them when they're through, but what if you like a girl and she likes you? That's what I'm talking about. What makes it right or wrong in that situation?"

"I had the same challenge with Julia. I don't think the desire was any different than it is today, but I do think it's tougher now because our culture and society are no longer supporting the right answer. If everyone is doing it, sleeping together, living together, and times have changed, isn't it now okay versus those outdated, old-fashioned rules?"

"Isn't it different?"

"Just because a lot of people are doing something doesn't make it right. If more people drank a poison, would it make it less dangerous?"

Jamiel thought for a moment. "No. It would make it more dangerous because more people would be hurt."

"Right. For me, it came down to three things. First is: What is the moral thing to do? If you believe in God, it's pretty clear that sex was meant for a committed marriage. So we have to decide if we are going to honor and trust His plan or ours. I had to think about this a lot when Danny was your age and asking the same questions. If you think honestly about the natural design of sex, that plan is pretty obvious."

"What do you mean?"

"Well, we find women attractive for a reason. Every physical feature we find attractive is tied to a woman's fertility and health as a mate to produce healthy offspring. Even though there is more to sex than making babies, it is what the natural design is all about. We may try to block it with artificial means, but that's not the natural design, nor is treating a woman's fertility that attracted us to them like a disease. We're not being honest when we deny that sex is for *both* bonding and creating new life, not just one."

"You can't expect to have a baby every time, though!"

"No, but that gets to the second item. What is the responsible thing for a man to do? People talk about 'safe sex,' but no contraception is a hundred percent effective in real practice. The majority of women having abortions used contraception. Thinking of people's whole lives, from a baby on up to old age, what percentage of those lives do you think it's okay to bring into the world with no father, no committed family?"

Jamiel thought of growing up without a father and how hard his mom had to struggle. He also thought of all the young girls, not ready to give their babies what they deserved, getting pregnant. "I guess there isn't one."

"Did you know that the pill is a Group One carcinogen? Or that there are tens of millions of new cases of STDs each year in the US alone, and most aren't preventable with birth control? It wasn't until I was talking with Danny that it hit me. If sex was saved for marriage, all children would be born into a committed family that would care for them, and there would be no STDs. So, I had to ask—what would a responsible man do?"

"Take a cold shower."

Gus laughed. "Or maybe focus on the third thing. What is the most loving thing to do? What do you want when it comes to that girl you want to spend your life with? What does she deserve? Is she worth waiting for? Should that level of intimacy be part of something more special, more sacred, more honest?"

"More honest?"

"Sure, when you have sex, you are telling a woman that you are giving your entire self to her, but that would be a lie outside of marriage. The good news—instead of this being about a 'No,' it's really about a much bigger 'Yes' that I thought Julia deserved. Julia was worth waiting for, no matter how much part of me didn't want to wait."

"I can tell that you believe that. But I don't think of my mom as a bad person in any way."

"I don't either. Most young people are uninformed. Most young women are used when their hearts are full of what they believe is love. We make mistakes, and while I don't think she would trade you in for anything in the world, I'll bet she wishes you had a dad around."

"Yeah. Me, too. We've never even talked about him."

"Maybe you should."

Chapter 40

Even though it was a school day, Jamiel felt upbeat when he woke up. Summer was coming fast. He and BJ continued to work out with both Father Tom and Gus on their basketball game and could feel the difference. The only conflicts seemed to be figuring out how to connect with his lifelong friends from Lenox, and how to deal with Marnie's continued refusal to talk with him. Both issues bothered him.

After school, he changed clothes and made his way down to Lenox Street and found the gang in their usual spot "guarding the gates."

"My, my, my, if it isn't the Asphalt God slummin' it again," commented one of the boys.

"What's been up, man?" greeted Halfway.

"Been busy with school and fixin' up a new sled," responded Jamiel as he half-hugged him.

"I heard about that. Chevy SS? Sweet ride."

"Hey, Jam, they're startin' up that tournament they used to have at Ramsay. You know, the one they stopped after that brother got knifed. Long time ago, but I think they want to foster some more love in town. Five large to the winnin' team."

Jamiel's eyes widened. "Five thousand? Who can play?"

"Anyone from the South End, Rox, Dot, and the Pan. For the brothers to make them feel better about keeping us in this craphole. You gotta play on our team, man."

"You got that right," came a voice from behind.

Jamiel turned to see Leonard, Ricky, Trig, and Bronx walking up to join the rest of the gang. "Sure. I got someone I would like to play," Jamiel responded as he clenched hands with Leonard.

"If he ain't from Lenox and looks like Casper, he's out."

"But he's really good, and he lives in the South End."

"He's out."

Leonard put his arm around Jamiel's neck and tugged him away from the crowd, with Ricky following. "What's up lately? Spendin' all your time hangin' around the white folks makin' you forget who you are? If we don't stick together, they win. Loyalty matters."

Jamiel wasn't going to debate Leonard. Getting to know and see people who happened to be white may have changed how Jamiel felt about that individual, but it didn't change the larger problem Leonard was talking about, even if he didn't agree with the approach. "I know."

Ricky stared directly into Jamiel's eyes. "Lately, you don't sound like you know or act like you know. We hardly even see you anymore, man."

Leonard put out his arm and moved his brother, Ricky, back from Jamiel, who was not backing down. "We just need to know where your loyalty is these days. To that old cracker landlord of yours? To that Grant Manor girl of yours?"

"She's not my girl."

"Exactly."

"Look. I told you why I was there that day. Nothin' to do with her brother or anything that went down. She won't even talk with me. I've been nothin' but loyal to you. Trust goes both ways." Anger and adrenaline filled him.

When he reached his house, he sat on the porch to cool off.

Gus saw him sitting and climbed the steps. "Anything you want to share?"

"Not really. Just a run-in with some friends."

"Are they friends? Or just boys you grew up with?"

"What's the difference?"

"Friends want to stay friends. They want to know your side. They want what's best for you. They trust you."

"Well, they certainly don't trust me. One side thinks I went to Grant Manor to tip Marnie's brother off the day he was shot, and the other side thinks I was there to get him killed."

"When emotions and hate are running high, I guess it's hard to trust anyone."

"Gus, they were talking about starting back up this basketball tournament at Ramsay, and the next thing, they're telling me I'm hangin' around with white people too much. Maybe that last part is true, but they're questioning my loyalty, and they don't trust me."

Gus didn't respond.

When Jamiel glanced over, he could tell by the narrowing of Gus's eyes that he was deep in thought. "Mr. Busbi, I mean Gus, did I say something wrong? I didn't mean anything about that 'white' comment."

Gus got up and headed down the stairs. Without turning around, he said, "It wasn't that. Don't worry; it's not you. I just need to go in."

At the moment, Jamiel felt as if he was out of sync with everyone.

After a quiet dinner, his mother asked, "What's up, honey?"

"Nothin' really."

"I can tell. You've been up lately, but something's got you down today."

"The world. I think it's time I stop followin' and start doin' what I think I want to do."

"And what does that mean exactly?"

"I don't know." Jamiel stood up and started toward the stairs. "Thanks for talkin'."

Celia shook her head. "Sure. I only wish I knew what we were talking about."

Jamiel decided to go up to Gus's apartment, the same stairs he had feared to climb such a short time ago. If Jamiel had asked himself a couple of months ago who he would go to for advice, he would never have said Gus Busbi, but now he realized that's exactly whom he needed to talk with.

Gus didn't say a word as he let Jamiel in.

Jamiel sat down at the kitchen table. "I'm thinkin' of playing in that tournament. It's five thousand dollars to the winners."

"It's gone up."

"You know about this tournament?"

Gus nodded.

"Is there something about it you don't want to talk about? Did I say something?"

"No."

Jamiel could feel the heaviness of the cloud hanging over Gus. "Gus, you can talk to me about anything."

A half-smile made its way to Gus's mouth, but it didn't reach his eyes.

"Was Danny in this tournament? Is that it?"

"I told you that Danny became best friends with Anthony from Lenox Street. They played at Ramsay all the time, and I worked with the guys on their game, but having Danny and I there never sat well with some of the gang leaders. Anthony never let us know, but they put a lot of pressure on him to have Danny stop playing on their turf. He didn't. The tournament had teams from a lot of the neighborhoods representing the gangs in each of those neighborhoods. As Anthony and Danny's team kept winning and moving up, the rival gangs got angrier."

Gus hesitated as he drifted back to that warm summer evening game under the lights. "The team from Grant Manor was playing a real physical game against Anthony and Danny's team in the semi-finals. As the Grant Manor team started to fall behind late in the second half, one of the guys watching on the sidelines put a knife into Anthony's side after he scored a layup."

Jamiel could see the painful emotion in Gus's eyes as he continued, "No one...knew anything had happened as he staggered back onto the court and then collapsed, blood running from his side. All of a sudden, there was chaos, screaming, and then an all-out brawl between Grant Manor and Lenox Street Cardinals gang members. I was able to grab Danny and get him out of there before anyone went after him."

"Damn. That sounds scary as hell. I've never heard this story. Is that why they stopped having this tournament?"

"I think so," said Gus in a quiet tone. "Anthony died on that court, and Danny was killed two days later."

"Oh, crap. I'm sorry."

Gus's eyes were closed as Jamiel put his hand on his shoulder.

"I'm so sorry, Gus."

Chapter 41

Saturday morning, Jamiel was learning how to sand, use Bondo, and get the body of the car ready for the all-important paint job. "Gus, I've been thinking about your son. I'd like to play in that tournament, in his honor. I'd like the winnings to go to a scholarship fund in his name or something at St. Francis to remember him by."

Gus's eyes watered, the old man visibly moved by Jamiel's desire to honor his son, someone he had never met. "That means a lot to me, Jamiel. It does. I'm just afraid of you putting yourself at risk.

"We definitely need to see about that, but if I can get some guarantee, I would like you to coach us."

Gus let out a long exhale. "I'll have to think about it."

"That's all I'm asking, Coach," responded Jamiel with a hopeful smile, putting some extra elbow grease into sanding a rust spot.

To Leonard's disappointment, Jamiel recruited some neighborhood players who often didn't get the respect of many of the other Lenox Street players. Now that school was out, Father Tom let them use the gym to play. As they showed up for their first practice, Gus appeared at the door and made his way to center court where they gathered. "So you want to win a tournament, do you?"

"And five thousand bucks while we're at it!" added one of the recruits.

"Well, you're going to have to work for it—and you're going to see some rougher play than you may be used to. Winning will be about more than the money to many of these players, and hopefully to all of you."

Jamiel said, "We're up for it, Coach."

Gus extended his hand. "Are you up for it as a team?"

All six players in the circle put their hands on Gus's. "As a team!"

"Sounded kind of wimpy."

"AS A TEAM!"

"Let's play a little three-on-three to see what we have."

Jamiel noticed Gus watching each player and taking mental notes of their skill level, tendencies, strengths, and weaknesses. After a few games, Gus pulled them back to mid-court. "There's no black or white on this team, only a team. I noticed BJ open several times, and he didn't get the pass that would have been the right play. *So*, who's committed to playing as a team?"

Everyone raised their hands.

"Okay. I saw some good stuff out there, and I saw a lot of work ahead of us, too. The tournament starts in ten days. Who can make it here every day?" Everyone raised their hand, except for BJ.

BJ said, "I'm supposed to start a job working with Angelo here this week."

A voice at the door said, "I think I can get a delayed start for you, BJ. Good to see you found the best coach in town. Listen to him, and you might be champs," said Father Tom, stepping out of the shadows.

Each day, they worked on coordinated plays, spacing, passing, boxing out for rebounds, and team defense. Gus took them through game scenarios and how to create an advantage in each situation. Most importantly, he impressed upon them the need to be disciplined when the other teams played rough. "Don't lose your temper if you get hit hard and the ref doesn't call it. And complaining won't help. Just get back by winning the next play. A defensive stop here, a steal there, a fast break, and an offensive rebound alone could mean eight points a game. Play each play as a team, and don't get down no matter what. If we do that throughout the tournament, you can win!"

This was the side of Gus that Father Tom tried to describe to Jamiel once. He was energized and commanded their attention and respect through his presence, his knowledge, and his respect for each of them. Even the most skeptical on the team became a believer as they showed noticeable improvement in working together as a team playing against a few practice teams Father Tom and Gus were able to bring in on a few occasions.

It was a great early summer day for the first day of the Ramsay Memorial Tournament that would run for four consecutive Saturdays until the last remaining of the sixteen teams entered was left standing. There was already a large crowd of spectators for the first of eight games. The Lenox Street Cardinals would play Heath Street in the first game, and Jamiel's team, called DnA for Danny and Anthony, would play the second game against Orchard Park, luckily an ally of Lenox Street.

The atmosphere was festive, but there was tension in the air with rival gangs in the same area, despite the police presence. The first game was often sloppy but an easy win for the Cardinals, despite not having Jamiel to anchor their team. During the game, Jamiel could feel the anger in Leonard's stare as he defied his command to play with the Cardinals and to leave BJ out of this.

As they readied to take the court to warm up for the second game, Gus pulled them together. "Remember what we practiced. Play hard defense to stop them and generate your offense. Don't let anything get you rattled and play as—"

"A TEAM!" said the players in unison as they clasped hands.

There was a loud booing sound as the DnA team took the court, and Jamiel knew it was because BJ was the only white player in the tournament. Jamiel was well aware that the booing could also be a message to him, but he didn't feel fazed. As the ref tossed the ball for the tip-off, BJ jumped to tip the ball, and the opposing players bumped him enough to throw him off balance, causing him to land hard on the asphalt, with no foul called. Jamiel picked him up, but they were down 2-0 with a quick basket by Orchard Park.

No matter how many times Gus instructed them not to get rattled by the aggressively physical play, it was throwing them off, and they were quickly down by 8-0. Jamiel pulled the team together. "Now that they think we don't know what we're doing, let's start playing our game." The humor broke the tension, and on the next play, there was a quick pass on the wing to Jamiel, who dribbled behind his back, making a 360-degree turn before he tossed a high, floating pass above the rim that BJ slammed home. Despite the score by the white guy, the crowd couldn't help making a collective "whoa" sound. The team got back into their rhythm and confidence and coasted home to a comfortable 36–24 win in front of an impressed crowd.

The DnA team stayed the entire four hours to watch each of the games, taking note of whom they may be up against next. While their confidence had been boosted by their first win, they realized that the teams going into the next round would be much tougher competition in more ways than one.

Chapter 42

Jamiel and Gus spent Sunday afternoon prepping and taping up the car to get it ready for applying the primer coat. They had bought a car door and hood from the junkyard for Jamiel to practice applying paint with the sprayer for even coats without drips. It was worth the investment. As they worked, they talked about strategy for the next tournament team they'd be facing—the Greenwood Street Posse, a rival of the Lenox Street Cardinals. Even though the DnA team was not the Cardinals, everyone on the team, except BJ, was from the Lenox Street Projects. The Greenwood players were strong, aggressive, and very physical. They agreed to keep the ball passing quick and crisp on offense, to cut off passing lanes, and to box out aggressively on defense, all things they worked on with the team at practice that week.

Saturday morning came around fast, with everyone anticipating the remaining eight teams to play aggressively competitive games. Neighborhood spectators were there early, and the atmosphere was festive with loud music and the buzz of conversations. The first game pitted the team from Grant Manor against Mattapan. The match did not disappoint. Great passing, outside shooting, and a few monster dunks brought the crowd to their feet. In the end, the Grant Manor team was too strong and won. Jamiel had paid close attention to the two main talents on the team. The second game was no less entertaining, with the Columbia Point Dawgs soundly beating the team from Heath Street.

Jamiel's DnA team was up next. They watched the confident elbowings and bumping of bodies going on by the Greenwood Street Posse before the game even started, which only hardened their resolve to win. As practiced, they moved the ball quickly around the court with passes that led to open shots and a quick 8-2 lead, causing frustration for the Posse players who huddled for a timeout. Jamiel listened to Gus as he glanced up and noticed Reverend Rich across the court watching the game. His presence made him want to play even harder, but he didn't recognize the man standing with him. The stranger was tall and broad-shouldered with a goatee, and his eyes were fixed on Jamiel. It unnerved Jamiel for several moments as he missed his next two jump shots and gave up on one of the Posse players who drove right by him for a score to tie the game. Jamiel kept glancing over at the mystery guest who was still looking his way.

The inbound pass came to Jamiel, who dribbled smoothly down the court. He probably had the best ball-handling skills in the tournament, and it showed as he wove in out of Posse players trying to lunge for a steal. With a quick no-look pass to BJ and then back to Jamiel, he slammed the ball through the basket with power that brought a loud cheer from the crowd and an elated reaction from Reverend Rich and his companion. Jamiel stole the inbounds pass for a quick basket and then hit two pretty-looking jumps shots for a 16-8 lead. By the time the clock ran out, DnA had won the game by ten points and sent an angry, arguing Posse team home.

In the final game, Lenox Street beat the Dorchester team handily, and much of the crowd stayed to congregate while others dispersed.

Leonard walked over to Jamiel. "Nice game, my man. Should have been for your home team, though. I know the Dawgs and Grant Manor are against us. Are you?"

"Cool, it's competition, a game, not war."

"I told you before; it's not a game! It's turf. It's respect. It's survival. You're with us or against us!" Leonard turned away without waiting for a response.

As Jamiel went back to congratulate his team on a well-played game, he noticed the man who had been standing with Reverend Rich talking with Leonard. The exchange seemed controlled but not overly friendly.

Gus took the team out for pizza and game planning. "It looks like we will be facing the Lenox Street Cardinals. Watching their games, they will be a tough team to beat. But I also think we can win."

When they got home, Jamiel said, "Gus, thanks for all your mentoring. I know it's probably not been easy to go to these games. I just wanted you to know how much I appreciate it. What do you think of our chances now?"

"It depends. If we play our game all out, I think you have as good a chance as the other three teams, even with their size and experience."

"We won't let Danny down."

Gus nodded as he headed to the backyard, and Jamiel went into the house to let his mother know about the game. They sat and talked for a while. His mom smiled the entire time she was listening. When he got up to fill up his glass from the kitchen faucet, he stopped talking for the first time since he arrived home. He noticed someone walking down the driveway to the backyard, the stranger who had been at the game with Reverend Rich. "There's a guy who was at the game today, and now he is talkin' with Gus. Actually, they look like they are arguing about something. Mom, should I go out and see what's going on? To make sure Gus is okay?"

Celia came over to the window to watch. Gus was shaking his head and waving to the man to leave. "Gus seems especially upset, maybe—" Celia froze mid-sentence as the man turned, and she could see his face. All of a sudden, his mother doubled over the sink and breathed in and out with shallow breaths.

"Mom, what is it? Are you okay?"

She put her shaking hand to her face and turned back out, but the man was no longer in the driveway. She made her way to the kitchen table and dropped in the chair.

"Are you feeling sick?"

"I just need a second. I need to think."

"So, you're not going to faint or anything?"

"No, no. Don't worry."

"Well, what is it then? I've never seen you like this."

Celia peered down and rubbed her thumb against her hand, staring at the table. "I'm okay. I was just feeling overwhelmed for a moment."

"By what?"

No response.

"Who was that man in the driveway?"

Celia slowly lifted her gaze from the table and peered into her son's eyes. "It was your father."

"What?! My father's been around, and you haven't told me?"

"Your father hasn't been around. I haven't seen him since I was carrying you. No one would tell me where he was, and he didn't want to see me."

"And I guess he didn't want to see me either," Jamiel said angrily as he climbed the steps two by two to his room until he lay face down on his bed. He felt a sense of rejection and worthlessness, confirming his fears over all those years. Why did he show up now? Gus had been more of a father to him over these months than his real father had ever been in his entire life. What was he doing showing up when he's already grown up? A tear rolled down his cheek, but he still felt anger and fear more than anything.

He could hear his mother's footsteps as she slowly made her way up the stairs. What was she feeling with the shock of this unexpected visit?

She tapped on the frame of Jamiel's open door.

"What?"

"Can I come in?"

"I guess." He turned his head. "What's going on?"

"I don't know, son. I really don't know."

"That man was at my game today. I've never seen him before, but he was staring right at me. He was standing with Reverend Rich."

"Reverend Rich? Huh."

"What are we going to do? And why was he arguing with Gus? Tell me what's going on."

"I'm as confused as you are."

"Then tell me the truth about what you do know. No holding back to protect me anymore."

His mother nodded and glanced up, as if in prayer. "I grew up in our old neighborhood. I never really knew my own dad, your grandfather, either. He was shot and killed when I was very young, and my mother never talked about him. She just pulled herself up and tried to raise us right. There was this boy who was several years older than me that I always liked. I couldn't tell you exactly why. I just saw something in him I was attracted to, but I never let him know and didn't think he even knew I existed. He used to play ball at the same park as you, and he was quite a player and shooter. I think that's why they called him, 'Sure Thing'."

"What was his name?"

"William Bennet. He went by 'Willie,' but I called him Will. He had a very tough family background, and he started getting involved with a bad crowd; I mean *really* bad. He seemed to get tougher and angrier when he got involved with the Lenox Street gang. A gang war had killed off the heads of the Cardinals, and with his presence and leadership, he became the leader of the gang—a gang involved in drugs, robbery, and worse."

"How could you like a guy like that?"

"No excuse, but I was pretty young and naïve. I would imagine there are friends of yours from the old neighborhood that aren't so clean, but you can see the other side of them. Under that tough, angry exterior, I just felt like there was someone worthwhile—something he just didn't know or believe himself."

Jamiel got up and sat on the side of his bed, holding his head in his hands. "I feel awkward asking you this, but where did I fit into this?"

"You fit here with me and in whatever God's plans are for you."

"You know what I mean, Mom."

"By the time I was seventeen, he started to notice me, but not so anyone else would know, and I didn't tell anyone how I felt. I just really cared about him and worried as things in the neighborhood got more dangerous with drive-by shootings, fights, and arrests. At that time in my life, I thought I had no options to go anywhere—no college, no good job, but maybe I could be with this guy, someone who didn't think he would live to see twenty-five. He met me alone at one point and let me know how he felt about me, but he didn't want me getting involved with someone like him. He thought I deserved better, and there was no future for us. He thought I should date someone like his brother, Anthony, and—"

"Anthony? Will was Anthony's brother?"

"You know about Anthony?"

"The Anthony that was friends with Gus's son, Danny Busbi?"

Celia tightened her face. "Yes."

"Did you go out with Anthony?"

"No, we were friends, and he was the only one who knew I liked Will. He had befriended Danny through basketball, and they became very close. Anthony found a family with Danny's family. It was much more than basketball."

"Wait a minute. You've known all along that we were living in Danny's house?"

"Yes. But I didn't plan it. I was desperate to get you into a healthier place to live and go to school. I've seen those neighborhoods chew up so many promising young men and spit them out—and worse."

"Does Gus know who we are?"

"No. No one alive knows that you are William Bennett's son. Not even my family knows."

"What do you mean by 'no one alive'?"

Celia stood up from the bed and nervously paced back and forth. "Will didn't like his brother Anthony hanging around with Danny. He was angry at the racism that kept him in the ghetto. He was probably a good enough ballplayer himself to play in college, but he took another path, one that he didn't want Anthony to take. But he didn't want him hanging around with the enemy either. They fought often about it, but Anthony wouldn't back down. So, Will aimed his ire at Danny and let him know it every time he showed up at the courts to play. He became especially explosive when he found out from Anthony that Danny liked me."

"What?! Did you like him?"

"I did, but not in that way. I was too taken with your father to be attracted to anyone else at the time, even if Will would never date me. I'm ashamed to say that your father and I were together only once, but I'm not ashamed of the gift of you." Celia closed her eyes tightly as memories apparently flooded back. "There was the basketball tournament, and Will wouldn't let Danny play on the Lenox Street team. Against Will's threats, Anthony and Danny pulled together their own team. This didn't sit well with the rival gang's team, either. Danny was the only white player in the tournament. You have to understand, in a world where blacks owned literally nothing, the tournament was something that was theirs, and Danny represented an assault on that reality."

Jamiel remembered Gus talking about the tournament. "Were you there at the games?"

"I was there. Anthony and Danny were both outstanding players, and together they seemed impossible to beat. They made it to the final game—"

"Was it against Lenox Street?"

"No, Lenox lost on a last-second shot against Grant Manor in the previous round."

"So, Anthony and Danny were playing against Grant Manor in the final?"

"Yes, and Grant Manor hated everything Lenox Street. They also seemed the angriest about playing against a team with a white player on it and were brutally rough with him during the game. At one point, one of the players pulled Anthony aside and chided him to 'get the cracker out of the hood.' Anthony just stared him down and played harder against the dirty tactics of the Grant Manor players."

His mom's voice cracked as tears streamed down her cheeks. Jamiel could tell that she was now shaking as she continued.

"Ah—when it looked like Anthony and Danny's team was going to put this final game out of reach on a layup shot by Anthony that landed him in the crowd—I just remember screaming when Anthony staggered across the court holding his stomach with his hand on his bloodied shirt. He collapsed at mid-court, and Will pushed through the crowd to watch Anthony and all his promise die."

Her body dropped to the bed as she cried, and Jamiel held her, cradling her head with the palm of his hand. "Are you okay?"

She continued sobbing as she nodded, but didn't say anything.

"Gus told me about Anthony. He said Danny was dead two days later?"

"Yes." He could hear in a muffled voice.

"By Grant Manor?"

No sound came from his mother.

"Mom?"

She couldn't utter a response.

Jamiel let her lay there as he went outside to sit on the porch to clear his head. His father had been ten feet away from him, and he didn't even know it. As he walked around to the back, he peered up at Gus's apartment and wondered how he was doing. On the narrow flight of stairs, it hit him like a ton of bricks why Gus had the visceral reaction when he looked at him—he could see his dad in him. He turned around on the creaky steps to go back down before Gus heard him, but the door opened. "Jamiel?"

"I just wanted to know if you were okay, but then I thought you might not want to be disturbed." He could tell that Gus was already disturbed as his brow furrowed.

"Yeah, maybe this isn't a good time."

Jamiel felt a sigh of relief, avoiding any conversation that let him know who he really was, but then he turned back. "Gus. Are you sure?"

Gus stood at the top of the stairs and squeezed his eyes shut for a second. "Come on up."

Sitting at the kitchen table, Jamiel watched the leaves outside the window, dancing to the breeze's movements. "Can I get you a tonic?" asked Gus.

"Sure."

"Root beer okay?"

"Yes, thanks."

As Gus poured him a glass, Jamiel asked, "I, um, saw someone in the driveway. Was he giving you trouble?"

Gus sat down, taking the chair next to the window where the sun streamed in. "I was shocked to see him—here of all places."

Jamiel didn't say anything and let the silence fill the room until Gus allowed him into his thoughts.

Gus exhaled with a long breath, and his voice cracked as he continued, "It was, um—it was the man that killed Danny."

A sudden rush of panic and shame ran through Jamiel's entire being. His father had taken away everything from this man Jamiel cared about more than he had realized until this very moment. He could see Gus's eyes well up as he remembered that day. Not that he probably didn't think of it every day, but now the painful memory would be more vividly set in Gus's mind. Jamiel had to push aside his own conflicted feelings and his instinctive denial that this was his father they were discussing.

"Why was he here? Shouldn't he be in prison?"

"He was just released on parole. I was informed that he was out, but I never expected him to have the nerve, to have the gumption, to come into this yard and talk to me."

"What did he say?"

"I was so angry and upset when I saw him approaching. I kept telling him to leave. I thought he was trying to say he was—that he was sorry."

"Do you think he was, I mean, really sorry?"

"A little late for that. During the long trial, he showed no remorse at all. He stared directly at Julia and me with nothing but the hatred and contempt he showed Danny."

"I don't know if I could forgive him either." Jamiel wondered if he could forgive his father for what he had done, for leaving his mother to struggle alone, and for never being there for him as a father. This stranger was someone who did more harm to people he cared about than anyone he knew. "Gus, why did he do it?"

"I told you about Danny's friend, Anthony, being killed by a stabbing at the tournament. That was Willie Bennett's younger brother. Willie was a dangerous and volatile leader of the Cardinals gang, and he had ordered Danny to stop hanging around with his brother, especially not to play in that tournament. He wasn't the only one upset by Danny's playing. The team of a rival gang was about to lose to Danny and Anthony's team, and that was when someone in the crowd stabbed and killed Anthony. I'm pretty sure Willie blamed Danny for his brother's death."

"What about blaming the person that knifed him?"

"I don't know. Maybe his pent-up anger for Danny and the loss of his brother just pushed him over the edge? He came to the house and shouted for Danny from across the street. Danny was heartbroken by the loss of Anthony, and we were all planning on attending his funeral the next day. Danny went to talk with Willie, never expecting what was going to happen. Julia was sitting on the porch, and I was in the house as Danny stepped onto the street, approaching Willie. That is when—" Gus squeezed his eyes tight again as if he was feeling the pain of the bullet entering his own body. His voice cracked with pain. "That is when I heard an explosion, a loud shotgun blast." Gus sat quietly, and Jamiel put his hand on his shoulder. "I ran outside, hoping it was something different, a car backfiring or something, but there stood Willie with the sawed-off shotgun in his hand and anger in his eyes. Julia was screaming as I ran to grab Danny's body."

Jamiel watched the tears stream down Gus's cheeks, and Jamiel couldn't hold his own tears back.

Gus struggled to continue, "I couldn't believe it. I cradled him as the blood poured out. I peered up at a man that showed no sign of remorse, only hate."

"Oh, my God. I can't imagine how difficult this has been to live with all these years. I'm so, so sorry about your son, and for your wife, and especially for you, Gus."

Gus lifted his head with wet red-rimmed eyes and stared directly at Jamiel.

Jamiel didn't feel as if he belonged there at this moment. Something was wrong, and Jamiel was the only one who knew what it was.

"I think I need some time alone."

Jamiel nodded and stood up. He reached out to shake Gus's hand but instinctively hugged him instead and then left Gus to his memories and conflict, while he pushed his own away. Now he understood why his mother couldn't bring herself to tell him who had killed Danny.

Chapter 43

When the team met up at St. Francis gym for practice on Monday, Gus didn't show up to coach. Jamiel took the lead to try to break down the key things they needed to do on both offense and defense. Father Tom dropped by to watch and helped when he realized Gus wasn't there. After practice, Tom asked Jamiel, "Is Gus feeling okay?"

"I don't know. When I saw him yesterday, he was in tough shape."

"Is he sick?"

"Not physically, but I'm worried about him."

"I'm confused. Did something happen?"

"My f— a man came by to see Gus, and they got into an argument."

"What man?"

"The man who killed Danny."

"What? What did he want?"

"I think he tried to apologize, and Gus told him to leave."

"I see. Gus has struggled with this for many years, and now he is dealing face to face with it.'

"What do you mean, Father Tom?"

"Gus was a man of strong faith. Love and forgiveness are at the center of that faith, and he cannot bring himself to do either."

"How can he forgive someone who has no remorse?"

"We are asked to love and forgive even those that hate us and wish to do us more harm."

"Who asked us to do that?"

"Christ commands us to love our enemies and to be forgiven as we forgive others, not to judge or condemn, but to love and forgive. Gus can't bring himself to forgive the killer, and he feels it's putting his soul at risk. He doesn't want to be a hypocrite if he can't do it sincerely, but he doesn't believe the killer has any remorse. I think Gus believes it will dishonor Danny to forgive someone who isn't sorry for what they did."

"Well, how *can* you?"

"It's not ours to judge or administer justice. God will do that. It's our job to love or wish the best for those that are lost and even to forgive our enemies. Just as Jesus did on the cross."

"Would it be easier if that man was sorry, truly sorry for what he did?"

"Yes, it may be easier if the man is sorry for what he did, but the forgiveness should be unconditional."

When Jamiel got home, he found that his mom had arrived from work earlier than usual. "How did practice go today? How was Gus?"

"He didn't come. How are *you* doin'? This must be hard for you too, Mom."

"Jamiel, I'm sorry."

"What are you sorry about?"

"I've felt so sorry that you had to live your life without a father, and that's my fault. I'm sorry that I never told you about him, but he made me promise that I'd never tell you that he was in prison. I just never knew where he was sent. He didn't want you to be ashamed of your father. And I'm sorry for not finding out yesterday how you were feeling. I can't begin to imagine what it's like to be seventeen and find out your father is alive and what he has done."

"I think I'm in denial. Gus is in pain, and that is real to me. This man that you say is my father has never been a father to me. He did nothing in life other than destroy a good family. And I don't think he's sorry at all for it. I feel nothing but anger for him."

Celia nodded and hugged her son.

The next day, the team showed up to work on their strategy. Gus showed up, and Jamiel met him at mid-court. "I'm glad you came, Gus."

"I've been letting that man beat me for too long now. It's time to live, for Danny, for Julia, for me—and for you."

Jamiel waved the other players over, and Gus said he was impressed with the game plan they had developed and the plays they were working on.

By the time Saturday came around, the team felt ready for a tough challenge—the Lenox Street Cardinals.

There would be only two games that day for the last four teams remaining in the tournament. The size of the crowd and the buzz seemed bigger than the first two Saturdays. Grant Manor played an aggressive first game and managed to beat the Columbia Point Dawgs by five points. Emotions were high after the loss, and there was a brawl on the court that was quickly broken up by the police.

The Lenox Street Cardinals took the court with their heads up and appearing very confident and ready to play their game, which was a physical style of play that pushed the boundaries of the rules. They were stronger and intimidating, carried a chip on their shoulder, and were intent on winning at any cost.

Gus reminded his team if they followed through on what they practiced and didn't let the players ruffle them, the game would be theirs. As they took the court, there was loud booing from one side of the spectators. Leonard gave Jamiel as stern a look as he had ever given, and someone gave BJ a pretty good bump as he stepped on the court. As they were ready to tip the ball, Jamiel noticed a confused Gus staring at Willie Bennett in the crowd before he quickly turned his attention back to the game and gave Jamiel a confident nod.

Jamiel and BJ moved the ball with quick, crisp passes around the court to avoid the physical defense of the Lenox players. Jamiel scored first on a nice jump shot and glanced at his father, who was watching with Reverend Rich. Why was Reverend Rich spending time with his father? On the next play, BJ was knocked to the ground, allowing for an easy layup to tie the score. The prettiest play came when Jamiel committed his defensive man to a move, followed by a great cross-over dribble and layup, a move Father Tom had spent time working with Jamiel on. The score see-sawed back and forth with a tie game, leaving the Cardinals with four seconds to score and win.

Leonard had moved to the baseline and grabbed Jamiel's jersey. "This is where you prove your loyalty. Are you with us or against us? You know what happens to those who are against us."

The Cardinal player made a bullet bounce pass to their best scorer to seal the victory, but just as the ball skipped on the asphalt, Jamiel anticipated the passing angle and poked the ball the other way, retrieved it and glided in for an authoritative slamdunk just as the buzzer sounded. The crowd went crazy with the dunk and the win by this underdog team. While Jamiel wanted to see Gus's reaction, he instinctively glanced over to where his father had been standing, but he was no longer there. He was surprised by his disappointment that Will might have missed the last play.

When he turned toward Gus, he could see his father trying to talk to him, but they began to argue. Jamiel hesitated to make his way through the crowd to where they were. It didn't seem like the time or the place to introduce himself to the father he had never known, to the man who abandoned his family and responsibilities. He didn't even know if he wanted to meet him.

Leonard was now standing next to Jamiel. "We could have used a player like you on our team. Just as a warning, you might want to be careful in the final game. The word on the street is that they think you were responsible for Tyrell's death. Grant Manor always tries to settle its scores."

Jamiel's heart pounded, and he could hardly hear as he let what Leonard had just said sink in. This was supposed to be a sport, but not to the players of these games.

He glanced back up towards Gus. The confrontation seemed to have gotten more heated. Gus dropped to the ground. Had his father hit him or worse? Jamiel sprinted to the spot he lay and dropped to his knees. "Gus! Gus!" Was he dead? There was no response as he held him in his arms. He lifted his head and glared at the man who was his father and shouted, "What did you do?"

Willie turned, grabbed one of the police officers, and an ambulance pulled up within a few minutes. Reverend Rich drove up with his car and yelled to Willie and Jamiel to get in to drive to the hospital. As they drove to the hospital, there was an awkward reality which everyone was aware of, but didn't know the others were also aware. Instead of addressing it there and then, Reverend Rich filled the silence by talking about the traffic and the best route to get them there for the short ride to Beth Israel Hospital.

They sat in the emergency room waiting area, each one alternatively looking up at the other, but never at the same time. Finally, a doctor came out into the waiting room. "Who's here for Garibaldi Busbi?"

Jamiel shot up. "I am. Is he alive? Did he have a heart attack?"

The doctor put his hand on Jamiel's shoulder. "I'm Dr. Argeros. He's okay. His blood pressure was very high, and I think he fainted and hit his head in the fall. We'll know better what's going on when he regains consciousness."

Thanking the doctor, Jamiel then walked out of the waiting room entrance and started for home. He didn't want to talk to Reverend Rich or his father at the moment. He was upset for a long list of reasons and needed to clear his head. As he walked, he could hear a voice closing in on him.

"Jamiel, wait, wait." Jamiel slowed his pace as the huffing sound reached him. He stopped and looked into his father's eyes for the first time in his life.

"Do you know who I am?"

Jamiel nodded as he glared at the person he had long hoped to embrace.

"I'm sorry. I've thought about meeting you for seventeen years, and this isn't how I wanted it to be."

"I'm sorry too. Why did you wait seventeen years?"

Willie's shoulders slumped. "I don't know how much you know."

"I know you left me without a father, and mom without a husband. I know you didn't care enough about me to have me when you were ready to be a real father. I know you killed an innocent boy for something he didn't do. I know you left a good man broken without a second thought or any remorse. What else do I need to know?"

Willie winced at what Jamiel had just said. "There are a lot more things I'm not proud of that I could add to your list. When I went to prison, I wasn't the man you deserved for a father. I didn't want you burdened with the shame for the man I was. I did exactly what you said, but to say that I have no remorse is no longer true." Tears filled Willie's eyes. "I carry the weight of Danny's death and his parents' sorrow on my soul every day."

"And you show that by putting Gus in the hospital? He doesn't think you're sorry. You've had seventeen years to tell him how sorry you are, but you didn't bother. You had seventeen years to let me know you cared about me and Mom, but you didn't. You're not part of our lives because you chose not to be. Now you want to flip the switch and be forgiven? Gus is ten times the man you will ever be to me."

Without waiting for a response, Jamiel turned, first slowly inching away and then at a faster clip, noticing that his father didn't care enough to follow.

Chapter 44

The next day, Jamiel went to the hospital to visit Gus and found him sitting upright in his bed. A big smile came over Gus's face. "Hey, shouldn't you be practicing?"

Jamiel rested his hand on Gus's shoulder. "Can't practice without a coach."

"I think you are ready to coach and lead this team. I think it will be the toughest match so far. They're a lot older and stronger than you, and they have a few really good players."

"Let's worry about you. What are they saying? Are you going to be okay?"

"Sure. Sure. As much as I prayed for it in the past, I'm not going out that easily."

"What happened?"

"A mild stroke, and I blacked out and hit the noggin pretty good. Good thing I have a hard head like you. They think it will last me for a while longer. Sorry I didn't get to tell you how well you played. That was quite a game."

"Never mind the game. Isn't a stroke bad?"

"I just need to watch my medication—and my temper. I can actually go home tomorrow. Maybe Mike can come over, and we can get some more coats on that Chevy? I'll ask him when he takes me home." Gus handed Jamiel a few pieces of paper with writing and diagrams all over them.

"What's this?"

"A few notes for playing Grant Manor in the finals. Something to work on with the boys."

"Gus."

"Yeah, Jamiel."

"The man you were with?"

"I don't want to talk about him. He keeps trying to talk about being sorry, but I don't believe him. I think he's trying to get rid of the guilt instead of being truly sorry."

"Maybe. You don't need to get upset again."

On his way back home, Jamiel thought about that morning's church service. Marnie still wouldn't talk to him. Did she think that he had only gone to see her that day to help her brother get killed? During the social hour after service, Reverend Rich had disappeared with his mother for quite some time. When she came back, Jamiel could tell that she had been crying, but she didn't talk about it on the way home. She seemed deep in thought.

That afternoon, the team practiced at St. Francis. The rest of the players had no issues with Jamiel leading the coaching responsibilities. They went over the papers Gus had given to Jamiel to try to decipher the plays and recommendations. Across the top was written: *BELIEVE IN YOURSELVES. I DO!*

After a good practice, Jamiel pulled BJ aside. "I never apologized for givin' you a hard time when you first arrived."

"Don't worry about it. You've more than made up for it."

"You're a real friend. I love playing with you, but I care about you now, and I don't want you to get hurt."

"What are you saying, Jamiel?"

"I'm not sure if you should play on Saturday. The Grant Manor players are no Girl Scouts, and there have been threats about you playing in the tournament. I'm afraid of it coming to a head in the final game when things will be red hot."

"I know. It's been more than the physical stuff going on, but they have seemed almost more angry at you. Should *you* be playing?"

"I can't let them beat me with intimidation."

"I wasn't thinking about intimidation. I was thinking of something worse."

"I know. I have to play."

"Then let's win or go down together."

Crazy Texan, thought Jamiel. As they stepped outside, Jamiel noticed two men walking with Father Tom at the end of the driveway. It took him a second to recognize that it was Reverend Rich and his father. What would they be doing at a Catholic Church, never mind talking with Father Tom? Too many conversations going on that he didn't understand.

On Monday, Gus was home early and able to get around slowly. They set up a chair outside the garage so Gus could watch Jamiel spray the primed doors, frame, and hood the bright red he had selected with Gus. It was all worth the hard work they put into it, especially because of the time he got to spend with Gus. Afterward, before heading to practice, he went through some of the strengths and weaknesses of the Grant Manor team, where they could leverage their own strengths and minimize their weaknesses.

After practice, Jamiel drank a tall glass of water at the kitchen sink and was surprised to see Father Tom coming out of Gus's apartment and walking past the window. He thought, *He could be just checking up on him, but something's going on.* Jamiel jumped onto the porch and then the sidewalk just as Father Tom came around the corner of the house. "Father Tom!"

"Hey, Jamiel. How's the coaching going?"

"Goin' all right. Did you see Gus—I mean, Mr. Busbi?"

"Yeah. He seemed to be doing good, just a little tired."

"What did you two talk about?" queried Jamiel.

"Just some personal stuff. You really care about him, don't you?"

"Sure, personal stuff? Meaning, mind my own business?"

"Well, I wouldn't put it that way."

"You talked to my father the other day. Is that none of my business too?"

"You saw that, did you? I thought you were in practice. Yes, I did meet your dad."

"And Reverend Rich?"

"And Reverend Rich. I've met him before at an ecumenical meeting. I like him a lot. He seems to like you quite a bit, too."

"Can you tell me what you talked about with them?"

Just then, Celia came up the drive from work.

Father Tom nodded to her. "Hi, Celia. Good timing. Jamiel was asking some questions that you might be interested in. Can we go in and talk?"

They sat in the living room, and Tom started, "I just talked with Gus. He's still pretty upset about Willie Bennett coming to see him. What I didn't know and what I still think he doesn't know is that Jamiel is Willie's son."

Visibly taken back, Celia said, "Um, if Gus doesn't know this, how did you find out?"

"I received a visit from Willie and Reverend Rich Obasi. Reverend Rich visited Willie at Walpole MCI every week for the seventeen years he was incarcerated, and they had a very interesting journey to share."

Jamiel stood up. "No offense, but why did they want to share it with you?"

"Willie had tried to talk to Gus a few times, but Gus isn't interested in talking to Willie. He's been understandably upset, and they thought that I may be able to help."

"And did you?"

"I wasn't able to get very far and didn't want to excite him during his recovery by pushing too much. I just told him to try to be open."

His mother sat on the edge of her seat. "What did Will tell you when you saw him?"

"Well, they've been on this journey together, so they both shared how angry and belligerent Willie, or Will, was when he entered prison and for many years afterward. Reverend Rich never gave up on him and visited every week until they were able to talk about life, about true manhood, and believing there is a God who loved him and had a purpose for his life. It took many many years for Will to believe there was good inside of him and that he could be forgiven."

Celia closed her eyes and cried. "Reverend Rich pulled me aside after church to tell me how much Will has changed. He now follows Christ, but—I—I couldn't let it in. I believed there was something special in Will—but I don't feel like I can risk believing that again. I couldn't let Jamiel get hurt if it weren't true."

Jamiel was fidgety. "How do you know you can trust this guy?"

Tom replied, "I can understand your caution and need to protect each other and yourselves. It's a healthy instinct. I have talked to a lot of troubled men who have believed they were going to change, only to fall back into the same old habits and patterns. It's more common than doing the real work of change and taking responsibility for yourself. The difference with Will is that he has had a complete change of heart. He knows that God is on his side and at the center of his life. The man who left that prison is not the man who entered it. He's now the man God created him to be. I've been doing this for some time now, and I can tell when it's authentic. I think he's the real deal—but he's having a hard time letting Gus know that he's truly remorseful for what he did to Danny, Julia, and Gus."

Shaking his head, Jamiel said, "I don't know. I don't know how you can change that much. How can he expect to be forgiven for what he did?"

"This is not my place, but I could tell how sorry he was for not being there, not being there for you, Celia—not being there as the father you needed, Jamiel. He knows that he cannot go back in time to fix what has been done, but he would like to talk with you about what might work going forward."

Jamiel clenched his fist and pounded the table. "What?! So, he wants to waltz in and play house now, like nothin' happened? Like I didn't miss having a father for my entire childhood? Forget it."

Celia got up and put her arm around Jamiel. "Thank you, Father Tom. I think we just need to step back and process what's going on."

Father Tom stood up and shook her hand. "Jamiel, remember— anywhere, anytime, for—"

"'—any reason.' I remember," Jamiel responded as he recalled sitting in the holding area at the police station in the early hours of the morning waiting for Father Tom to pick him up. He was also thinking about how Gus might feel when he found out his true identity.

Chapter 45

Over the next few days, Jamiel worked the spray gun, with Gus's guidance only when needed. He finished the last coat for the two wide, black rally stripes on the hood and trunk and stepped back to admire his work. For that moment, it helped to take his mind off everything else.

"Outstanding job, Jamiel. We can get all that paper and tape off, put on the wheels and finishing touches, and I think we're there. I'm proud of the job you've done here. Very impressive," said Gus with a smile.

"It will be more impressive if it runs, too!"

Gus still couldn't make it to the gym, but he worked on plays and areas of focus with Jamiel to take to St. Francis and work on with the team. Gus made a final push to say how concerned he was for Jamiel's safety. "Jamiel, I don't know if playing this game is worth the risk. I'm very worried."

"I know. I talked to BJ about it, and we want to play. If we quit and forfeit because they intimidated us, we will always regret it."

"It's not the game I'm worried about."

"I know, Gus. I talked to one of the cops, and they are going to have more officers there for the last game." He paused, glanced across the yard a moment, then stared Gus in the eyes. "Gus, there's something that I need to tell you, but I don't want to upset you."

"I don't think you can get me more upset than I've been. Don't worry about whatever it is. I trust you."

"I don't know if you should. The man that came by to see you the other day, the man that killed your son—"

"Is your father."

Jamiel's mouth fell open. "How—how did you know? I didn't even know until recently."

Gus ran his hand through his hair. "I've known for a while. When I first met you, I knew it bothered me to see you for some reason. I just could never understand why, and I had no reason to feel that way about you. When I saw him across the way at the game, I was shaken up, but it became so obvious who you looked like, and I finally understood."

"You don't hate me? You're not angry?"

"I could never hate you, Jamiel. You aren't responsible for what he did, but your mother has known all along, hasn't she?"

"Are you mad at her?"

Sighing, Gus dropped a rag on the car's hood. "No. Your mother is one of the nicest people on this earth. She's tried to look out for me, perhaps to make up for Danny's death even though she wasn't responsible. I don't blame her for not telling you. Maybe it was part of Someone else's plan?"

"And I thought you were just a cranky old buzzard."

"I am," said Gus with a smirk.

"So, what do we do?"

"We finish your car. We win that tournament. And we move forward."

"What about my father?"

"How do you feel about him?"

"I don't want anything to do with him. He was a gangster that did no good. He's a killer that destroyed real people's lives. He used my mother and left me without a father for my entire life. Why would I feel anything about him but disdain?"

Nodding slowly, Gus chose his words carefully before replying. "Jamiel, you have a lot of emotions to work through, but take it from this cranky old buzzard—spending a life hating him will only rob you of your life. I've done it for too long, and the only ones it hurt were Julia, myself, and everyone I've known."

Stunned, Jamiel asked, "Are you saying that I should have a relationship with him?"

"I'm just saying not to let the anger and resentment eat you up like it has me. That's all."

"So, what are you going to do—forgive and forget?"

"I know I can't forget, and I just can't forgive. I can't do it. When he came, he acted like he was sorry, but I can't believe him. Deep down, I just can't. The way he did what he did. The expression of hate he gave Danny after he killed him in cold blood, and then the complete lack of remorse afterward, just doesn't leave room to believe he's sincere. I can't cheapen Danny's memory that way."

When Jamiel and Celia ate dinner that evening, they were both quiet. From her red eyes, he could tell his mother had been crying. She was antsy and couldn't sit for long in any one place.

Jamiel knew she couldn't sleep that night because he couldn't either. Emotionally, the answer just wasn't that easy.

Friday felt like a better day because of the car. With all the tape and protective papers removed, they put on the wheels. The car came out better than Jamiel had ever imagined. He had a photo of the same model and paint job he wanted, but that car didn't have the hours of his sweat and hard work that this car had. As he sat inside, with his hands on the wheel and Gus in the passenger seat, Jamiel realized that it wasn't the car that he loved, but the time he had spent with Gus working together on it, the talks they had, the friendship they forged, and the man it helped him to start becoming.

"Well, driver. Start her up."

Jamiel said, "I don't have a key."

Gus laughed and pulled a set out of his pants pocket. The set of keys was on a rabbit's foot chain that had a medal with Jamiel's name on it. "I think these might work. After all, it's your car now. You earned it."

Clutching the keys, Jamiel smiled and started the engine. It purred but had enough sound as he revved it to feel how powerful the engine was.

"Let's take a spin and keep the shiny side up if you don't mind."

Jamiel pulled carefully out of the driveway in the meticulously restored bright red sports car that he never believed he would ever get close to owning. The driving lessons from Gus had given him the confidence to drive and respect for everyone else on the road, even if this thing could go fast. They drove by Mike's house and beeped the horn, bringing Mike out with a wide grin on his face. "My, my, my—that's a sweet set of wheels you have there, Mr. Russell."

Jamiel couldn't get the smirk off his face. "Do you want to hop in for a ride?"

"Some other time. I think this first ride was meant for you and that hitchhiker you picked up. It came out pretty nice, didn't it, Gus? I told you he could do it," Mike said with a chuckle.

They drove by BJ's apartment to get his excited reaction. Then they drove down Lenox Street and slowed to a crawl as they passed the steps with a number of the boys congregating. Leonard and Ricky were sitting but didn't get up with the others who admired the shiny buffed exterior. As Jamiel received the momentary adulation of the spectators, he glanced over at Leonard and wondered if Leonard ever really cared about him.

When they returned home and backed the car carefully into the garage, Jamiel turned to Gus. "Gus, I want to thank you for everything you've done for me. It's been like having a dad, not that I know what that's like," he said with a crooked smile.

Gus's eyes brimmed with tears. He nodded, then spoke hoarsely, "I think you should get a good rest tonight for the game tomorrow. I'm sorry that I can't be there in person, but I'll be there with you in spirit."

"I know you will. I know you always will."

Chapter 46

When Jamiel got to the game, the buzz of the huge crowd seemed ready for an all-out battle. He noticed that the Grant Manor gang members had staked out their territory under one basket end-line while the Lenox Street Cardinals were gathered under the other. The ref was working with the police to push the spectators back from the edges of the court to give the players room to operate. Jamiel's mom was sitting with Mike in his truck so that they could watch safely. Reverend Rich and Father Tom were standing on the sidelines together. Jamiel found himself scanning the crowd to see if his father had come, despite the rejection he had given him earlier. He didn't see him as he gathered his teammates for final game prep.

Just before taking the court, Jamiel felt a presence behind him. His defensive reflexes kicked in, and he turned quickly, thinking it might be someone from the Grant Manor team out to get him. Instead, it was his father.

"Jamiel, I wanted to wish you luck. I've watched you play, and I can't tell you how impressed I've been with your game. Give 'em hell."

Jamiel fought his instinct to say something hurtful or sarcastic, but he just nodded and stepped onto the court. The crowd had grown, and he could see Leonard, Ricky, Halfway, Mal, and even Trig with his hood over his head, staring directly at Jamiel but not cheering him on. As he turned toward the other end-line, he got a stare down from Grant Manor leaders, Tookie Walker and Fat Fingers Williams. The stare made him think as if they would be willing to shoot him on the spot to get payback for Tyrell's death.

BJ readied himself for the tip-off and received a hard bump from the Grant Manor center sending him a signal. The ref raised his hand with a warning. Jamiel could hear the Grant Manor center say to BJ, "I wouldn't be playing today if I were you, redneck." BJ didn't respond.

Jamiel and the other players jockeyed for position before the ball was tossed up to begin the game with a loud set of cheers and boos from the crowd. The tension in the air was explosive as BJ won the tip to Jamiel, and they started to bring the ball up. Jamiel put his fist up and they ran the first play they had worked on, rotating the ball and running screens to get mismatches on defense until the ball went into BJ. He faked a shot and made a nice pass to Jamiel as he cut to the basket for a layup until he was hit with force from behind, sending him hard to the asphalt. Grant Manor was sending a clear message that they were going to intimidate and play dirty to win this game at any cost.

Getting back up, Jamiel pulled his teammates together. "Don't get fazed, no matter what. We can take a few bumps and bruises."

The Grant Manor team had enough players to commit as many hard fouls as needed to muscle their way to a win. They also had some very good ballers, who could score and play hardnosed defense, making this challenge a tough one for the DnA team. Despite the long odds, Jamiel's shooting was outstanding, and BJ was making a huge difference under the boards with rebounds and tip-in baskets. BJ received some of the hardest fouls and constant taunting and even death threats from the Grant Manor side of the crowd. Jamiel noticed that he didn't let it faze him as he continued to stay focused.

The score was tied 30–30, with ten minutes left on the clock. Grant Manor team was yelling and getting nervous as Jamiel & Co. wouldn't go away, despite the hard play. Jamiel could sense the anger on Tookie's face as he screamed expletives at the team. He remembered how serious Leonard was when he said this wasn't a game; it was something much more than that to these gangs, and here was a rag-tag team with two teenagers pushing them to the brink—and one of them was as white as the puffy clouds in the blue sky above. The expression on their faces said they couldn't let this happen.

When DnA took a four-point lead off of a tough jumper from the corner and then a sweet-looking dunk by Jamiel, Jamiel caught his father cheering hard while Tookie was having a fit yelling at his guys. On the next play, BJ was playing tough defense on the Grant Manor center under the basket next to Tookie, who was yelling, "Bang the hell out of that, Casper!" Just as the player went up with his shot, BJ timed his jump perfectly to block it and then dove into the crowd to try to save the ball. As he hit the ground surrounded by spectators, Tookie leaned down as if to hit him, but someone in the crowd grabbed his wrist and bent it back, forcing Tookie to pull back. BJ quickly got up and darted back on the court as the crowd covered up anything that was going on. Jamiel felt panicked as he glanced over to see Reverend Rich and Father Tom gesturing encouragement, but he no longer saw his father on the sidelines.

With thirty seconds left in the game, Grant Manor was able to get a stop on defense and bring the score within one point. The crowd was as vocal and tense as they had been all game. As one of Jamiel's teammates tossed in the ball to BJ, the pass was deflected and stolen by Grant Manor, who scored and put Grant Manor up by one on an easy layup.

Jamiel pulled the team together. "We only have five seconds to win this thing. We can do it. We just need a clean inbound's pass high to BJ. BJ will fire the ball to whoever is open down the court. Just take whatever shot is open and let it fly."

Being overly careful about the pass, the DnA player stepped on the line when he made the pass, getting a whistle from the ref and awarding the ball to Grant Manor. All the Grant Manor team needed to do was to inbounds the ball and run the clock out to win the tournament and the five-thousand-dollar prize. Jamiel could see Tookie holding his wrist while yelling at his player to get the ball in. The ball was tossed high for their tallest player to catch, and as it floated in slow motion into the air, everyone turned their head to watch it land in the tall guy's hands for the win, but Jamiel jumped as high as he had ever jumped and tipped the ball forward, chasing it in a sprint as it skipped down the court, with several players in pursuit. His long strides allowed him to reach the ball first, pick it up and slam it through the basket with authority just as the end-of-game buzzer sounded.

It didn't seem to matter who the spectators had been rooting for, the crowd jumped and erupted with cheers at the unbelievable play and dramatic end to the game. Jamiel's teammates picked him up as he held onto the game ball and held his other hand high in the air with a genuine smile of elation. Mike beeped the horn as Celia was now standing on the sideboard, cheering wildly. Father Tom and Reverend Rich hugged each other, and now he could see his father again, smiling proudly. Tookie and his soldiers moved toward his father, but it was too crowded for them to get to him. Jamiel could see Tookie pointing his finger at his father and making a threatening gesture as the police came between them to move everyone along.

The crowd had thinned out a bit as Jamiel made it to the sideline, where he got handshakes and pats on the back from Father Tom and Reverend Rich. Father Tom yelled above the crowd noise, "I told you I made a good choice of captain for next year's team!"

Jamiel grinned and responded, "My agent will be getting in touch with you since my market value just went up."

Celia wrapped Jamiel in a tight hug as Mike patted his back. Celia turned and noticed Willie standing next to them. She peered up at him as if she were still that eighteen-year-old girl still in love.

"CeCe. How are you?"

"Hello, Will. I'm glad you came to watch. Maybe we can talk afterward. I'd like to."

Willie nodded and turned to Jamiel. "Jamiel, you played a heck of a game. I know it might not mean much coming from me, but I was proud to watch you play. Congratulations," said Will.

Jamiel nodded, feeling confused about how to respond. He would have loved to have had a father come to his games to cheer him on, to teach him how to play and develop confidence, to encourage him when he got down, but who was he to show up now and expect him to be happy? Jamiel became angry. *Yeah. You weren't important enough to be with, but now that you've won five-thousand dollars, I'm proud to be your dad.* Jamiel remained silent, the moment became awkward, and so they split up to make their way to their respective homes. Jamiel made sure that BJ was safely on his way before he rode home with Mike and his mother in the middle.

When they got home, Jamiel ran up the stairs to Gus's apartment and knocked several times but heard no reply. He started to panic, thinking that Gus may have had another stroke or a heart attack. He remembered where Gus kept the key and quietly opened the door, in case he was only napping. "Gus," he said in a soft voice but saw no one in the kitchen or living room from the doorway. The bathroom door was open, and he tiptoed to his bedroom and saw nothing but a made bed and a Bible on the nightstand.

Standing in the center of Gus's quiet apartment, Jamiel scratched his head with one hand as he held the Ramsay Park Tournament trophy in the other. There were open letters all over the kitchen table, but Jamiel didn't want to pry into personal stuff. He closed and locked the door and slowly descended the staircase, feeling disappointed that he couldn't share the news with the person with whom he most wanted to share it. The first time he left Gus's apartment, he couldn't do it fast enough, but now he felt sad to be leaving.

Chapter 47

The morning sunlight filled Jamiel's bedroom as he felt the relief of nothing to do. Then he heard his mother call up the stairs. "Leaving for church in fifteen minutes. I hope you're just a quiet dresser this morning!"

Jamiel jumped up. "Almost ready!" he yelled as he scrambled to put on his clothes while he shook the sleep from his eyes.

It was a sunny day and a pleasant morning for the stroll to church. "Are you really goin' to meet with that guy?"

"Your father? Yes. I think it's only fair to hear him out and give him a chance. I feel like I got a second chance to be judged differently by others, not everyone, but those who cared. I don't know what will come of it, and I'm very nervous."

"When are you goin' to see him?"

"I asked him over to the house after church. You don't have to be around. This was my choice. You'll have to make your own at some point."

Jamiel's shoulders slumped as he thought about seeing him again and Gus's reaction if he did.

After church, Reverend Rich approached Jamiel. "Congratulations again, King of the Asphalt."

Jamiel blushed and grinned.

"I'm sorry the interactions with your dad haven't gone well. I think you might feel very differently if you give him a chance. I know there are years of hurt and broken trust, but try not to judge a man only by the things you are aware of. Sometimes there is more to a man than what we can see from the outside."

Nodding, Jamiel didn't argue as Reverend Rich patted him on the shoulder and moved on to talk with other parishioners. Suddenly he heard a voice from behind.

"Hi, Jamiel."

It was Marnie. Jamiel flushed with uncertainty. "Hi, Marnie. I've wondered how you've been doing."

"I just wanted to say that I'm sorry that I was upset with you and didn't trust you. I've talked with Reverend Rich about the conflicting feelings I've been having and all the things I'm hearing—but I realized that they never sounded like you. I let my fears stop me from giving you a chance."

"I appreciate that—and I'm so sorry about your brother. I've had Lenox Street guys telling me I was there to tip-off Tyrell and other people telling me I was there to get him killed."

"So, why were you there that day?"

"The back and forth drive-bys were getting crazy dangerous. I heard about something that might happen that day, and I wanted to get you out of there, just in case. I didn't want you hurt in this crazy war."

"So, you didn't actually want to ask me out then?"

Jamiel scratched his head, his heart pounding. "I did. I was feeling a bit shy, but that kind of forced the issue."

"Well, if you ask me proper again sometime, I might just say 'yes'." She took his hand for a second and gazed into his eyes in a way that seemed like she trusted him again, and then she said goodbye.

Jamiel found his mother and asked again when his father was coming by.

"He should be there shortly after we get home. Why?"

"I was hoping to catch Gus beforehand. He wasn't home when I tried to see him yesterday."

"Maybe he was taking a nap? I think he's still recovering from his episode last week."

"Maybe."

As they turned the corner to their street, they saw Willie sitting on the front steps. Jamiel wasn't sure if he wanted to talk with him.

Willie stood up and smiled. "Hey, Jamiel. CeCe, thanks for being willing to talk. I know it's been a long time, too long to expect anything, but I'm glad to see you both."

Celia grinned. "Why did you keep where you were so secret? Strict orders to everyone not to let on where you were all these years?"

"I was ashamed. You both deserved better, and I thought it was best for you for different reasons."

"We can talk about it inside."

"Okay. I'm a little worried. That Grant Manor gang seemed more than angry at the game. I stopped the guy Tookie from knifing that white kid on your team. I almost had to break his wrist to take that blade from him."

His mom's mouth fell open. "Are you thinking they'll come after you?"

"I'm not worried about me. They said something about evening the score with Jamiel. Something to do with Tyrell's shooting?"

Her eyes grew wide with a look of panic. "Oh, my God. What can we do? Should we call the police?"

"I talked to some of the officers at the game, and they agreed to send some extra patrols over here for a while, but I don't think it will stop Tookie, by the look on his face. He was pretty angry, and I think I embarrassed him by the knife incident in front of his soldiers. I would have wanted revenge myself, back in the day."

Jamiel peered across the road that opened up to an intersection. It was still quiet on a Sunday, and the black Cadillac that pulled up a minute earlier was still sitting there idling. "I don't like the looks of that ride over there."

Just as Jamiel finished speaking, the doors with the black tinted windows opened up, and Tookie and Fat Fingers stepped out and started approaching the house across the empty street. Willie whispered to Celia and Jamiel, "Slowly, go into the house. Don't look back. Just go in and call the police."

"I'm not runnin'. We need to straighten this out," said Jamiel with a stern voice.

"I think their idea of straightening this out doesn't include talking. Go in *now*."

Tookie and Fat Fingers got closer, and the tension in the air thickened. Just as Celia moved to grab Jamiel to climb the porch stairs, Tookie reached his hand over his shoulder and pulled out a Barretta sawed-off shotgun from a holster behind his back. Pointing at them, he said, "I wouldn't move if I were you."

Jamiel chided, "Let her go in. She's not part of this." His legs were shaking, and the fear of being shot again ran through him like a knife, but he couldn't let his mother get hurt.

"She can watch from the porch, but not in the house."

His mother tried to pull Jamiel, but she was forced to climb the steps alone. "Please don't do this!" she screamed as tears fell from her cheeks onto the porch floor.

Willie stepped out onto the street to create some distance between any shooting and Celia. Despite his order for Jamiel to stay behind, Jamiel stood next to his father as his stomach clenched.

"Jamiel had nothing to do with Tyrell's death," said Willie with a firm tone.

"I've heard otherwise. We are here to settle all scores today."

"I told you the other day; he's not part of the score to settle."

"That may be, but our first order of business is with his old man. That's right, we know who you are—old-time leader of the Cardinals—and old-time rival of Grant Manor. How about that? Embarrassing me yesterday was probably enough, but I'm here to settle the score for Kyrie."

Jamiel asked, "Who's Kyrie?"

"You shut up until I'm ready for you!" snapped Tookie with an angry glare. "Your old man here didn't just shoot that white baller for gettin' his little brother killed. He also killed my uncle, Kyrie. He may have stuck your little bro like a pig, but he was still my uncle and Grant Manor. So for old time's sake—"

Just as Tookie raised the Barretta and began to pull the trigger, Gus, who had heard the commotion, suddenly appeared, stepped in front of Willie, and the ear-piercing blast hit him point-blank, propelling him to the ground with a thud.

Panicked, Jamiel dropped to his knees beside his friend's bloodied body and screamed, "Gus! Gus!"

Tookie moved to shoot again but pulled the gun back as the sound of police sirens made their way down the street. Before they could scramble and jump into the getaway car, the cruisers arrived, their guns drawn. Tookie dropped the Barretta to the pavement and raised his hands along with Fat Fingers.

"Gus, what did you do? Why?" Jamiel sobbed from deep within his soul. "Gus! Hold on! The ambulance is coming."

Celia was screaming, and neighbors came out onto their stoops or peered out their windows to see what the commotion was about.

Gus lay in Jamiel's arms as blood poured from his midsection, and he gazed up at Jamiel with a fondness Jamiel hadn't felt from any man. "Jamiel. It's okay." Tears came to his eyes. "It's okay. I love you like my own son. I was dead before I knew you, and then you helped me feel alive again." He coughed and choked several times as he spoke and reached out his pointed finger. "I want to tell you something important. That man right there is your dad. I think you should give him a chance to be the dad you still need."

Willie knelt down, and Gus looked straight at him. Gus said, "I'm sorry."

Willie's eyes widened with surprise as his cheeks tightened. "You're sorry? I'm the one who's so sorry. I can't blame you for not forgiving me."

"I'm sorry because I didn't give you a chance. I just didn't believe you cared or that you were sorry at all." Gus grimaced and coughed again.

"Mr. Busbi, why do you believe me now?"

"When you came to see me, the expression in your eyes was so different. Father Tom tried to tell me how much of a changed man you were, but I couldn't believe it. I wouldn't believe it. I couldn't forgive you if you didn't care about what you did to Danny." Gus choked and coughed again, saying, "I was wrong."

"But what changed?"

"Yesterday—" Gus labored to breathe.

Jamiel said, "Don't overexert yourself."

"Jamiel, listen—this is important to you and to me. Yesterday I spent the day reading every one of the letters your father wrote to me over all those years. I wouldn't open them before, but when I did, I saw the change over years of letters and how sincerely remorseful he was—and I saw a real man that should be your dad."

Gus gripped Willie's sleeve. "I—forgive you—for everything. Please take care of Celia—and your son."

Jamiel held Gus and cried, "Don't go, Gus!"

Father Tom knelt beside them. "I heard the commotion and ran over. Gus."

Gus nodded, and a teary-eyed Father Tom made the Sign of the Cross on Gus's forehead and bent over to listen to his confession. He gave him absolution before saying the prayers of the Last Rites.

Gus was holding Jamiel's hand as he clutched Father Tom's arm. "Maybe I can see Julia and Danny now. I feel ready."

Jamiel gripped Gus's hand tighter as Gus's grip loosened, and he breathed his last breath. A small breeze picked up as if to take him away.

The ambulances had arrived, but it would not be to save him; he had already done that himself.

Father Tom put his arm around Jamiel, and his father rubbed Jamiel's back. Father Tom said, "He loved you so much, Jamiel. He could see in you the extraordinary young man that God created. You gave him such a great gift—that was yourself."

"He wouldn't be dead if it wasn't for me," cried Jamiel, his eyes burning.

"He wouldn't have been alive if it weren't for you. You helped him with the greatest struggle in his life and gave him the reason to confront it. He came by yesterday to go to Reconciliation and then to Mass to receive

Communion for the first time in many years. It meant so much to him to be reconciled with God and his own soul. He was at peace for the first time since losing Danny. He told me how much you meant to him and how he now believed your father was a good man."

"Tookie was going to shoot him, and Gus purposely stepped in front to protect him. Why would he do that?" It hit him that his gang friends would never do that. Without Gus and his mother, he probably would've ended up like his friends from the old neighborhood, on the road to prison. Heck, he should already be in prison for the crimes he committed, but he knew his life would be different now to make up for them.

"No one has greater love than this, to lay down one's life for another."

They stood up as the police dispersed the crowd, and ambulance EMTs put Gus's body on a stretcher.

Jamiel peered up at his dad, no longer with hate or resentment, but a reason to give him a chance.

****

Willie stood on the sidewalk with his arm around Celia and his hand on Jamiel's shoulder as he watched them take Gus away, the man who forgave him with his own life despite having lost everything he cherished because of him.

****

Jamiel thought, *If Gus isn't in heaven at this very moment smiling down on us, then no one is.* He would miss him dearly, but for the rest of his life, he would also cherish every second of the time they had spent together.

Acknowledgments

The story of Gus Busbi and Jamiel Russell started percolating in my mind as I was writing *The Father's Son*. It ended up being a timely story about a relationship between two men looking past their differences and struggles in life to find something profoundly worth the effort. I wanted to share my gratitude to those who encouraged me and helped to shape this story, including all the patient editing support from my wife, Joanne, and from Ellen Hrkach and Michelle Buckman. Many thanks also to beta readers Florence, John, Jerry, Jason, and Wayne, and to the three men I admire most for always being there.

About the Author

Jim Sano grew up in an Irish/Italian family in Massachusetts. Jim is a husband, father, lifelong Catholic and has worked as a teacher, consultant, and businessman. He has degrees from Boston College and Bentley University and is currently attending Franciscan University for a master's degree in Catechetics and Evangelization. He has also attended certificate programs at The Theological Institute for the New Evangelization at St. John's Seminary and the Apologetics Academy. Jim is a member of the Catholic Writers Guild and has enjoyed growing in his faith and now sharing it through writing novels. *The Father's Son* was his first novel. *Gus Busbi* is his second.

Jim resides in Medfield, Massachusetts with his wife, Joanne, and has two daughters, Emily and Megan.

Published by Full Quiver Publishing
PO Box 244
Pakenham, ON K0A2X0
Canada
www.fullquiverpublishing.com

Made in the USA
Coppell, TX
06 September 2021

61870629R00134